Run for the

Money

Jon Gregory

This story would not have been possible without Paul Chutkow, his input, ideas and encouragement have been priceless.

Sonya, you never had a doubt – thank you sweetie for putting up with the process.

And Mom and Dad – so much you have given me that is immeasurable.

*"It is double the pleasure
to deceive the deceiver."*

Jean De La Fontaine
(1621-1695)

Chapter One

He rebooted the computer. Nothing changed.

Rebooted again; the empty account page stared back.

Still in his formal shirt, slacks and black shoes, Travis bolted down the stairs from his flat, through the still lit foyer and into the chilly night air. Sweating despite the cold wind, his breath misting in front of him, Travis fumbled with his keys, unable to focus on anything except what he knew he had to do.

He backed out of his driveway and looked in the rear view mirror; his face was ashen, washed out under the amber street lights. He sped towards his office, jumping red lights, tires screeching over the metal cable car tracks embedded in the asphalt of California Street.

The Embarcadero waterfront echoed with the sounds of a working port; foghorns, fishing trawlers, produce trucks, and a steady hum of graveyard shift traffic on the Bay Bridge above. Travis parked in front of the 14 story building and swiped his pass card into a slot at the front entrance. The door hissed open.

A security guard sat with his feet up on the front desk watching a reality show on a 10-inch monitor; cackles of laughter echoed in the empty lobby. The guard looked up as Travis ran by holding up his ID card.

"Are you working late or getting in early?" He asked.

Travis faked a smile and headed to the elevators. The new security system in the building would generate a log of his entry and exit based on the card he'd scanned.

Within moments he was at his desk on the 10th floor offices of his employer, Hastings & McCloud, pounding at his keyboard. It was possible there was a problem with his home computer, or a random glitch in the system. He typed in his security code and logged into the trading account. Nothing. There had been no glitch at home; the money was gone.

A few moments ago Travis was a player in the game of money, on the threshold of seeing his deepest ambitions fulfilled. Now he was on the outside looking in, with one question... *Where was the money?*

Foghorns from the Bay penetrated the silence. On the large windows around him the eerie fluorescent glow of the office lights bounced off the glass

He picked up the phone.

Chapter Two

He dialed Reg's number one more time. Nothing. *Why wasn't his voice mail picking up?*

Travis spent the next hour trying to get Reg on the phone, placing calls to the back office tech people in New York to see if there was some kind of system-wide problem with the office computers while pacing around his cubicle.

His rushing thoughts stopped...*there had to be a signed document to move the money.* Contrary to popular belief, large sums don't move across the world with a phone call. Every movement of funds has to have an authorized signature, either in fax or hard copy. Compliance and legal departments insist on paper trails and it was now clear to Travis why.

Travis had spent the last four months putting clients into Reg's hedge fund; a half million here, a million there. So far he had put over 50 million of client funds with Reg.

The procedure was simple. Travis had opened a trading account in the name of RC Partners, and as he put client money in the account Reg would phone in or e-mail the trades. Most of the action took place just before a Fed meeting. Late-night overseas trades were entered by the London branch. Travis would get the commissions on the trades and keep track of the accounting, while Reg took a management fee and a percentage of the profits. The last time he checked, the balance was over $54 million-- funds his top clients had deposited over the prior four months.

He walked to the fax machine behind the front counter to look for evidence of a signature that would've had to come through authorizing the wire transfer. While it was Reg who made the actual trading decisions, the funds were held in a branch account meaning the money would had to have been moved by a Hastings & McCloud employee acting on signed, written instructions from Reg. Digging through the usual stack of legitimate customer requests to move money, gift shares of stock to charities, cut checks to third parties, Travis found the incriminating document. It spelled out in specific language that the entire contents of the trading account were to be wired to Banco de San Juan, Calle San Francisco, San Juan, Puerto Rico. The bank account was identified only by a ten digit number.

At the bottom, scrawled in sharp, angular letters was Reg's familiar signature Reginald Crae, Attorney in Fact.

———

Travis reread the document on his way back to his desk. He sat down, rubbed his eyes and took stock of his situation. He forced himself to start thinking in linear steps, to get some movement on this. Anything that felt like action, no matter how ineffective, would be better than staring at a computer screen hoping the digits would change.

He made a list.

First, where was Reg?

Second, the back office people in New York knew of no system-wide problem that would show an error in account activity or balances.

Third, the money was now in a bank in Puerto Rico following signed instructions by Reg.

He wrote down two possibilities: Either Reg was involved in some sophisticated offshore investment requiring the funds to be in Puerto Rico - or he had stolen the money.

At 3:30 a.m. Travis placed a call to Banco de San Juan.

After several attempts he got someone who spoke English.

"I'm looking into a wire transfer that was made to your bank last night. If I give you the wire number can you help me with the specifics of this?"

"Yes, and who am I speaking with?"

He hesitated....

"Sir?"

"Travis Black."

"Of course, why don't you read me what you have and we'll tell you what we can." The voice was cultured, the English clear, traces of a Spanish accent. He sounded ready to help and for the first time in hours Travis felt as if he wasn't chasing a phantom. He read off the wire numbers and the account number from the faxed document he held in his hand.

"Very well, and your password?"

"Excuse me?"

"Your password sir, you would have given it to us when you opened the account."

Travis started to stumble, caught himself, "It seems I've forgotten it…I have so many of these accounts."

"I see. As you know, we set it up this way for your protection to avoid just anybody calling in and inquiring about your account."

"All right, without the password what can you tell me?"

"Nothing you don't already know. Funds were wired into this account last night. I'm sorry sir, that is all I can say without your password."

"Can you tell me how the account is registered? Who the principals are?"

"Please sir, if you could somehow find that password I will be at liberty to help you. Unfortunately I must attend to some other business, please call me back when you find it."

"Wait!"

"Yes?"

"Don't you have a way of helping people that have forgotten their password?"

"Yes, you'll need to come in to the bank for that."

"But I'm in San Francisco."

"I see. The prompt here says it would be the license plate of your first car. Does that help?"

Travis knew this would get him nowhere. He took a frustrated stab in the dark with his plate from college.

"8L33067"

"I'm sorry sir, we're not…how do you Americans say…not in the same ballpark. Now if you'll excuse me."

The line went dead.

Travis went to the bathroom and splashed cold water on his face. He paced back and forth, desperate for anything to grab hold of. He looked at himself in the mirror under the merciless glare of fluorescent lights; fast growing whiskers shadowed his face, sunken wild eyes stared back. His short, dark hair stuck out at odd angles. Leaning his hands on the counter he moved closer to the mirror and peered deeper into a face he didn't recognize.

What is happening?

Hours went by as Travis retried everything he'd already done. He typed Banco de San Juan into the computer's search engine and came up with nothing he could use.

Placed more calls to Reg, nothing.

Checked his last e-mail communication with Reg looking for clues to what was on his mind. Nothing.

He went over his list looking for something he hadn't thought of yet while dawn light crept into the windows. Early arriving employees made their way out of the elevators in chattering packs, shouldering computer bags and gulping from Starbucks cups.

One of the first to arrive was Marc Fletcher, Travis's squash partner. They crossed paths as Travis headed back to the bathroom.

Marc looked Travis up and down, not sure whether to laugh or offer help, "What the...? Did you sleep here or what?"

"I couldn't sleep. Thought I'd come in and get some things done...didn't realize how late...I mean, how early it was."

"You don't look so hot, Travis."

"I know...I'm going home to get cleaned up."

Travis headed to the elevators.

Ignoring the comments and glares from a river of people he was swimming against, Travis leaned against the back of the elevator, let the doors close him in and thought through his next move. Reg not answering his phone meant he'd have to go see him in person; there was too much at stake. Travis had been to Reg's office several times in the beginning of their relationship. It was where they had filled out the paperwork to get things started and it housed the computer systems Reg used to follow the markets.

The markets had over an hour before the 6:30 opening bell. Brokers with east coast clients usually got in at 5:30, while the heavy traders who relied on overseas market action to give them an indication of the US markets filed in shortly before 5. Travis tried to act nonchalant as he faced the throngs heading into the front doors. It was an impossible act for a disheveled guy in a tux.

He drove back up California Street and over to Clay. The traffic had mushroomed into Monday morning intensity. Cable cars rang and vibrated. Hurried pedestrians read smartphones while waiting at red lights.

Travis double-parked in front of a two-story Victorian home which had been converted into offices. The sign poking up from the small, manicured lawn in front had the names of architects, therapists, and an accountant, as well as several other urban professionals. The foundation was covered with traditional plantings of hydrangea and purple Lily of the Valley blossoms. He ran up the steps, opened the heavy wooden door and walked down the familiar hallway.

On the right an office door was open.

One of the tenants Travis had seen on a previous visit, a therapist, was listening to headphones while pecking away on a laptop. Further down on the left he came to Reg's door and knocked. The same antique brass number 3 was nailed to the door.

But something about the door was different.

He tried the knob. It was locked.

He walked back to the therapist's office and knocked on the doorjamb. The man didn't look up. He was balding, with wisps of gray hair over his ears. His eyes were hooded. He was typing as if in a trance. "Excuse me…" Travis knocked harder. The man's face snapped up, startled, pulling the headphones off and standing all in one motion.

"What is it?"

"Have you seen Reg Crae, the man down the hall?"

"Who?"

"RC Partners, he rents the office down the hall from you."

"No, can't help you, sorry." The man went back to his headphones and started adjusting them.

"Wait, I've got an emergency, can you give me the landlord or the property manager's name? It's urgent."

Without answering, the balding man rummaged through a stack of business cards. He copied down a name and number on a piece of paper, tore it off the pad and handed it to Travis. "The owner is an Asian company, this is the property manager." He put his headphones back on and resumed typing.

Travis called the number from his cell. The number had a San Francisco prefix and belonged to a Kent Bristow. "*You have reached the offices of Bay Property Management…we're not in at this time…*" he hung up before the recording finished and went back to Reg's door.

He stood there looking at it, wondering what was bothering him and tried the knob again, this time harder, pushing in on the door. There was no give, only the solid barrier of a locked door.

"Can I help you?"

Travis looked up. A man was walking down the hallway. He looked young, wore an olive colored suit and juggled a briefcase, a leather bag, a coffee cup and a ring of keys. "I'm looking for the guy who uses this office, Reg Crae…have you seen him?"

"Afraid you're a few days late, he moved out Friday and I moved in over the weekend."

Chapter Three

Travis stared. His mind circling around what he'd just heard.

"Moved out?"

"Yep, his lease was up and I was next on the list. Getting a space like this hasn't been easy. I've been on a waiting list for months. Now if you'll excuse me..." He stuck his key out and put it in the door. It was at that moment Travis realized what bothered him about the door.

The knob was different.

When he'd visited Reg here before, the knob had been an unusual chrome-plated one that didn't match the others in the hallway. This one was an authentic brass model that fit the Victorian décor of the rest of the building.

"Wait...do you have any idea where he went?"

"According to Kent, he's the property manager...nobody knows. Kent had to put in a doorknob from one of the rooms upstairs, seems this guy changed knobs as soon as he took over the office and nobody could get in. Kent never noticed it until Friday, though."

"How long ago did he move in?"

"Kent said he was only a short timer; a few months then gone."

Travis tried to peer inside the door... "Do you mind? Could I just look in here for a second, this is starting to feel like a bad dream."

"Go ahead, I'm just getting set up myself." They both walked in.

Travis couldn't believe his eyes.

He stood in the doorway and stared, speechless. Bookshelves that had held volumes of finance textbooks alongside bound conference notes and corporate financial reports were now empty. The wall behind the desk was bare; faded outlines of the spots where Reg had hung framed documents showing his education, awards and photos. Nails that had held pictures were still stuck in the wall. The desk, once overloaded, was bare. The credenza was barren; the three computer monitors and flat-screen TV running the financial channel were gone.

"I won't take any more of your time," Travis said. "I need to go."

"No problem, I hope you find what you're looking for. Did this guy take money or something?"

"You could say that."

"Here's my card, let me know if I can do anything to help." Travis looked at it, not noticing the name, the words *Executive Coach* embossed in gold lettering stood out.

"Yeah, thanks." Travis walked down the hallway and out into the street. He pulled his cell phone out of his pocket, hit send again and left a message with the building manager.

Just keep moving forward.

Travis knew who he had to turn to.

Chapter Four

He turned off Nob Hill, down Divisadero and onto Lombard towards the Presidio. Alcatraz Island seemed close enough to touch as the rising sun brought out the rocky outcroppings and concrete ruins.

Near the famous Presidio military base stood a board-and-care facility with a monthly tab of $15,000 and a two-year waiting list. Everything was covered including a full medical staff, outings, transportation, and a gourmet chef. The rich came here to live out their last days, and Travis came here to see the man who got him his job with one phone call.

Travis walked through a front porch designed to make the place feel like a private residence; potted plants graced the brick steps on both sides, stained glass inserts on the front doors portraying images of golfers, hunting scenes and sailboats. A brass WELCOME placard was nailed to the wooden frame above the door, the doormat was plain straw. The front receptionist gave him a smile of recognition,

"Hello Travis. Phil was just asking about you the other day. How's the market?"

Travis hated this question even on a good day, this morning he could care less. "Good, I guess. Look I'm kind of in a hurry. Is he in?"

"Sure, just register here and go on back."

Travis signed in and walked down the main hallway. He passed the lonely, wistful stares of unvisited elders watching whoever came through the door. They looked as though they would talk to anyone, including Travis. He picked up his pace, turned the corner and knocked on a door. A gruff voice inside said to come in.

Phil had been a broker with a major Wall Street firm's San Francisco branch for over 50 years. Old pros still called him to pick his brain. He sat on the board of several foundations and he was known as "the guy that got out at the top". While most others were trying to squeeze the last dime out of the dot-com bubble, Phil saw it for what it was. He'd seen manias before and knew that when it was time to get out the door wouldn't be big enough. He bailed early, got his clients out and retired.

At first everyone thought he was a fool - too old to understand the *new* economy. As the *new* economy and tech stocks sank into a death spiral it became obvious that the old rules still applied. There truly was no substitute for wisdom and experience in this game.

He was an old friend of the family who had gotten Travis into his career with one phone call. Travis still called him Uncle Phil.

He opened the door. Phil was sitting in a leather chair, remote control in hand, trying to dull the volume of the financial news network. He had a full head of white hair and a face tanned and deeply lined of a lifetime of golf and sailing. His granite gaze stared down old age in a battle to the finish. He wore a button-down shirt, knit tie and wingtip shoes, still dressing the part and ready for anything.

Phil stood up. "Travis, good to see you, my boy." Phil's voice sounded like walking on crushed rock; solid, calm unwavering, a welcome sound to Travis.

They hugged, Phil slapping him on the back. Travis closed the door and sat across from Phil.

"What the hell is this? You never wear a tux to see me! I feel like I'm at my own funeral." This was followed by a raspy cough.

"I've got a problem."

"Problems…the things that get us out of bed in the morning," Phil hitched his pants up and sat back down. "Spell it out."

Travis related the events of the last few hours. Phil listened patiently, glancing once or twice at the TV screen. He asked no questions until Travis had finished.

Only when he was sure Travis was done did he ask a question.

"Have you told Dick?" Dick Callan was Travis's manager.

"No," Travis ran his fingers through his hair, the exhaustion of a sleepless night invading his system. "I wanted to talk to you first. I'm lost here, Phil. Nothing like this has ever happened to me."

"I wouldn't think so. How long have you been at this? A year or two?"

"Four years. I can remember the day you took Dick and me to lunch like it was yesterday."

"Me too. It seems like you were just starting to get the hang of this." Phil was unshaken, a rock. Travis was reeling from what was beginning to look like a meticulously plotted sting against him and his clients; Phil acted as if they were talking about his golf swing.

"I don't know what to do."

"First, tell Dick. Let me ask you some questions though."

"Go ahead."

"What the hell is with this trading account? Most of these hedge guys have a separate account for each client, making this *very* unusual. How did it happen?"

"The way Reg explained it was I would move funds into the trading account from my client accounts, and he'd do all the trades through me. I would get the commissions on the trades, and he'd take a management fee and a percentage of the profits. It was a slow time for me, Dick was crawling down my throat to open accounts, and I was desperate."

"How did you meet this guy Reg?"

"I first met him in his office. He seemed sophisticated enough, knew his way around trading overseas bond futures. He seemed calm, driven, and so focused on making money for his clients that he didn't have time to raise the money to get his hedge fund up to the size it needed to be, and that's where I would come in. Reg could devote his time to trading and research, while I would bring in the client money. This would elevate Reg's fund to a level where he could become a more serious player in the international markets, getting exposure to circles of influence only big money had access to. Nothing seemed out of place… I thought it was a perfect fit."

Travis recoiled at the sound of his own words. This had been what he saw as his ticket to the elite corps of young superstars who graced the covers of trade and financial magazines. These were guys who turned down prospects without a second thought while the others spent their days cold-calling strangers and bugging CPA's for referrals.

Travis felt that he had come to trust someone who'd played him, teased him with visions of money, recognition, a key to the game where the big cats played. Reg had vanished, vaporizing any evidence of his existence.

Travis brought himself back to the moment…"He was referred to me by a client, or so he said when he called me. His story sounded legit. I was anxious to get hooked up with money managers, like you had told me you had done, so I went to go see him."

Phil shook his head, "It was a different time when that worked for me. Those were the days when you scratched their backs and they scratched yours. Nobody complained. Now everybody wants to squeeze you guys out of your last buck, making you jump through hoops while they watch."

Travis leaned forward, elbows on his knees. He struggled to push away the thought that he had allowed himself to become the pawn in Reg's game.

Phil went on with his questions. "Did you ask Dick about this? That's what managers are for, to keep things like this from getting too big, out of control. I would have thought you'd at least come to him and lay it out before going ahead with it."

Travis stared down at his feet. His voice cracked, "No."

Phil leaned in closer, "Did Dick even know about this arrangement?"

"He signed the paperwork, didn't ask too many questions. The truth is, I think he had bigger things going at the time and didn't look too closely."

"That's gonna bite him in the ass now. He could be in as much trouble as you, or even more when it comes down to it."

"How?"

"He signed off on the paperwork. That's why they have these guys, to make sure this doesn't happen and if it does they have somebody to pin it on. He's guilty of what they call 'lack of supervision'. The best thing you've got going is his signature." Phil paused, looked at Travis sideways, "Now wait a second; are there any papers that should have been signed by him but weren't?"

"No."

"Have you told me everything? If you want my help I need to know you're not leaving anything out."

Travis shook his head, "No, that's everything."

"Go tell Dick what you told me, then call me and tell me what your next move is. Dick has to be in the loop for you to get out of this. But call me just the same. If you're in a jam, I know some people who've dealt with things like this before."

Phil sat back and folded his arms.

"Why don't we call them now instead of me going to Dick?"

"Tell Dick will ya?" Phil slapped his knee, startling Travis. "That's the first step; get this thing moving through the proper channels. That isn't too hard, is it?"

"Suppose he fires me on the spot. What then?"

"Kid, that is the *least* of your problems."

Chapter Five

Travis raced out of the parking lot, ran red lights and cut off pedestrians hurrying back to his office; once he got there he sat in his car in the underground garage and held back tears. The exhaustion of being up all night and reliving the story for Phil was starting to wear, and he still had to face Dick.

The branch manager was ex-military, running the office like he thought it was some kind of battleship. Travis gripped the steering wheel and put his face in his arms, he could smell the fear in his sweat.

Walking through the office again he almost forgot he was still in his tux until he saw his reflection in the glass doors opposite him. By now his co-workers knew something had to be up, watching him as if through a glass cage, avoiding any eye contact. He made his way to Dick's office and peered in the door. Dick was winding up a phone call, looked up at Travis and did a double take before motioning him to sit down.

The office was decorated as an extension of Dick's ego. Photos of him on his sailboat, group pictures of his naval unit in front of a gunboat, Dick in scuba outfits, Dick parachuting, Dick shaking hands with the head of the New York Stock Exchange; diplomas and certificates were strategically placed within view of whoever was sitting in front of him.

In a transparent power play, the visitor's chairs in front of the desk were sunk low, giving Dick the psychological advantage of looking down on whoever sat in them.

Travis sat and listened to Dick's side of the conversation while he finished his phone call, "Fifty million, huh? How long did that take?"

Dick had close cropped gray hair, cold steel eyes, and a hard set jaw that rarely smiled. He was wearing a heavily starched white shirt, striped tie

15

and a diver's watch. Travis couldn't remember seeing him in any other color shirt except white.

"Uh, huh," Dick went on. "They know who it is yet?"

What the...? Did Dick already know? Travis looked at Dick's face for a sign, eye contact, an accusing glance.

Nothing.

"They can track these things a lot faster these days. All the footprints people leave with computers, they should be able to find out in a day or so."

Why wasn't he looking at me if he already knew...?

"Have you talked to anyone from the SEC?"

Pause.

"Okay, I gotta run. One of my big hitters just walked in my office wearing a tux, must be important." He laughed and hung up, the smile vanished.

He looked at Travis, "So what can I do for *you*?"

It was not a friendly question, more like what he had to say to get Travis out of his office.

Travis got up, "Mind if I close the door?"

As he did so, he noticed the gaze of Dick's assistant and other co-workers lingering just outside the door.

"What was that conversation about? It sounded kind of bizarre." Travis sat back down. His voice quivered, he held his hands together to keep them from shaking.

"The branch manager of the LA office has an insider trading case on his hands. One of the branch's offshore accounts put 28 million dollars into Caribou Software on margin two days before a merger was announced. The client made over 22 million bucks in two days on inside information. The manager's nervous because the adviser might be implicated in this. If that happens, the manager usually gets hit with a fine or a suspension."

Travis's throat felt thick, the muscles constricting.

He swallowed and leaned forward.

"Do you remember that hedge fund manager I started to do business with?"

"Vaguely. Wasn't he supposed to generate a bunch of commissions for you?"

Travis nodded.

"What happened? Did he lose all the money?"

"Worse. It looks like he stole it."

"Give me that account number." As Dick said this, he leaned over his desk, pulled his keyboard closer, put on glasses and raised his head to peer through them. Travis had known the account number by heart for months; Dick typed in the numbers as Travis spoke.

Dick struck the enter key with enough force to bounce the keyboard on the desk and sat back in his chair. The color drained from his face.

Control quickly returned. Dick leaned forward and ripped off the glasses in a well-rehearsed motion. "Why don't you tell me how in God's name you let this happen?"

Travis sat back and let out the breath he'd been holding. He let his mind take him back to the beginning, the day of the phone call from the mysterious hedge fund manager Reginald Crae.

Travis found it easier to talk if he kept his eyes on the patterned carpet while he told the story, avoiding Dick's glare.

"I originally got this call from a man who said he was referred to me from my client, Mrs. Hanratty. She was in Europe for a few months so I couldn't call her to thank her for the referral, anyway this guy has me go out to see him at his office."

"This being this Crae fellow."

"Right. So I get to his office in Pacific Heights, it's all wired up with trading monitors, phone lines, the whole set up. He tells me he's been running this hedge fund for wealthy investors, and has made a lot of money specializing in certain types of transactions."

"What kind?"

"Treasury-bond futures and option strategies that he'd do in front of the fed open market meetings. The fed meets about every six weeks, and that's usually when he makes most of the money. He had an uncanny ability to make money for his clients off of the volatility that came after an interest rate move."

"What did he want with you?"

Travis sat up as he continued, "He was new at this and didn't have a large client base. What he was looking for was somebody to raise money for him so he could concentrate on his trading. He kept talking about needing a bigger pool of funds to get into some overseas transactions he wanted to put together; but he didn't want to take his eye off the ball to go out and market himself."

"Why you?"

"He said he heard from Mrs. Hanratty that I was a straight shooter so he made me an offer: I raise money for him, he does these trades through me, and we both get what we want. I earn commissions, and he gets a bigger hedge fund to manage."

"You check this guy out at all?"

"Yes, his track record was right on target, and everything seemed legit…"

Dick held up a hand, "You know we offer hedge funds that are already sanctioned by our due diligence people. Why did you have to be a hero and go do this on your own?"

"I know, it's just that this arrangement sounded like it was my ticket to the next level. There are lots of brokers that hook up with a money manager early in their careers and it pays off, sometimes big. I thought this was my opportunity. Plus, you were putting a lot of pressure on me at the time to get my production up. I needed this."

"Gimme a break. Go on." Dick leaned back in his chair and crossed his arms.

The speaker phone on Dick's desk blared with the voice of his assistant, *"Mr. Callan, I have Rex on line two…"*

"No calls for a while please, tell him I'll get back to him." Dick looked back at Travis, and cocked his head in condescension, "I'm listening."

"We set up this trading account. The idea was, I put client money in there, he manages it, and we'd handle the accounting and get the commissions."

"Sounds like a very unusual arrangement, I can see how you'd be vulnerable to get sucked into this. It's too bad you didn't check him out more thoroughly, or better yet, use one of our in-house hedge funds."

Travis winced, blame closed in on him. Dick's innuendo painted a clear picture that Travis was going to be solely responsible for what happened.

"How much money did you put with him?"

"I moved about 54 million dollars of client assets into the trading account."

"I assume you had them sign some kind of trading authority and power of attorney papers that gave Reg carte blanche to do what he wanted with the money?"

Travis nodded.

"And I assume you got me to sign these authorizations?"

Another nod, this one slower.

Dick looked down at him like a school teacher about to send a student to the principal's office.

"You're so far in over your head you don't even know…"

Travis stared blankly at Dick. He needed to get Dick on his side but he felt like he was slowly being led to the gallows.

"I need to know what to do here. The money was just wired out last night. What can we do while the trail is still fresh?"

"What do you think, you're Sherlock Holmes or something? You think you've got problems now? My ass will be in a sling because of your greed and stupidity. In case you forgot, we have our annual audit on Friday. This shows up and I get slammed for what's known as 'lack of supervision'. That means a fine, possible suspension, and with the size of this the SEC and the FBI will be snooping around. Since you've never had to deal with them, let me just tell you…when those guys show up with their laptops and thick

18

glasses, you'll feel like you're in a snake pit. It really gets fun when the press digs in."

Dick leaned forward, put an elbow on the desk and pointed his finger at Travis, "You may think we're in this together, but I swear to you I'll make sure you go down for this one. The only thing you have going for you right now is my signature is on all the paperwork, and that makes me as guilty as you. I don't know how I let those slip by, I'm sure it happened when I was putting out fires around here and was too distracted to give them the attention they deserved. I've got better things to do around here than babysit idiotic brokers trying to take short-cuts and making my life miserable."

Dick stood up, hands on his hips, the skin on his face tighter, tendons sticking out from his neck.

"Between you and me, you're taking this one up the ass. Now get out of here and let me talk to our ops manager about this. Stay in your office."

Travis went to the men's room to hide and get his thoughts together. While the session with Dick confirmed everything Travis had to fear, in some strange way he felt better that the initial confrontation was behind him.

He looked in the bathroom mirror, rubbing his unshaven, hollow, sleep-deprived face, and decided the first chance he got he'd have to go home and take a shower, eat something and regroup. He knew he needed to stay close to the office until Dick talked to him again, meaning he had to do something to pass the time. Travis splashed cold water on his face, dried his hands and walked back to his office.

As he sat down he noticed he was followed closely by his assistant, Daphne.

"Got a minute?" She smiled as she asked this, and without waiting for an answer, sat on the client chair across from his desk and crossed her legs.

Travis was about to say no, but when he looked at Daphne he saw something he'd never paid attention to. She was giving him a flirtatious look for the first time in the four months she'd been there. Her skirt was hiked up and for a split-second Travis forgot what he was going through.

"Sure, what's up?" He looked at her legs as they crossed again, at the same time trying to pretend he was still looking in her eyes.

She kept smiling.

"Is everything okay, Travis?"

"Some trades have gone against me, nothing I can't handle." He waved a hand in the air as if his problem was a small insect.

"How are things with you and Beth?"

He hadn't thought of his girlfriend since he pulled up the account last night.

"Not that great, now that you ask. Can we talk about this later? I'm kind of up against it right now."

"Sure." She walked out, and he watched her legs from behind as she did.

Daphne looked back and smiled.

The phone rang.

"Hey Travis, Dave Simmons here. Got a sec?"

Dave was one of the original investors in the hedge fund.

Sleep deprived, straining to focus, "Sure Dave, what's up?"

"Anything you need to tell me?"

Did he know…?

"Excuse me?"

"The big Fed meeting coming up. Do you have any idea how our hedge fund is set up for it?"

He covered the mouthpiece with his hand, held his breath and closed his eyes.

Travis let the breath back out before talking, "He plays it pretty close to the vest, even with me. I don't really have anything to tell you."

"You still feel pretty good about this guy?"

"Sure, why?" The line was crossed. Once the deception began it would multiply.

"I was thinking of putting more money into it, do you think that's a good idea?"

Yes on any other day, add to the winners, get rid of the losers, keep upgrading the portfolios. "Let's hold off until after the Fed meeting Dave, I don't want you to get over concentrated in any one investment, no matter how good it looks."

"Okay, but keep me in mind. I have some money that I want to put to work."

"I'll have something for you in the next day or so."

They said their goodbyes. Travis sat back in his chair and punched up his computer screen, looking for something to occupy his thoughts until he could talk to Dick again. He saw nothing but the white noise of stocks drifting on a trendless day.

His interoffice line rang, Dick. "Come in."

Travis stood in front of Dick's desk.

"48 hours."

"Excuse me?"

"That's how long you have to get the money back." Dick sat smugly in his leather chair, dripping condescension. "You get it back here in 48 hours and we pretend this never happened, saves your ass and mine. If you fail, I have no choice but to terminate you. After that I'll put you in front of this thing so I don't take the fall. Any contact between you and this firm will be severed immediately, and you'll be under the jurisdiction of the FBI as well as the SEC."

Travis stepped back, reaching out to the bookcase to steady himself.

"How would I even begin? I mean, I'm as much in the dark as you are, the account's empty, what do you want me to do? Fly to Puerto Rico or wherever this guy is and put a gun to his head?"

"I've briefed our ops manager Wendy on all she needs to know to put you in touch with our back-office people. They're the ones who can give you the best shot at tracking this. What I need you to do is keep the big picture between you and me. We don't have time for any of the standard formalities such as SAR's, background checks and so on. You bring my name into this or any conversation we've had today and you go down on the spot for this. They will be looking at me to see what I knew and when I knew it. Right now, as far as you're concerned, you haven't told me and you're pursuing this on your own. Are we completely clear on this?"

Travis could only nod. The words Dick was saying wrapped around him and crept under his clothes. He shivered, tightening his grip on the bookcase.

Dick went on, "Don't tell anybody the whole story, just enough to get what you need from them. My ass is still on the line here and since I'm giving you this break, you can return the favor by keeping a lid on this. It's almost as if somebody knew my audit was coming up, and that I have as much to lose as you do…idiotic compliance people will be all over me. I should have seen this coming. Why my bonus has to be tied to what punks like you do is beyond me. When the audit is over you and I are going to have a long talk."

Travis shifted, unsure of what he was supposed to do. "So I get with Wendy and call the back office?"

"Do what you have to do, Travis." Dick picked up his glasses, put them on and dialed the phone. He stopped halfway through the dialing and looked at his watch, "47 hours and 58 minutes - use it wisely."

He walked down the hall and into Wendy's office. She was on the phone and motioned with her hand for him to sit down.

She finished her conversation, folded her hands on her desk and looked at Travis. Wendy was a young, perky redhead and her large glasses made her look like she should be working in a library or a research lab. She was usually nice enough to Travis in a warm, maternal sort of way.

The warmth was gone.

"Got a minute?" Travis asked.

She looked up without answering.

"I need to start tracing a wire transfer that was made in error. We need to get the funds back here and it doesn't look like it'll be easy."

She held up her hand. "Here's where we are on this. I put a trace on the wires Dick gave me and I expect to hear from our back-office people in New York later this morning as to where the money is. Dick can tell me where to go from there."

Travis let out a breath for the first time in what seemed like hours. "Okay, what do you need from me?"

She shook her head, "Give me at least an hour though. These back-office people are slow, and it's lunchtime back there." She put her head down and picked up a pen, started writing as if he were no longer there.

Chapter Six

Travis went to the garage, pulled onto the street and headed to Phil's again. Although Dick had told him to stay in the office the idea of killing hours while evading questions from clients and co-workers felt like he'd be walking in quicksand.

Driving the BMW felt like the only thing he had control over. Banking through the tight turns, shifting down on the hills in San Francisco, this was something he could do well. Putting the vehicle through its paces gave him a brief respite from the glaring fact that his career was dismantling before his eyes.

The receptionist signed him in again and told him to walk back. Phil was surprised. "Twice in one day? You'd think you were trying to get into my will or something. Did you talk to Dick yet?"

Travis nodded, "He gave me 48 hours to get the money back and he has our back-office people working on it as we speak. You sure were right about Dick, all he cares about is how this will affect his bonus."

"He's from the old school Travis. He's the first one to talk about principles and ethics…" Phil held up a gnarled finger, "except when it comes to him."

Phil sat back and let this sink in before continuing, "What happens after 48 hours?"

"If I don't get the money back I'm fired, charges are filed, the SEC gets brought in, the works."

"Remember, I know some people that can help with this kind of thing. Think you'll need a little more muscle than those back office clowns?"

"Dick mentioned something about an SAR. What's that?"

Phil waved a hand to brush the thought away, "It stands for suspicious activity report, and it's *way* too late in the game for that. It puts on record that Dick was looking into this and went through the proper procedures. I tell you, he is out to cover his ass - and his ass alone. Don't worry though, there's a way through this. Think of it like crossing a river... the other side looks fine...it's just those treacherous rapids and slippery boulders we have to get through to make it."

Travis slowed his pacing, the tensions of the last hours felt smaller at the sound of Phil's voice.

"What do you have in mind?" Travis asked.

"Let me make a call. I have a guy owes me a favor. He knows his way around this sort of thing."

"Who is he?"

Phil leaned back in his chair and looked up at the ceiling, "His name is Chaz. He used to work in international banking until he got involved in a money laundering scheme with some wealthy Middle Eastern types. He ended up taking the fall and spent five years in one of those country-club prisons. Turns out he kept all his connections and they respect him for keeping his mouth shut. Now he consults for international corporations on how to prevent illegal wire transfers, money laundering, and so on. He lives down in Puerto Rico. They say if money moves, Chaz can smell it. Let me see what he can do for us."

Phil placed a call, got a recording, looked in his address book and dialed another number. Chaz answered.

Phil smiled at the sound of Chaz's voice, "Yeah Chaz, still kicking around the retirement home... No not golf, I'd rather beat the old farts around here at poker and use the money to take the nurses to the clubs downtown."

There was some laughter, more small talk and the requisite catching up before the reason for a call out of the blue. Phil briefed Chaz on what Travis had told him, and Chaz asked him questions such as who was involved, names of accounts, and times of transfers. They promised to keep in better touch with each other, and Phil gave him his retirement home number as well as Travis's office phone before hanging up.

"Well, what'd he say?"

"You're screwed."

Silence.

"Just kidding. Look, he'll make some inquiries and call you back at your office. You'll be there, right?"

"Yeah, thanks Phil. I have to get back anyway."

They said their goodbyes and Travis headed back to the office.

As Travis walked back onto the 10th floor the curious gazes from his co-workers had no effect on him anymore. He had no time for this and it dwarfed in size to his real problems.

He sat at his desk and pretended to look busy while he waited.

After what felt like an eternal wait as the minutes dragged, a call came in. Chaz.

"Can you get the original wiring instructions and read them over the phone to me?"

The voice had a slight British accent, possibly South African. It was the voice of a hunter, shoot-to-kill.

"Sure, hold on."

Travis went to Wendy's office and told her he had someone at headquarters who owed him a favor and could he see a copy of the wiring instructions. She reached over to the in-basket on the corner of her desk, pulled out a manila folder from under the documents on top and handed it to him.

At the bottom in dark strokes lay the telltale signature of Reginald Crae. Though he'd stolen millions with the stroke of a pen, he hadn't done anything legally wrong since the account was in the name of Reg's hedge fund, with Reg as sole trustee. The firm had simply received wiring instructions from a trustee and followed them efficiently. This occurred tens of thousands of times a day all over the world.

In any brokerage firm this kind of wire would need a manager's approval. Since it was wired Friday afternoon Dick had already left and Bernie the assistant manager signed off on it. Bernie didn't know what he was doing anyway and was more concerned about his afternoon tee-time than filling in for Dick. Everything went as if conceived and plotted by a cold, calculating mastermind.

Travis went back to his desk and picked up the phone.

"Okay, got it."

"Read me the bank name and routing numbers."

Travis held the slip of fax paper and read off the page, "Banco de San Juan, Account SE-1489558, routing number 1440-035699."

"Okay, and the exact amount of money?"

"It just says 'all available cash'."

"I need to know exactly how much he got."

Travis looked up at the account activity on his computer, a task he'd done dozens of time since the night before in the hopes this would all go away.

"Here it is: Fifty-four million, three-hundred sixty-seven thousand, nine-hundred fifty-five dollars, and 35 cents."

"I'll call you right back. Stay there." The line went dead.

More waiting.

The broker next to him hung his arms over the partition dividing the bullpen offices that Travis shared with the other newer brokers. Private offices on the perimeter were reserved for only the higher echelon, the big hitters, the guys who Travis thought he would be like...until today. "So what's your big hedge fund guru doing in front of the fed meeting?"

Oh God...

"Is he betting they raise rates?" The broker persisted. "That worked pretty well last time."

Travis spoke from the part of his mind reserved for lies, "He hasn't made any moves yet, seems to be laying low."

"Probably not a bad strategy. Whose research does he use?"

"He goes it alone, you know. Like most of these guys he's a maverick, a lone wolf." He wanted to walk away from this conversation but he had to sit there and wait for Chaz to call.

"You feel good enough about this guy to keep putting money with him?"

When was this going to stop?

The phone rang.

Kent, the property manager.

"You're looking for information on Reg Crae?"

While he was glad to get out of the conversation with his co-worker, the broker was still hanging his arms over the partition while Travis had to talk to Kent.

He turned away and lowered his voice.

"He seems to have disappeared and he has something of mine. I was calling to see if you had any idea where he is."

"It doesn't sound like I can add much to what you already know. He paid for six months in advance, Friday was his last day and he was gone by noon. He kept quiet, never a complaint about him from any of the other tenants."

"Did he leave any forwarding address?"

"Nothing. He had a P.O. Box on the lease agreement, but other than that I'm afraid I don't have much for you to go on. Did he do anything illegal while he was a tenant?"

"It looks that way. Didn't he have a deposit coming back that he wanted you to send to him?"

"No, see he paid six months in advance, which is unusual. A cashier's check if I remember, so I didn't ask for a deposit under that arrangement. What exactly was he doing, can you tell me?"

Travis looked at the broker next to him, standing there idiotically waiting, no respect for confidentiality.

"I can't go into that right now, but I may have to call you back later."

"Do you want me to contact the police? On the other hand, I really should get our attorney in the loop on this. It sounds like that's my next move from a liability standpoint."

"Don't do that."

Travis tried to stare down the guy next to him. It was obvious he smelled blood in the water Travis was swimming in and he hung around to watch the mauling.

"Don't do what?" Kent asked.

"Call the police."

"I'll leave that one up to you, but I will call our attorney and see how he wants to handle this. Is it alright if he calls you?"

"Sure."

Travis hung up. The co-worker came back over to the partition and leaned over, "Trouble there, big hitter?"

"Just a little issue with a speeding ticket." He pretended to dial the phone again to get this guy away from him.

When would he be able to stop lying? The charade pulled at his nerve endings. He wasn't sure how long he could do this, let alone keep track of who he'd told what lies to.

The phone again. "Hello, Travis Black."

"Okay Travis," Chaz started, "you sitting down?"

The broker was still there, waiting. Travis put his hand over the mouth piece, "Can you excuse me for a few minutes? This is an important call."

The broker sipped his coffee, made a cursory move a step or two away but still within earshot.

"What is it Chaz?" Travis brought his voice down to a whisper.

"Anything you want to tell me sport?"

"Excuse me?"

"Come on, don't waste my time. This is a favor for Phil. I don't know you and right now that suits me just fine. But you start jerking me around I'll make sure your head never stops spinning."

Travis covered the mouthpiece of the phone and hissed at his coworker, "Do you mind?"

He moved a step further, sipped his coffee and pretended to look away.

"What the hell are you talking about?"

A pause while it sounded like Chaz took a breath before saying what he wanted to say.

"Now would be a good time to tell me if you're in on this."

"What?"

"Level with me now or I walk away. Are you a part of this? I'm not here to arrest you, but I *absolutely* need to know before we go any further."

"Know what? What are you getting at?"

Travis turned his head and saw Dick and Wendy headed his way.

"What I'm about to tell you will answer all these questions."

Stopping front of his cubicle, Dick looked at his watch and put his hands on his hips. He and Wendy stared at Travis.

"Go on."

"The money was wired from the hedge fund into an account in Puerto Rico, from there it moved to the Cayman Islands…"

"Okay…" Travis didn't know what was coming next. "What else?"

"The account it went to in Puerto Rico is a corporate shell…"

Chaz's voice tightened.

"…*in the name of Travis Black and Associates.*"

Travis squeezed the phone until his knuckles were white and looked up at Dick.

The room began to spin.

Chapter Seven

The words ripped through him like a hot bullet. Dick stepped forward, "Anything you want to tell me Travis?"

Travis couldn't open his mouth. He pretended to put Chaz on hold and left the phone on the desk.

"Travis, have you got anything?"

It took every ounce of will just to get a coherent sentence out, "Nothing yet...why?"

"Wendy here says you asked for the wiring instructions, any progress?"

"Waiting on some people to call me back...anything on your end?"

Wendy spoke up, "Our internal fraud division is in touch with the wiring department, they're getting the names the funds went to so they can start pursuit. Right now it looks like it went to some shell corporation but it's the name behind it that they want."

Travis listened, trying to hear what was coming. It was difficult to read them, *did they already know?*

"They think they'll have something in a few minutes."

Travis blinked, staring, speechless.

Dick went on, "These things always take longer than you want, to us it's meaningful but to them it's something standing in the way of lunch. Let's keep each other informed of any new data we get when we get it. You with me Travis?"

Wendy looked at Travis, the unsaid accusations carved into the icy glare.

"Of course."

They walked away.

Travis put the phone back to his ear, turned his head away and down towards the level of the desk.

His words came out in a desperate hush, "I'm still trying to process what you just told me Chaz. Why the hell is the money in my name?"

"Hold up there, it's not in your name. It was put in your name first. Now it's somewhere in the Cayman's."

"I need you to explain what this means."

"You've not only been ripped off, but you've been set up. Whoever did this wants you to be a suspect while they finish getting the money out of the Caymans, that way deflecting suspicion away from them and on to you. I hate to say this but this guy's a pro Travis. He's covered all the angles."

"What do we do now?"

"You're okay until your internal fraud division finds this out. Once it gets back to your local manager you're pretty much going down until you can prove you didn't do it. They'll put the hammer down hard at first, and…you need to know…it's going to get worse before it gets better."

"But I didn't do anything!"

"I know, but to them it looks like it. I'd lay low if I were you, let me keep working this on my end. Meanwhile stay near a phone, and give me your cell number."

Travis gave him the number, hung up and called his girlfriend Beth at her office. The voice mail picked up. He tried her cell, same result. He decided to get some air and walk to her office.

She worked a few blocks down the street and he needed the diversion. Travis poked his head into Wendy's office. "Just stepping out for a few, call me on my cell if you hear anything." Wendy looked at him but didn't answer.

Beth worked at one of the trendy graphic design firms just off of California Street. They had survived the dot-com bust and were highly sought in the ever changing sneakers and jeans fashion business. Some of their designs and images had won prestigious awards and Beth was one of their top designers. He put his hands in his pockets against the chill of a San Francisco morning and walked the two blocks.

Looking down California Street to the bay, a thin wisp of fog had been left hanging over the water. Dark, crawling shadows of tanker ships sliced through it on their way under the Bay Bridge from Oakland. Foghorns, seagulls, cable car bells, these sounds were lost on Travis as the weight of what he was into crawled around in his head. Mulling over the events of the last hours made him want to run. Run until he couldn't run anymore. Run his lungs out, then run further.

He quickened his pace.

Travis entered Beth's building where a security guard asked him to sign in. As he did so he briefly thought of putting down a fictitious name, keep

Beth out of this. *What if they found out he visited her, would they arrest her too?* He stayed with his name, handed the clipboard back to the guard, went to the elevators and punched in the fourth floor.

He walked through the frosted glass doors of Cutting Edge Designs, went to Beth's studio which was a well lit room overlooking the Bay Bridge, drafting tables set at an angle, computer terminal with a screen saver scrolling across, pencils, colored pens, angular drawing tools, and the smell of art. On the walls hung previous designs from designer jeans ads, framed, looking out, teasing you.

Beth was nowhere in sight.

Travis walked over to the reception area and asked the girl behind the desk where Beth was. When the girl opened her mouth to speak Travis was caught off guard by a pierced tongue with a pea sized silver ball stuck right in the middle of it. He'd lived in the city most of his adult life but this was still something he couldn't get used to.

"She uhh, wait, you're her boyfriend, right?"

"Yes."

The girl with the pierced tongue took a pencil and started twirling her ink-black hair with it. Her pasty white face, black lips and vacant stare made Travis feel he was in some kind of strange dream.

"It's kinda weird, she hasn't been in today, and we haven't heard from her. Usually she's pretty good at letting us know. Is she sick?"

"I don't think so, I was with her last night and she seemed fine. She's usually here by nine or so right?"

"Yeah." The girl looked at the clock on the wall, it was well after ten. "I don't know, can you, like let us know if you hear from her?"

Travis was trying to put all this together, *who could he talk to? Where was Beth?* He stared at her, not knowing what to say or how to respond.

"Sir, are you all right?"

"Excuse me?"

"You look like you're not feeling well, do you want some coffee or water?"

"No. I've just had a really weird night."

"Nice outfit." She smiled, looked him up and down as she said this. Travis looked down and saw that he was still in his tux.

"Okay, can you call me if you see her as well?"

The drive to Beth's flat was only a few minutes and it was that brief lull in traffic between the morning rush and the lunch fest. He gunned up California, over to Webster, double parked in front of the familiar redone façade that blended in with the rest of the buildings on the street, and pressed the buzzer to her flat.

No answer. He pressed the other buttons…nothing.

The building was mainly a young professional residence, and the few neighbors he had met were not the type to be at home on a weekday morning. He stood there, paced in front of the door and tried her home number on his cell again, nothing.

He was ready to get back to his car when and an older well-dressed Asian couple wheeling several plastic grocery bags in a rickety folding cart shuffled to the door and fished out a key.

"Excuse me, you live here? I seem to have left my key at the…"

Silent, they went about letting themselves in as if he were invisible. He followed, they didn't hold the door nor did they make it hard for him to get in. They picked up their pace in an effort to distance themselves from someone who they didn't understand, and was now in their building.

Travis raced up the flight of stairs to Beth's second floor flat and knocked on the door.

No answer.

He knocked harder, tried the knob, nothing.

He hadn't reached a stage with Beth where she felt like giving him a key, and she didn't have one of his. This arrangement worked, yet Travis was starting to realize he had come to depend on Beth as a sounding board for his work. She had been supportive, encouraging to the extent that he wanted to do better *for her*. Being with her had become part of the reason he wanted to get to the next level, not so much to impress her but to meet the high expectations she had of him.

He knocked again.

The door next to hers opened and an older lady peered out still in curlers. Travis looked over at her and started to ask if she had seen Beth. The woman pulled her head back in and closed the door, locking and sliding chains from inside. *What the…?*

On his way up he'd noticed the sign on apartment number one had said 'manager'. He went back downstairs and knocked. A male voice answered, "What is it?"

"I'm a friend of Beth Wagner's, she's in one of your flats upstairs. Have you seen her today?"

"No."

"It's kind of important, anything you can tell me?"

"Nope."

Travis hated this part of the city. In San Mateo, down on the peninsula where he'd grown up people talked to you, helped you. Up here it was every man for himself and keep your troubles away from me.

He got back in his car, peeled away from the curb and started asking himself questions out loud. *"Where the hell had she gone? Did she even give a shit about me?"*

He rounded the corner onto California Street and headed back towards the office, the main entrance to the garage looming into view as he crested the top of Nob Hill. In the background behind it the sparkling waters of the bay changed from the morning gray to the bright blue that it would stay until dusk.

What Travis saw next brought cold fingers under his collar, gripping his neck. In front of the building were three police cars with lights flashing, parked at angles to block entrance or exit from the garage. Three men in suits stood next to them, pointing to the street and back to the garage. Two others, in blue police uniforms, were stringing wide yellow tape across the entrance. In large black letters it read, 'Crime Scene- Do Not Cross'.

Chapter Eight

T ravis made a quick left turn into an alley filled with newsstands, florist kiosks, and delivery trucks. He pulled out his cell and called Daphne on her direct extension.

"What's going on up there?"

Brief silence. "Why don't you tell me."

"What? I'm not kidding, what's going on up there?"

"Where are you?"

"What is this? You gotta trust me Daphne, whatever you're being told I did isn't true. Are the police up there?"

"I can't talk right now." The line went dead.

It seemed like only seconds had passed and the landscape was now treacherous, rocky, slippery. Travis decided to go home, get some things and either drive around or check into a hotel and lay low. The last thing he needed was to get arrested before he could find the money. He backed out of the side street, maneuvered around a delivery truck going the opposite way and headed the other direction up California Street. Checking his rear view mirror revealed the same police action he'd seen moments ago.

Travis picked up his cell and dialed Chaz.

"The cops are outside my office Chaz, what do you think's going on?"

"Are you in the office?"

"No, I went out for a few minutes, came back and the entrance has three police cars in front of it with guys in suits wandering around."

Travis jumped a yellow light, narrowly missing a bus as he crossed Van Ness.

"This can mean only one thing. They've somehow found out that the money was in your name and called the authorities before you could flee."

"I don't understand, Dick said I had 48 hours."

"Things have changed. That was before he saw the account titled in your name. It started out that Reg was the bad guy, now they think it's you and are moving accordingly. What are you doing right now?"

"I'm going home to get some stuff and check into a hotel for a few days, lay low and stay away from the cops. I'm just turning the corner now, I'll call you back once I…"

"What is it?"

Travis had stopped the car a block from his apartment and slouched low in his seat. The speed with which this was escalating had Travis reeling.

"The cops are in front of my place. There's three cars, lights flashing, what the…?"

"Stay calm Travis, just back away from the situation and let's keep our heads about us."

"That's easy for you to say, you're down in the Bahamas while I'm turning into a fugitive everywhere I look, I didn't do what they think I did and I can't even get into my own place. You expect me to stay calm? I don't even know you!"

"Travis, I've been where you are now. I don't know how much Phil told you about me but you've got to trust me here. Stay in control and back away from the situation."

Travis backed his car away and into a side street, turned around and pulled away from the scene.

"Okay, I just have one problem. How am I supposed to get this money back if the cops are after me? I can't even get to my office now."

Chaz's voice stayed calm, reasoned, while Travis spat questions in desperation.

"The situation has simply escalated to another level Travis. There isn't a problem out there that can't be solved."

"What do you want me to do, find the money with my cell phone? I'm stranded out here Chaz."

"Stay in your car, keep driving. Don't do anything out of the ordinary, keep off of bridges, don't use your credit cards and I'll call you back in a few minutes. I have an idea."

"Why keep off of bridges, you think I'm gonna jump?"

He heard Chaz let out a short breath, a chuckle in the face of danger.

"The toll booths have cameras mounted over them that take pictures of your license plates as you drive through. You're a fugitive Travis…start thinking like one."

Chapter Nine

Travis went back to Phil's. He and Chaz stood out as the only two people who trusted him, believed him, who wanted to help. He pulled into the lot and parked in the far corner where he would be shielded from the main entrance by a delivery truck. He tried Daphne one more time.

"Please don't hang up on me."

"Give me a reason not to."

"I didn't do it."

"Okay, sure, but you wired the money to yourself, tell me what I'm supposed to think." Her voice was hushed, echoing through what sounded like her hand over the phone.

"I was set up by Reg Crae."

"The hedge fund guy?"

"Yes. He wired the funds to an account in my name then to some other account in the Cayman Islands. He did this to throw the scent off of him, and you have to believe me I had no part in this."

"Sounds like a good story."

"What? This isn't a story, why would I be calling you trying to clear my name if I did this? Don't you think I'd be in the Caribbean by now collecting the money if I stole it? Can't you see?"

Travis checked his rear view mirror for any sign of a police tail. He turned around and backed into the spot to have a better view and afford a quick exit. Chaz's words echoed, *'You're a fugitive Travis, start thinking like one'*.

"I want to believe you Travis, I really do."

"How can you not? My life has just been flushed down the toilet and I'm on the phone trying to get you on my side."

"You just want to know what's happening up here, that's why."

"You have me there, I do want to know. I also need somebody on my side, I have no idea where Beth is, this guy that can help me lives in the Bahamas, and I'm sitting here in a parking lot trying to convince you I'm not a thief."

"Where's Beth?"

"Not a clue. This is all too weird, it's like the world has conspired against me all in the same 24 hour period. I'm in the twilight zone."

"Did she mention anything that might give you an idea where she went?"

"Nothing."

From where he was parked he could see the main street traffic through the trees lining the sidewalk, as well as anyone who pulled into the lot. He couldn't tell if it was his paranoid imagination or if it was natural for police cars to patrol the area. None pulled in, however enough drove by to keep him on edge.

"It's like the 10 minutes before the O.J. Simpson verdict around here."

"What do you mean?"

"Nobody's working, there's plainclothes cops walking around, your computer's been taken apart and some guys took it to the conference room to look at the hard drive I guess. And Dick's strutting around in a panic."

"How did all this get out?"

"The way I hear it is Wendy traced the wire herself, found out it went into your name so she went to Dick. He said to sit on it for 48 hours and see what you could come up with. Then she said 'either you call the cops or I do, we've been ripped off and I'm not standing around while you try and collect a bonus for looking the other way'."

"Did you actually hear this?"

"No, some others did, but you know how this stuff goes, gossip like this travels fast."

"What else do you know?"

"They've passed out these forms for all of us to fill out saying how we know you, what kind of relationship we have with you, where we were Friday night and Sunday night. Also, they got your phone records. There were a bunch of calls to the bank in Puerto Rico that your money went to."

"I had to make those calls for Reg, every so often he'd have me call them to verify wiring instructions for some euro dollar investments he was planning."

"That doesn't make sense. Why would he have you call down there when you could make the euro investment from the trading account anyway?"

Travis sat in his car, the events of the last twelve hours firing in his brain in random sequences trying to make sense out of the tiniest inconsistency, tying anything and everything together and coming up with the same conclusion…he had become the patsy, the fall guy, the one who would be going down.

"Come to think of it, he never did wire money or use that account until now. It's like he wanted those calls to show up on my phone record to further implicate me. This thing goes way deeper than I thought."

"What are you going to do?"

"I don't know, I may turn myself in and let the cops work it out, or try and get this guy in the Caribbean that I've been in touch with to come up with something. The cops have my place staked out, I need to lay low, have a plan, maybe check into a hotel. I'm sort of driving around trying to come up with answers."

"Why *wouldn't* you turn yourself in?"

"I'm probably going to, I just can't do it right now. I didn't do this and I feel like I've got guns pointed at me and I don't want it to get any worse. I'm just driving until I decide what to do. I need some time to think."

The line was silent as he sat there mentally watching his life hit an atom splitter while Daphne took in what she could, sorting out who and what to believe.

"So…you need a place to stay?"

"Yeah."

"I've got room at my place, why don't I get some food on the way home, meet me there, I'll run out and get you some clothes. You can hang there until you come up with something."

"You would do that?"

"I told you I want to believe you, I do, and I want to help you."

"I don't know what to say, that's probably the best news I've heard all day."

They made arrangements, she gave him directions, Travis hung up and called Chaz.

"Any new developments for me? You said you had an idea, I need something to go on."

"I've tracked what happened, and this guy has done this before. I still have some pretty good connections in money laundering, and Reg is a pro. His scam is so simple, yet takes steel nuts to pull it off. His genius lies in its simplicity." The traces of professional respect as Chaz talked were not lost on Travis.

"Alright, let's get back on track here…can we get the money back?"

"Yes, but you need to get down here to do it, this can't happen over the phone."

"I need to go to the Cayman Islands?"

"Puerto Rico to be exact."

"I thought you said the money's in the Cayman's."

"It is now, but this guy has a pattern, he's found some bankers he can trust, he uses them regularly and he doesn't alter his moves. This is where you need to start trusting that I know what I'm doing."

If Travis left the country now he might as well turn himself in. He'd look like a fugitive on the run who just stole over 50 million, and in trying to undo what Reg had done he'd get himself arrested at an airport.

"I'm turning myself in, let the cops sort all this out." As these words left his mouth he felt the waters part, his breathing came easier, weight cascading off his shoulders.

"There's just one problem with that."

"What?"

"I'll let you in on a few secrets about money laundering."

"I'm listening."

"Not only has Reg stolen your clients' money, but he has to 'wash' it so to speak, so that when he brings it back into the US it will appear to have come from legitimate sources. If he tries to move the money in increments of less than 10 grand at a time to stay under the radar of the IRS and the DEA that'll take him years, by then he knows we'll track him down…not to mention it's a pain in the ass. That means making 4 deposits every day in different banks for 5 years. What guys like him do is channel the money in blocks of several hundred thousand here and there into mutual fund accounts, online casinos, brokerage accounts, shell corporations set up exclusively for this purpose, and so on. The effect is the money stays liquid, yet he's not moving cash so the IRS doesn't notice, and it ends up in places that are legitimate holding places for sums of that size. That completes the laundering cycle, it's clean, untraced from its original source, and usable in very short notice."

"Won't he have to fill out those forms the IRS uses to declare more than $10,000 in a transaction?"

"Those are only required with cash, cold hard currency. This money is being moved over the wires and it's done all day and night around the globe."

"Won't they be able to trace the funds back to their original source?"

"What they'll find is that money was moved from the trading account to your name in Puerto Rico, then to a shell account in the Cayman's, then back to Puerto Rico, and finally to these accounts in the US. Is there anything more they need to nail you? I know you feel foolish for getting sucked in but believe me, it happens to the best of us and you're up against someone who stays up nights planning this."

"But won't they see Reg's name on the account in the Cayman's? That could clear me."

"Based on his past moves, he has a step in the money laundering process that shakes the trail anyway. Even if you could prove the account in the Cayman's has his name on it, from there the trail will vanish as if he were walking through a river. Meanwhile, you are left with nothing."

"I still don't see why I shouldn't let the cops sort this out."

"It's very simple Travis. While you're down at the police station trying to explain this, Reg will be moving the money from the Cayman's back to Puerto Rico, into a different name, and from there to these mutual funds and online casinos. The money will be dispersed into forty or fifty different places in as many different identities while you're still getting fingerprinted. My advice to you is clear your innocence and get the money back for your clients instead of handing yourself over to the cops. The money will be vanishing literally as they take your mug shot. If not then, it'll happen while you're being strapped to a lie detector."

Travis was silent, his mind piecing together exactly what he was involved in. It was clear that no matter which way he went this was a defining moment of decision making that would change everything.

Chaz went on, "Do you have any idea what the odds are for recovering the money once it's dispersed into all these little accounts scattered from here to Jersey? Zip. Use your head sport! The money's ready to disappear, the cops have a suspect handed to them with all kinds of incriminating evidence, how could you want to do it any other way? This is where you show yourself and your clients what you're made of. Reach down inside and find the strength Travis, I've been where you are right now, and I can save you all kinds of anguish and dead ends."

"What's in this for you Chaz?"

"I was wondering when you'd ask that. Let's just say I owe Phil a big favor and he asked me to help you out to square things up. He thinks a lot of you, and that's all I need to hear."

"I still don't like it. I come clean, tell my story, they handle it."

"Yeah, and the money's gone. You're in jail while they ask you what you really did with it, and your clients… while they might not say it to your face will hate you for the rest of their lives. They will always wonder, 'did he take it?' Did he hide it somewhere?'."

Travis kept thinking. The fork in the road was dark on both sides, the images Chaz brought up put a spin on this he hadn't seen before.

"You really think I'll go to jail even though I didn't do it?"

"Look at it from their side Travis, phone records, bank accounts, it looks like you've spent months planning this. Your prints are all over it in a manner of speaking, and they don't want to chase down to the Caymans, they want to wrap this up, open and shut, prosecute and move on. Keep in mind that Reg is a pro Travis, you've been set up good, he's way out of your league and believe me you don't want to go down for him. If you're going to take a fall then make it for something *you've* done, not him."

"Why can't you take what you're telling me to the cops?"

Chaz laughed, "They would no sooner listen to me about things like this than they would Bernie Madoff... I'm still a bad guy in their eyes and I'd rather not expose myself to them any more than I have to."

Silence, the mind-bending dialogue twisted itself into an overload of nerve endings, pulling him from both ends.

"There's just one more thing Travis."

"What's that?"

"I told you Reg has done this before, right?"

"Go on."

"If he follows his past moves, he'll move the money from the Cayman's back to Puerto Rico tomorrow, and then start dispersing it out the following day."

"And...?"

"And, this means Einstein, you've got 24 hours to make your move."

"My move?"

"I'll walk you through it, and be with you the whole way, but I need you down here, and preferably with a female accomplice. Are you game?"

Silence.

"There's the hard way and the easy way Travis. The easy way has you plea bargaining out of jail and the money's gone. The hard way has you down here in 12 hours getting your clients money back."

Travis didn't speak.

"Stay focused Travis. Time stops for no one."

Travis looked around the parking lot, watched a homeless guy take a seat across the street and set out a cup with a cardboard sign. Travis threw his head back and sucked in, then let it out slowly through pursed lips.

He remembered hearing something from one of the older guys in the office about most of life being the result of just a few split second decisions. His mind echoed the sounds of crime: cell doors closing, cameras flashing, gavels pounding, ratcheting handcuffs.

"I'm in."

Chapter Ten

Travis locked the car and walked into Phil's place. Before he could tell the receptionist he wanted to see Phil she looked up and smiled, "Three times in one day, this is a treat."

Travis mumbled hello, signed in and walked down the hallway. There was an antiseptic odor he hadn't noticed on his last visit, he ignored it, kept his head down and focused. Travis was realizing that by concentrating all his thoughts into what he was doing that very second he was more effective. It was when he stopped to contemplate the big picture that his abilities diminished, focus blurred into a grainy image. *You're a fugitive, start thinking like one.*

The door to Phil's room was partially opened, from inside he could hear the TV broadcasting the financial channel. The clanging of the closing bell on the New York Stock Exchange was the first audible clue Travis had in hours as to the time. It was now 1 pm and he hadn't eaten since last night. Phil looked up.

Long since retired from the business of trading stocks and bonds, Phil had settled into a daily routine driven by years of consistency, and Travis walked in to look at a dapper old man who still had a life to live. "Ah Travis, what news do we have from the world of high finance?"

Phil was sitting in his lounge chair finishing up a sandwich, wiping his mouth with a cloth napkin. Travis sat on the opposite chair.

"I didn't even notice the market today, how'd it do?"

"Up 30. Cut the crap, what's going on with you and Chaz?"

"It looks like I'm going down there to get the money back."

"About what I expected. Chaz doesn't waste any time when it comes to things like this. When he's made up his mind he usually doesn't sleep until the job's done. Why haven't you gone to the police?"

Travis explained Chaz's insight into how Reg had truly set him up, and how important swift action would be in the world of money laundering. He couldn't really see any concern on Phil's face that this was the wrong line of reasoning. In an odd way he found this reassuring.

"So what do you think? Am I doing the right thing?"

"If it was anybody but Chaz I'd say no. You need to realize Chaz isn't well thought of by the authorities in this country. If you went to the police you'd implicate yourself further by the mere mention of his name. He's a 'the end justifies the means' kind of man if you get my drift. But you're in good hands, the best. If there's any one man that should be helping you in this, it's him."

"He said he was doing this because he owed you a favor."

Phil didn't respond, dismissing the comment as if it was never said.

"When do you leave?"

"As soon as I can. Chaz said to bring a female accomplice if possible, why do you think he said that?"

Phil laughed, the laughter turning into a coughing fit, sputtering. "One thing you need to know about Chaz, do it his way. He has his reasons and you'd do yourself a favor to follow his instructions. I'm sure he's got something up his sleeve that you or I would only see in the movies."

Travis felt the fleeting but familiar sense of progress again. Phil's encouraging words and obvious confidence in Chaz were giving him something to hold on to.

Phil downed the rest of his milk. "With Chaz living down there you have a stroke of luck. It's his backyard, and it sounds like that's where you need to base your operations anyway. I wish you all the luck in the world Travis. If I had known this kind of thing would happen to you I'd never have helped you get into this racket, but I feel it's my duty to get you in with Chaz and make this right. Your clients will appreciate this more than you can know, they're used to being promised the moon and delivered a pizza. It's the rare guy who can come through in the end…who has the courage to make the tough choices, he's the one they stay with. When this is all over Travis you'll have a valuable asset in what you've done, use it."

"You make it sound like I've already gotten the money back."

Phil stood up and walked over behind Travis, putting his hands on his shoulders, "You will son, I see no other outcome with Chaz on your side."

A nurse came in to take his lunch tray, and asked if he needed anything. Phil waved her off and looked at Travis as the door closed. "She wants me, could you see the way she looked at me?"

"She must be half your age…well, hey, keep trying anyway, it'll keep you young."

"Keep me young? It'll keep *her* young!"

They laughed awkwardly which led into an uneasy silence. "I've been meaning to ask you, how did you and Chaz get to know each other?"

"From the sounds of things I don't think you have time for this story, it's a long one and you've got to get down there. We'll catch up when you get back."

Travis hesitated, Phil noticed the look of uncertainty on his face, a man about to either redeem himself or turn into a fugitive. "Sit back down, let me tell you a different story…"

Travis pulled up a chair and sat backwards on it, arms hanging over the back. The drapes were pulled open, the afternoon breeze had picked up its pace emptying the birch trees of their last leaves. The sun hung low in the sky and warmed the room making Travis feel the first need for sleep since this started. Phil tucked his fingers under his collar and pulled at it, his face flushed to the color of apples.

"When I had been in the business awhile there was a new guy in town, actually over the bridge in Marin, he started to get a reputation as an up and comer. His deal was he'd meet these people in church up there and they began to trust him with their money. Seems in Marin County the people who have all the money are always looking for some kind of meaning in their lives, and he hung out in these touchy-feely places and made them feel like they were contributing to society."

"How?"

"His investments were always cloaked as these socially responsible, do good for the earth and save the children in India kinds of things. I'm not sure what his pitch was, but you'd have these bored couples who had all the money they need and no matter how much they spent they were never satisfied. Most of them seemed to need a higher purpose than driving a new car every year and flying to the south of France every winter. This guy's investments made them feel like they were saving the world without having to go to India and watch a six month old baby die of starvation or crawl around in its own filth. You see, there's saving the world the way Mother Theresa did it, and there's the other way…send a check. His investments appealed to these people."

"This doesn't sound unusual so far, lots of people are into socially responsible investing."

"There was just one problem with this. While these people are buying seven different kinds of cheeses to put in their kids lunch box and driving to soccer practice in their $100,000 convertibles, this guy's *spending* their money instead of investing it."

"You mean he told them he's putting it with different funds or other socially responsible money managers, but he's banking it for himself instead?"

"Yes, but spending not banking. Soon he's in his own mansion, has some horses, several cars, boats, his girlfriend has new jewelry and the clients thought he was just successful as a result of his high moral standards. This fed the machine further as he was living proof to these lifeless spenders that you become more successful by helping other people than by trying to help yourself. He was the validation they needed and the money kept coming in."

"Didn't the clients want to see results? Was there any suspicion?"

"He falsified statements, he was like a little league version of Madoff. He'd send out glowing reports on impressive looking letterhead with false account values, interest rates, the whole deal. When somebody needed to make a withdrawal he'd send them their money back, and obviously it was somebody else's money. A Ponzi scheme all the way."

"How long did this go on?"

"A good year or two. He started to get a big head, and like a lot of guys that do this he didn't know when to stop. After you own all these toys by misdirecting tens of millions in client funds, you start to need more to feed the beast. That's when he started hiring hookers, two or three at a time. He'd send limos out to pick them up, have all of 'em at once or do a little of the weird stuff, you know leather and handcuffs. That went on until he started to fall for this one hooker from Norway."

"He fell for a hooker? Who was this guy?"

"Name was Roger Benikoff, he was a little before your time."

"Why are you telling me this?"

"Stay with me Travis, you'll see. Anyway, the hooker starts to get the creeps because Roger is just not an attractive guy, he's got bad breath up close, didn't have the greatest looks and he starts to get more and more into the bondage thing. She likes the money, but to her it's just a transaction, nothing more. To Roger this was the real deal, he thought this was the woman that could solve all his problems.

She wanted nothing more than to be paid for what she did, and he kept shelling out more and more money to please her. First he bought her a car, then a beach house, meanwhile his girlfriend is pissed off and leaves him so he goes even more nuts. He proposes to the hooker several times, each time she says no he buys her something else, and then the money starts to run out. Like all schemes he had to have a constant influx of new money to keep the ball in the air, and as that slowed down and his spending kept spiraling out of control the house of cards started to fall."

"How did he get caught?"

"One of the checks he sent out to an investor bounced. Usually something like that can be fixed except it took Roger a few days to make good on the funds and the guy got nervous. This investor had sent a lot of people to Roger and he had his own retirement invested with him. Turns out the client was pretty well connected, so he calls a buddy of his who happens to work in the DA's office. They send someone out to investigate and of course Roger is completely unprepared for anything like this. He bullshits his way through the initial interview, tells them he won't talk without his attorney present, and so on."

"Then what?"

"As soon as the guy from the DA's office leaves Roger wires what's left of the money to Luxembourg. He'd stolen about 25 million, and ended up wiring around 5 million. He left the country that afternoon. Meanwhile the guy from the DA's office had seen enough, comes back with a search warrant the next day and the place is cleaned out. Computers stripped, files gone, not a trace. He would have gotten away with it but he had one weakness."

Travis thought for a second, "The hooker."

"Bingo. He sent for her. Can you believe it? The guy's halfway around the world, an overnight fugitive and he sends cash back to the US so his favorite hooker can join him.

Here's where I'm going with this. One of the investors in Roger's scheme was a doctor, a gynecologist or something. His pension plan was cratering in the stock market so he went with Roger's program to try and make up lost ground. Otherwise he might have to take money out of his own pocket to make his employees whole or he'd face charges of lack of fiduciary responsibility. You follow?"

"So far."

"So this doctor has over 2 million invested with Roger, hears about him skipping town and decides to take matters into his own hands. He calls a friend of his who knows about this kind of thing. The friend flies to Luxembourg and makes contact with the recipient of the money Roger wired. Turns out it's a diamond dealer who has converted the cash into stones for Roger to take to Italy, where he thinks he'll meet up with the hooker."

"Thinks?"

"Good, you're following this. The diamond dealer tells the friend all this because they know each other from some prior dealings, and the diamond guy thinks he's just bullshitting with an old acquaintance. Turns out the gynecologist told this friend he'd give him 20% of whatever he recovered. The friend is trying to track Roger, and pumping the diamond dealer for information. This friend is somehow able to get the hooker on the phone and tells her what he's doing. He says that her cut will be 100 grand and she'll never have to see Roger again. She tells Roger she'll meet him at the airport in Florence and jumps on the next plane.

Roger is beside himself, he can't believe he finally gets to spend time with the hooker of his dreams. He flies to Luxembourg, grabs his briefcase full of diamonds and heads for the airport in Florence.

She's there waiting for him wearing a fur coat he bought her, and just as they begin to hug each other the cops nab him. They cuff him, throw him against the wall and yank 2 million in diamonds from different pockets in his suit. Meanwhile a man is standing there watching the whole thing, smoking a cigar."

"The friend?"

"Chaz. He hands the hooker an envelope full of cash right in front of Roger, who began to cry right there on the spot. Chaz collected a few hundred thou for his work and that set him up. Turns out the doctor was on the board of a regional bank in San Francisco and recommended Chaz get put on retainer to take care of things like fraud prevention, money laundering, identity theft and so on. That, my friend, is the man who is about to help you. I would have no fears."

They said their goodbyes and Travis went to his car. He drove down from Presidio Heights onto Divisadero and the main entrance of the Marina Green, a popular grassy area with views of sailboats, dogs chasing Frisbees, runners, kite flyers, mountain bikers and the occasional rapper with headphones glued to his ears.

Travis grabbed a parking spot, walked up to one of the street vendors selling hot dogs and ordered a polish dog with extra sauerkraut, and enjoyed the first moment of peace in over twelve hours.

Food, away from the office, encouraging words from Phil and Chaz, Daphne on his side… this just might work. His cell phone rang. Dad.

"I've been trying to reach you all morning son, everything all right?"

"Yeah, fine, why?" *The lies, when would they stop?*

"At your office when I called they acted funny, asked me if I knew where you were, it was really strange, almost like you'd been fired but they couldn't say that. They kept insisting I tell them where you were. What's going on?"

"Not fired. Just working on a few big deals and some lines have gotten crossed."

"How's the hedge fund, he making me rich yet?"

Oh God, the last thing on his mind. "Don't know, he keeps it pretty tight before a fed meeting."

"Look, your mom's birthday is tomorrow and your brother's coming up from San Diego, you're still coming right?"

The danger of being focused is being focused. The rest of the world passes you by while your mind lasers in on what it needs to do, and they all wonder how you could be so forgetful. "Can't do it dad. I have to leave town unexpectedly."

"What? Where are you going that's more important than your mother's birthday?"

"I can't talk about it now, but I'll call her tomorrow, I promise."

The line went dead.

A late wind picked the salt spray off the water, gathering the bay into white caps. In the distance tanker ships stacked with colored shipping crates crept in front of Alcatraz.

Chapter Eleven

T ravis spent the rest of the afternoon preparing for a trip to San Juan. He made his way to a mall on the north side of Fisherman's Wharf where he ducked into a Banana Republic. The store was crowded and most of the customers looked caught up in the usual tourist activity of confused browsing. Travis found himself at a heightened sense of awareness. He could feel the hair on the back of his neck bristle at the slightest glance from a perfect stranger. He felt like a panther pacing in a cage; hunted, cornered, using his peripheral vision.

He picked out rugged, tropical, easy maintenance clothing, kept his sunglasses on in the store and refused to let anyone get too long a look at him. He brought his items to the front counter where a young tattooed hipster gave him a sullen look.

He gave her his credit card and just as she was about to scan it he realized this was a mistake.

He tried to stop her.

"Wait, let me pay cash instead." He reached out to grab her wrist and stopped as he realized how much attention this would attract. She looked at him, then glanced behind her toward the rear of the store. Travis looked and saw only mirrors on the wall.

She had just slid the card through.

"This card won't work anyway."

"Excuse me?"

"Denied, authorization denied."

Travis realized that in a wired up and plugged in world it's possible someone knew exactly where he was this instant. *You're a fugitive, start thinking like one.* He paid with cash and left without getting his change.

He made his way through the mall, trying various circling efforts to see if he was being followed. Satisfied, he made a quick stop at a shoe store to get some sandals and loafers, then slid into a men's room and changed out of his black pants and white shirt, tossing them and the black shoes into the garbage. It felt good to be in sandals and shorts, the feeling of being incognito gave him some reassurance. Finally he picked out a good sized carry on to avoid any luggage delays. Chaz hadn't said how long he'd be down there so he decided to prepare for a few days at the most. Travis checked his watch, Daphne would be getting off work soon.

He called her.

"They figure you've left the country somehow."

"You're kidding. I'm right here down by the..."

She interrupted him, "Stop. The phones, they were doing things with them earlier."

"I don't understand how Dick could think I did this when it was me who came to him and told him what happened. Would I do that if I was guilty?"

"I think he did mention that, but these cops like what they have on you, phone records, your name on the account, you know. They also found e-mails to the bank in Puerto Rico. It seems like the deeper they dig the more they like you as a suspect."

"Reg had me send those e-mails to set up a..."

The sheer genius of Reg's advance work washed over Travis as he realized the methodical, calculating steps that had been taken. Implicate Travis, divert attention, throw off the scent while he scattered the money in a hundred different places; pure, premeditated genius.

"You okay Travis?"

"Yeah, I just need to be done with this."

"What have you been up to so far?"

"I'll tell you tonight. Have they questioned you?"

Daphne hesitated. "Yes."

"Was it bad?"

"They came down hard on me, figured I must know either that you did it or where you are. After an hour or two I think they decided you did this all on your own."

"I'm sorry you're wrapped up in this."

"I know that. You've got bigger problems than I do though, they've frozen your credit cards and bank accounts."

"I found that out the hard way. I'm thinking we should meet somewhere else, they're probably watching your place too. Why don't we use cell phones, call me back."

The cell connection was made. "I guess a guy like you has to be pretty paranoid, do you think they tapped these cell phones too?"

"I don't know how to tell. Look, just meet me at that place I took you to lunch after you helped me with the Clark account. You remember?"

"Sure, Ern…"

"Shhh!"

"Right, almost forgot, what time?"

"Six." The line went dead.

Travis picked up some last minute essentials for the trip then he had to lay low. He still had over an hour to kill before meeting Daphne and found himself in the situation of feeling rushed and having nothing to do in the same instant. It was like waiting in line for a movie that had already started; restless, checking his watch, pacing, and none of this getting him anywhere.

He bought a magazine at the newsstand on the pier that also sold kites and models of cable cars, took it to a bench on the dock and sat down. He tried reading it but the words meant nothing. His mind raced back and forth while he gave the articles a cursory glance. He had so many questions pounding him that nobody knew the answers to. *What was Chaz's plan? Was it legal? What would happen when he got back to the states? Would anybody hire him after this? What and when should he tell his parents?* His line of thought was interrupted by the shuffling feet of a homeless man standing in front of him. Travis looked up.

The face was grimy, sad, weathered; the man had too many clothes on for the weather, and attempted a toothless smile as he spoke, "Got any spare change?"

Travis had no desire to argue, and there was something harmless in the man's face. He reached into his pocket and fished out a few ones, at the same moment coming to a shocking realization. He had almost run out of cash. *How the hell were you supposed to fly to the Caribbean with no cash?* He hesitated.

"You don't have to give me the paper, just some coins will get me through."

Travis looked at the beggar again, a man mere feet from him whose biggest problem could be solved with fifty cents. He saw the irony of life in this man's face and he gave him the only help he could. "You want money right?"

The man stepped back.

"You're down on your ass, begging for your next piece of shit meal and you tell me coins are okay?"

Nothing.

"Ask for the moon man! Don't ask for pennies, that's all you'll ever get. Ask for the big order, go for a twenty and see what they say. Half the time people just want somebody to tell them what to do, you be that guy…get it?"

The man blinked, unsure where this was going. He brought a soiled hand up to his cheek and scratched.

Travis gave him a dollar, "Look, I don't want to mess up your day, but take it from me, just go for it…ask big and let them decide how much to give you."

The man walked to the next bench.

Travis didn't know where that outburst had come from, he'd never talked to beggars before. He had the feeling he might as well pass on something that he had more of than cash…a little free advice to someone who would listen before flying down to San Juan to recover 54 million dollars.

He got up and headed to Ernesto's, a North Beach style restaurant a block away from the wharf. The dinner crowd hadn't packed the place yet and Daphne was already sitting at a table in the corner.

"Somebody's been shopping."

"I needed to get a few things since I can't get into my place." He decided to wait a little before talking about going to the San Juan.

Travis ordered a beer, put his bags next to the table and sat down. The main restaurant area was an eclectic collection of red gingham covered tables, empty bottles of Chianti with candle wax dripping down the sides, chipped ladder back chairs, and a wide plank wooden floor that looked a hundred years old. The artwork on the walls was a sort of vintage poster theme, and each frame was either too big or too small for the print. Large, dusty braids of garlic hung in the corners.

"My uncle Phil put me in touch with a guy down in the Caribbean who thinks he can get the money back."

"Why not just come clean with the police?"

Travis explained to her what Chaz had told him, and gave her what he knew of the intricacies of money laundering, wire transfers, and how little time they had.

"So you've decided to cowboy on down there yourself instead of going to the police. Have you really thought this through?"

"What would you do?"

Daphne sat back, her dark hair starting to fall into her face as the braids and pins that held it together all day came undone. Brushing it away from her eyes and pulling it back behind her ear, she looked at him, "Have you told me everything?"

"Yes, you still doubt me?"

"This whole thing seems so farfetched, they were dusting your keyboard for fingerprints, unscrewing the back of your computer, interviewing everybody in the office. I don't know any more than what I see on those TV crime shows but they seemed very thorough. Now you think you can go down there, meet up with this guy you don't even know and just take the money? Why aren't you willing to let the cops do their job?"

Travis looked around the room and leaned forward. "They *are* doing their job Daphne, and so far they've got one suspect, me. If I go to them they'll finally figure out after a day of questioning that I'm innocent, meanwhile Reg has spread this money in small accounts all over the country. Maybe they catch him, maybe they don't, and the recovery rate of getting the money back drops to zip."

"Are you more concerned about clearing yourself or getting the money back?"

"Both. They're intertwined, I get the money back and my name is cleared."

"Maybe it's not. Maybe they think you lost your nerve. Anyway with you leaving the country it makes you look even guiltier."

"My father has $500,000 in this thing. My best clients have sat across my desk and said 'Travis, if you think this is a good idea, we trust you'. They've told me things they'd never tell anyone else, sat in my office and cried while they went on about their mother in a rest home or their wife in the cancer ward, they bring in statements from other firms asking me to help them understand what they've gotten into. These people aren't just clients, they have handed their lives over to me and I don't just look at them as dollars and cents. They ask me advice about whether to loan their son money one more time, or what kind of trust to set up, they want to know if I think they have enough money coming in to upgrade their Alaskan cruise, these are the flesh and blood of my business. They think of me as a member of their family, I get invited to their son's graduation or I go to their parent's funeral. If I'm to live up to that I just can't sit here answering questions at a police station while the money they trusted me with gets scattered into a maze of laundering operations, when I have the chance to use a pro and get it now. And if I do turn myself in, who's to say the cops will believe me? They have a neat and tidy suspect, my prints are all over this thing; or…they *do* believe me, the money's gone, then I spend the rest of my career looking into the faces of those who trusted me as they sit and wonder, '*did he really take it?*' I've made up my mind. Sure it's radical, it's cowboy as you say, but it's the only outcome I can live with."

Daphne stared at him, seeing a side of Travis she never knew existed. "So tell me more about this guy down in the Bahamas."

Chapter Twelve

A lean man with prematurely white hair made his way through the crowded airport. His black turtleneck and black slacks contrasted with his hair, drawing glances as he walked up to the line leading to the metal detector. Sliding off his boots and Rolex, he placed them in a tray next to his satchel and overnight bag on the conveyor belt. He removed a slim laptop from the main pocket of the overnight bag and handed it to the attendant.

He made it through the screening as expected, and looked around the airport. Off to the side, walking his way, a well-muscled man in a tight fitting golf shirt and khakis approached, "Reg, good to see you. Everything go okay?"

They shook hands and headed to the departure gate. "Excellent Donovan, I'll tell you all about it on the flight."

The loudspeaker announced, *"First call for flight number 76 from Miami to San Juan Puerto Rico, all Gold Club passengers and those requiring assistance may board now at gate 6E."*

Reg strapped his watch back on, slipped into his boots and looked around for the gate signs. "This way."

Reg and Donovan walked past news kiosks, Starbucks outlets and shoe shiners on their way to the gate. "Any trouble on your end?" Reg asked.

"Nada, I've been laying low at the hotel on Miami Beach, your call came in, nobody followed me and I haven't talked to anybody since I've been down here. I'd say this is going smooth so far."

Reg picked up the pace, "You know I don't like to get too cocky until the money's in the bag so to speak."

Donovan nodded. Reg usually had to find something to disagree with and it was pointless to argue with him. "I've got us a Hummer reserved at San Juan, same guy that helped us out last time."

"Excellent …here's our gate." Reg steered their path towards the gate and handed the attendant his ticket, Donovan followed.

"Good evening gentlemen, enjoy your flight." She checked their passport photos, slid the ticket through the electronic reader and they made their way down the gangplank.

They boarded the plane, threw their carry-on luggage under the seats and settled in.

"So tell me, everything go smooth on your end?" Donovan asked.

"It's a little scary sometimes, but we're getting good at this. All the pieces fit into place. The timing was perfect, it worked like a Swiss watch."

"How much did we end up getting?"

Reg looked around, saw a few too many passengers for him to feel comfortable talking anymore, and held up five fingers. He closed his fingers and opened them again to make a four.

They both ordered champagne, and as the flight attendant announced the safety procedures Reg slid a book from the outside pocket of his satchel, leaned back and began to read.

Donovan reached over and closed the window cover as the setting Florida sun beamed into the plane.

Chapter Thirteen

The days kept getting shorter, and as happens in fall in San Francisco, warmer. It was the best kept secret from the rest of the country that the bay flashed its postcard images just as the tourists were leaving. The skies deepened into an electric blue arc of clarity, winds turned into breezes, and the locals crawled out of the coffee shops they'd been hiding in all summer. Daphne and Travis walked out of Ernesto's as the sun vanished, the air silent, balmy.

Travis put his arm over Daphne's shoulder, "Ever been to the Caribbean before?"

She moved closer to him, "No, and if somebody had told me this morning I'd be leaving tonight to help you recover fifty million bucks in the Bahamas I'd have said they were out of their mind. This is crazy, it's exciting and I want to help you."

"I'm glad you're not having second thoughts."

"Who said I wasn't having second thoughts?" Daphne gave him a sideways glance, her dark eyes played with him.

Travis looked down at her, took his arm off, "There's something we need to figure out."

"What's that?"

"If we're going to your house to pack your stuff we have to make it look like you're just coming home from dinner after work. If the cops are watching your house they'll be looking for anything out of the ordinary, any sign that I might be lurking nearby will bring you down also."

"What should we do?"

Travis thought for a moment, nervously looking at passerby, expecting at any moment to be slammed up against a wall and handcuffed. "Go to your place, act normal, pack your stuff in a gym bag and put on clothes like you're going to the health club. Meet me back at the garage underneath this restaurant," Travis pointed to the floor, underneath lay the cavernous garage of the massive Embarcadero center, "and we'll go from there."

"What are you going to do?"

"I need to find a place to get my stuff packed, I'll just do that in the car, then we'll take your car from the garage."

"I don't even go to a health club."

"Just *act* like you're going to one, fake it Daphne."

She looked at Travis as if it might be the last time she'd see him alive. He couldn't tell if it was pity or apprehension, but he knew he needed her now more than she needed him.

"It'll be okay, just act normal." He grabbed her around the waist and pulled her to him, she stepped in closer wrapping her arms around his neck. Her hair smelled young, unpretentious. She buried her head into his shoulder, his frustration mounting as he wished it were another time, another day. His eyes open, he looked over her shoulder at the slate colored waters beyond Fisherman's Wharf, the glowing digital clock readout over the entrance read 7:17PM.

His mind raced.

The onrush of time, ticking minutes adding up to the 48 hours Dick had given him, the short fuse Chaz had him on, thoughts of over fifty million dollars spreading out into cyberspace like drops from a sprinkler, unable to gather back into their original form. The blur of the last 16 hours dragged his thoughts through dark crevices of uncertainty over what lay ahead. Chaz's words echoed... *You're a fugitive Travis, start thinking like one.*

She squeezed him tighter.

The digital clock silently changed...7:18PM.

He pulled his head back, "We need to hurry."

Travis went to the Fisherman's Wharf parking lot where he'd left his car backed inconspicuously in a corner space. He threw his bags in the trunk, fished out a pair of khakis, sandals and a tropical shirt and headed to the public bathroom at the end of the lot.

Daphne found her late model Honda in the garage, gave the attendant the validated ticket from Ernesto's and turned towards Market St. She shared a loft with a girlfriend from college, and while that helped with the rent Daphne was finding herself more of the quiet loner than Vicky.

They had different hours, Vicky was a nurse at SF General hospital on the night shift, and their weeks went by with a few passings in the hallway while weekends were usually spent with Vicky at her boyfriend of the month's place, and Daphne crashing with romance novels, streamed videos and a weak attempt at the Treadmill which doubled as a laundry rack.

She walked up the flight of stairs to her second floor loft and put the key in the door. The ceiling fan in the main living area was on, she could feel the breeze and hear the whirring from a bent blade. When she reached over to turn the light on the switch on the wall was already in the up position. Someone had turned the fan on without the light, and she had to grope her away around the darkened apartment to turn on a lamp. In spite of Vicky being a slob, it wasn't like her to leave the fan on without the light.

Daphne moved diagonally through the left of the room towards an end table she knew had a lamp on it. Cautiously waiting for her leg to brush up against the coffee table to get her bearings, she stepped on a thick pile of what must have been a stack of mail or old magazines, they shifted under her feet and her exasperation grew at what an incompatible roommate Vicky had turned out to be. Her hand found the light switch as she snuck her arm under the shade. What she saw next pulled her into the twisted nightmare Travis had fallen in.

The entire contents of every drawer in the apartment were piled into the center of the living room. Pictures, documents, junk mail, books, magazines, maps, scribbled notes; all heaped into a swelling mound of the remnants of her life.

Daphne slowly backed out of the apartment, staring at the room in complete disbelief. She fished her cell phone out of her purse and called Travis.

"You won't believe what's happened."

"What?"

"My apartment, somebody's been in here going through everything, it's a total mess." Tears started as she continued staring at the pile.

"Are you still there?"

"Yes."

"Get out! Leave now!"

"What about my stuff?"

"Forget it, close the door, lock it, we'll buy stuff. Just get out of there."

"Why? I didn't do anything wrong."

"They want me through you, and they'll make your life miserable to do it. Get off the phone, get back to our meeting place, and stay focused. We have a plane to catch."

Daphne hung up, not taking her eyes off the piles that would take a week to sort through. She backed out the door, turned the ceiling fan off, left the lamp on and locked the door from the outside.

She'd looked forward to getting out of her pumps and nylons, taking a quick shower before meeting Travis, and her evening had been completely shaken from its original plan. Daphne walked back down the steps to her car, took her coat off and pulled away from the curb. As she did so she noticed in her side mirror a dark, late model sedan pulling away without its lights on. She accelerated around the corner and the car followed, only turning its lights on when they both turned on to Van Ness.

She decided to see if she was being followed, or being paranoid. Daphne made an illegal u-turn on Van Ness, heading north back to the Golden Gate Bridge. The sedan following her missed the turn, accelerated to the next intersection and squealed around the corner, its rear wheels hopping over the curb. Daphne turned right on a side street and gunned it.

The sedan did the same.

Daphne hit send on her cell phone, "I can't meet you Travis, I'm being followed."

"Are you sure?"

"Positive."

"Where are you?"

Daphne peered out the windshield as she held the phone to her ear, "I'm on Chestnut, just off Van Ness. What should I do?"

"You need to lose them. If you bring them to me I'm toast and so are you."

"I wish I'd never agreed to this."

"You'd still be followed. You couldn't go out of your house without this happening, they think you can lead them to me. You'd be in the same boat regardless."

"I know, but why me? It's not like I'm in this with you, as far as they know I'm just your assistant. What am I supposed to do now?"

Silence.

"Did you get a look at the drivers who are following you?"

"Not really."

Daphne continued down Chestnut and adjusted her rear view mirror, the sedan's headlights bearing down on her.

"Do they look like cops?"

"I guess, it looks like one of those generic sedans they always use."

"Here's what I want you to do."

Chapter Fourteen

Every turn Daphne made was followed by a shark like crawl from the sedan behind her. The streetlights and neon signs played on the windshield, the only glances she was able to get of the drivers were when their heads were silhouetted against the high beams of a car behind them. Her pulse quickened at the audacity of the plan Travis had laid out, making it a struggle to keep her driving pace normal. With the loops and u-turns Daphne made they had to know she knew she was being followed. She turned right onto Larkin.

The rarest commodity in San Francisco is a parking spot, especially one near where you have to be. The Hannah Day Spa was primarily a weekend tourist destination that catered to the tourist and business trade, and had arrangements with all the major hotels in the area. Parking in front was available because they were closing for the evening. Daphne pulled in front, locked her car and went inside. An unplugged fake waterfall was against the wall to the left, side tables and couches in the center, on the right wall were shelves of potions, additives, herbal supplements, and meditation music disks. The receptionist was shutting down a computer system behind the front desk and looked up startled, "We're closed, did you want to make an appointment?"

Daphne pulled her handbag strap further up her shoulder. "No, thank you. I know where I'm headed."

She walked past the desk and down a hallway leading to the rear of the building.

The receptionist stood up, "But, we're closed, you can't go back there."

Daphne quickened her pace.

The hallway was still lit, and had two doors on each side. There were wall hangings depicting mountain scenery, waterfalls, ocean settings; all looking to create a sense of calm. A thick, assaulting eucalyptus odor crept under the doors, each had names scrolled in calligraphy on rough, lavender paper. She passed rooms named Tantra, Shakra, Rapture, Essence. At the end of the hall a closed, unmarked door faced her. Daphne went through.

The receptionist followed, "Excuse me...what can I help you with?"

Daphne didn't answer.

The unmarked door led her into a utility room containing plastic barrels of oils, lotions, towels, sheets and odd looking sponge materials. She continued to walk through this room and out to a rear alleyway. A blue dumpster overflowed with black trash bags, empty cardboard boxes were thrown in a pile next to it. Around the corner she heard the sound of an approaching car. *Would the sedan have made it back here so quickly?*

From inside the spa she heard sounds of yelling. A man's voice followed by a woman's but she couldn't make out the words. The back door hadn't closed all the way, she heard footsteps down the hall, the receptionist shouting, "She walked back there like she owned the place, are you guys cops?"

Travis's black Beemer swung around the corner, headlights off, his window down. "Get in, now!" Daphne ran out past the garbage area and jumped in the rear door. Rear wheels spun, grabbing the pavement and rocketing them out of the back alley. The two men who had been following in the sedan came running out the back door, one went back in, the other watching Travis's car, running down the alley to keep it in his vision as long as he could.

"Are you okay?"

Daphne pulled her knees up to her chest and buried her face in them. "Yes, I'm scared, that's all."

"I know. Having you cut through there bought us a little time, they'll have to go get their car but we still need to hurry."

Daphne crawled over to the front passenger seat, "How did you know about this place?"

"Beth used to go there all the time, it's the first thing that came to mind as a way to lose someone in the city."

"You act like you've done this before."

He looked at her, then looked back in front. He shifted up as they pulled out of the alley and onto Sacramento Street, dodging pedestrians, passing dangerously close to buses and taxis.

He checked the rear view mirror.

"I haven't done this before, there's a lot at stake and I'm in this all the way. I don't know much about running from the law, but I do know it's either in or out. Half way gets us nowhere. You with me?"

She didn't answer.

"What color was that sedan?"

"I think it was black or dark blue, maybe even dark green."

"Maybe? I think? What kind of an answer is that? Maybe I didn't make myself clear, we *are* running from the cops and we *have* to get to the Bahamas tomorrow. If not, I'm in jail and the money is gone. I need you on my side here, you get it?"

The glare from Daphne had heat behind it. "Just take a look at my apartment and you'll see how into this I am. And the sedan, it's nighttime, they all look alike in the dark. If you don't cut your bullshit and give me a little respect and apologize I'm walking right now. *You get it?*"

Travis swallowed. *Why the hell did Chaz want me to bring a female accomplice?* "I get it, look, I'm sorry. I'm tense, that's all."

"Yeah, me too. But if this is going to work you need to cut me some slack, I don't have to do this and a little appreciation is in order." Her eyes still flared, but the burner had been turned down.

"You're right, you don't have to do this, and I appreciate it."

No change.

"Really, I do." Like most guys, he couldn't do this very well, so he just kept repeating himself.

She lifted her face slightly. "That's more like it, now let's lose these guys before we get nailed."

The tires screeched, Travis cut around a bright green city bus, fishtailing through the next block as they flew down Fillmore St. Daphne's head snapped back against the headrest as the RPM's picked up.

He cut left onto Lombard and made a beeline for the Golden Gate Bridge. Chaz had a plane waiting at the Napa airport, and at this time of day with no delays it would take less than an hour to get there. He kept his speed lower on the busy thoroughfare, passing Indian cafés, Basque restaurants, antique shops and on every corner, a homeless person holding up a cardboard sign. They were heading to the right as Lombard fed onto the bridge.

Travis glanced at the rear view mirror, "They're behind us."

Chapter Fifteen

Heading north onto the Golden Gate, southbound traffic stopping to pay a toll just to their left, the BMW opened it up and fired straight through onto the bridge. The bridge usually had three northbound lanes and two southbound lanes open, with the middle lane coned off for the bridge maintenance truck or emergency vehicles. Travis cut through the cones into the middle lane and shifted into 5th, the speedometer gaining on 70.

The sedan followed.

Bright yellow lights spanning the cables that draped from the two towers flew by them in a rush of dizzying speed while Travis concentrated on staying in the middle lane and getting off the bridge safely.

The lane ahead looked like a straight race track converging on the horizon. The hypnotic V shape of the coned track gave him a point of reference to hone in on as the car sped past 100 mph. Oncoming traffic gave him a wide berth while the cars he passed swerved away at the last second, honked, or didn't even notice him until he was several yards past.

He didn't dare look in the rear view mirror, the concentration it took to stay in the lane and navigate opposing traffic at speeds over 100 miles per hour was total. He knew this needed everything he had, and how far back the sedan was had nothing to do with how fast he could go.

White knuckled on the wheel, unblinking eyes using all their faculties of peripheral vision, Travis pushed the pedal, extending the distance between him and the sedan.

From the corner of his eye he could see Daphne move forward and start to say something, but no words came from her mouth. He looked over, looked back ahead, and saw it.

Straight ahead were the flashing yellow lights and bright headlamps of the maintenance truck. It was hard to make out the details at this distance, Travis remembered it usually lumbered along slowly, workers hanging off of each side and the back end picking up cones or placing them on another side of the lane to open up more room for commuter traffic.

The distance between them vanished at over a hundred feet per second, Daphne put one hand on the dashboard and with the other she grabbed the handhold over her door. The terror in her throat constricted, holding back screams she wanted to let out.

Travis glanced in the mirror.

They were still there, the unmistakable lights of the sedan trailing behind in the same closed off lane. He brought his speed down to 80, still passing the traffic on the right, but at a speed he could control. The sedan closed in from the rear.

The wide, orange truck grew in size with every second as they sped closed to each other in a head on course.

Daphne screamed.

He saw the opening. A Land Rover had just switched one lane to the right, in its place Travis swerved. He braked hard to meld into the slower throngs of tired northbound traffic just as the maintenance truck came up on his left. He changed back into the lane he'd been in, the truck now behind him, and became the first vehicle to be using the new lane heading into Marin. His ears waited for the inevitable while he continued to push the speed up as the highway curved into the rolling hills above Sausalito.

And then it came.

The sounds of metal against metal, tires skidding, horns, glass breaking. He looked back in the mirror. The sedan had missed the maintenance truck, but glided into the cars on its right as it swerved to avoid a head on. The multiple car pile-up at high speeds brought the 8 pm traffic on the Golden Gate Bridge to a complete halt in both directions.

Travis tore his gaze from the mirror, sickened… forcing himself to keep moving.

Daphne let go of her grips on the car, opened her eyes and let out her breath. She put her hand on her chest and tried to slow her breathing, eyes closed, mascara streaking down her face. "Could we be in any deeper?"

Travis kept driving. They were playing at a new level, at this altitude remorse or second thoughts would be lethal.

"Do you think they radioed ahead and there's some kind of roadblock in front of us?"

Travis was silent for a moment. They continued passing cars, but at a less noticeable pace.

"I'd bet on it."

"What do we do now?"

"Roadblock or not, this highway is crawling with cops. They nab speeders all day, and a black Beemer passing everybody else will bring them down like mosquitoes. I need to think."

The highway curved away from the Marin headlands and opened up a twilight view of Mt. Tam in the distance. Wisps of fog curled around its peak, the full moon glowed in the distance behind the dark peaks. Behind Mt. Tam, unseen from where they were, the cobalt colored waters of the Pacific slid onto the beaches.

Traffic opened up as the highway widened, Travis picked a spot in the fast lane.

"Let's look at our situation. Those guys probably radioed in when we left the spa, and again when we got on the bridge so we most likely have Marin county cops set up to stop us somewhere. We're running, they think we have over fifty million in stolen money, they've been through both of our places. I'm surprised we've made it this far."

Travis leaned forward and looked up at the sky through the windshield. "No choppers yet, you see any?"

Daphne looked out her window and the rear. She had to wipe mist off as the adrenalin flow from what they'd just been through brought the heat up in the car.

"I don't see any."

As the highway veered right they came to the first exit after the bridge, Travis cut across three lanes of traffic to the off-ramp which snaked into downtown Sausalito. Passing hillside bungalows overlooking the bay, corner restaurants and sidewalk art galleries, Travis slowed to match the pace of the seaside tourist attraction. As he pulled further away from the highway he heard sirens coming from the direction of the bridge. "We need to stay off the main roads. I might as well have a sign on my back with this car."

"What should we do?"

"We can't use back roads all the way to Napa. We need to do something else. Hold on."

Travis pulled up to one of the better known restaurants on the main street through town, Toma's. It had large picture windows overlooking the water, and one of the more accessible parking lots in the city. A large sign said it was for restaurant patrons only, and locals knew this hardly made up for the mediocre food.

The parking attendant walked up.

"Just follow my lead Daphne, I need your help here."

The man stood at the open window. "Are you dining with us this evening?"

Travis got out of his car, "Yes, let me just get a few things."

Travis walked around to the trunk, grabbed his bags and handed one to Daphne. He reached in his wallet for a tip, handed it to the attendant and walked towards the entrance. Just to the left of the door was the attendant's station, a stool, table, and a board with numbered hooks for the car keys. "This is where I need you, distract him, you left something in the car. Make it good."

Daphne walked back towards the BMW which had just been parked by the attendant on the far side of the lot. "Excuse me! I need to get something out of there."

The attendant looked at Daphne, and waited for her to retrieve whatever it is she wanted. She made an exaggerated display of bending over through the doorway, still in her business skirt and high heels, the attendant making sure to get a good view.

Travis quickly scanned the keys and noticed the set for a white Jeep sitting near the front. He looked around, leaned over and yanked them from their hook. Just then the door opened and a man in a suit came out and looked at him.

"Here you go, it's a silver Jag." With that he stuck a dollar bill and a claim ticket in Travis's face.

"Sorry, it's him you want." Travis pointed out towards the lot.

The man in the suit hailed the attendant, who came and retrieved the key from the set of hooks, then went to the other end of the lot to retrieve the Jag. Daphne ran up to him whispering, "I couldn't distract him any longer, that guy came out."

"I know, you did great, follow me."

As soon as the attendant sat down in the Jag Travis grabbed Daphne, headed for the Jeep, and stood on the passenger side. The jag backed out of its spot, Travis unlocked the Jeep, got in, threw the bags in the back seat and slid to the drivers' side.

He started the engine and pulled out slowly, timing it so the attendant was facing the front of the restaurant as he rolled the jeep out onto the main thoroughfare of Sausalito. He turned right.

She turned to Travis as they sped down the street, "Giving up the Beemer for this?"

"I think if we get out of this in one piece that will be the least of my worries. Besides, we're in too deep. We can't do this thing halfway, if I start letting up now then we're both in jail and the whole thing's a waste. This is all the way or no way, in or out, no stealing second with one foot still on first."

Daphne looked over at him. "Yeah, now that you can add stealing a car to the list, I guess you do have to start thinking like a fugitive."

Chapter Sixteen

Travis drove through Sausalito and re-entered Highway 101 two exits further north than where they exited. Traffic was lighter, the evening commute had thinned out and Travis positioned them in the middle lane at a speed matching the rest of the traffic. The moon took on a brighter sheen as the fog around it broke up, unveiling a clear fall night by the bay.

"How long do you think before the owner of this car reports it stolen?"

Travis looked over at her. *How the hell should I know?* "Don't know. It's not a bad trade if he gets the Beemer though."

They both laughed, the break in tension a welcome relief.

Travis's cell phone rang. Dad

"Travis, I need to know what you're up to…is there something you want to tell me?"

"Is there something you want to tell me?" These were words usually said by someone who knew, but wanted to hear it from you. Travis felt the final threads of whatever was keeping him together start to unravel. "I'm in a scrape dad, that's all I can tell you right now, but I promise when this is all done I'll tell you everything. You gotta believe me."

"Before I go believing you…" his father's voice was firm, unwavering. "…let me tell you a few things. The police called here earlier and after they were positive that your mother and I have no idea where you are, they filled us in on what they have found. Seems you're over fifty million dollars richer and have left town. Have you any idea what you're doing to yourself?"

"Dad, I didn't take it."

"So when the police tell me that your office e-mails and phone records all point to this account in the Caribbean that's in your name I'm supposed to think you're innocent? Don't get me wrong, I'll go to bat for you all the way if you are, but the evidence is pretty incriminating. Where are you now?"

"I can't tell you that dad. Besides, those calls were made and e-mails sent in the normal course of doing business for the hedge fund guy I've told you about before, and now they're being used against me. I've been set up dad, I swear to you."

"Okay, that explains the phone calls from your office, what about from your house?"

"What?"

"Your house, the police told us they searched your phone records and pulled your home computer records, seems these same call and e-mails were done from your home also. What am I supposed to think about that?"

"Dad, I didn't make calls like that from the house."

"Son, I *want* to believe you. I swear to you that I'll give you the benefit of the doubt, but you have to realize the evidence the cops laid out is convincing. Give me something I can go on, something to make your mother stop crying."

Travis heard her muffled sobs in the background, the pain of his helpless situation squeezing from all sides.

"I didn't do it, I've been set up. That's all I can tell you."

"Okay son, play it your way."

"I gotta go dad, I promise I'll fill you in. What else did the cops say?"

"They didn't say this, but I will. If you did this Travis they *will* find you and you *will* go to jail. You've got a chance to turn yourself in here before you get any deeper. As your father, my advice is to do that."

"Goodbye dad, tell mom I love her." Travis hung up and drove in silence. He turned off the highway and headed east onto the long, dark stretch of Highway 37 to Napa. Skirting the south end of Sonoma on the left, passing marinas that served the north bay on the right, and the barest beginnings of the vineyards this area was famous for, the drive was a welcome change of pace from what they had been through.

Chaz had given them a set of instructions with details as to how to approach the airport, when to douse headlights, and even which parking area to use. Travis pulled off the highway and onto a side road in the direction of the small municipal airport. The bright lights of the highway gave way to smaller, less frequent street lights as the country road crossed a flat, marshy expanse.

Surrounded by views of the blinking lights of Marin straight ahead, San Francisco to the left, and in front of them in every direction, the flat, dark surface of the still bay waters, Travis drove to the end of the road and pointed the car in the direction of west by northwest and flashed the headlights twice.

A response of flashing headlights greeted them across the parking lot towards the main runway. He drove towards it. The airport had a chain link fence separating the main parking area from the tarmac lined with arrows and numbers, and to the right were parked several small commuter and recreational planes secured to the pavement with cables hooked onto metal loops cemented into the surface.

The chain link fence had an opening on the right side which took them to an unloading area, Travis drove through it and parked next to an army jeep behind the nearest row of planes. Travis had seen the back of a man's head in the driver's side of the jeep as he pulled up; he cautiously walked over to the side and looked in. The man he saw was just getting out, had on a short sleeved khaki shirt, jeans, wore his blonde hair in a crew cut, and had the look of a rugged outdoor adventure tour guide. He held a clipboard in his hand.

"You must be the people Chaz sent." He greeted them with the reserved warmth of someone wanting to be sure he had the right people before going further.

He introduced himself as Scott, shook their hands, and Travis was relieved to see that Scott looked at him like he was just another guy taking a flight out of Napa. He helped them load the bags out of the car and into the luggage compartment of the plane while briefing them on a few necessary in flight rules.

He helped them board, then stayed outside to undo the tie downs and remove the chocks from under the wheels before climbing in and shutting the door.

The plane was a six-seater, two in front for the pilots, then two rows in the back with fold down armrests, not quite an executive jet, but comfortable. Scott put on his headphones, talked to the control tower and cleared them for takeoff. He maneuvered several switches on the control panel, then taxied out towards the runway. The whining engine revved up and the plane started to vibrate as they turned left to the runway.

Travis leaned forward, shouting over the noise in the cockpit, "Where are we going?"

Scott turned his head back, "Salt Lake City."

He accelerated the plane, lifting off to the south as the dark mountain range between Napa and the Pacific Ocean yawned back at them, falling away while the plane banked to the east.

Travis sat back in his seat once he could no longer see the glow of San Francisco. Nighttime flights showed little interest no matter where you flew, and Travis was too preoccupied with his thoughts to do anything conventional like read a magazine. The lack of sleep over the last 24 hours had crept up on him, and this was his first chance to get some.

Daphne had brought along a Cosmo and was skimming articles and sniffing perfume samples like this was just any other day. Travis envied her this, if only his mind could slow down, if he could just feel for a moment that it had jumped the track it was racing on and sit on the sidelines.

He pushed the button to recline his chair and gave sleep his best shot.

It must have worked, as the next thing he noticed was the plane starting its descent towards Salt Lake. His mouth had the grainy, stale feel of airplane naps, and Daphne was sleeping in her chair with the magazine still open on her lap. The lights of Salt Lake blinked in the distance, Travis looked at his watch and noticed it was just after 2 am. Chaz had promised them a Puerto Rican sunrise, it would be a push but enjoying a sunrise was something he couldn't justify until this was done.

Nothing else mattered.

The plane continued dropping, and as the change in pressure intensified Daphne woke up.

"I wish I could sleep like you."

She yawned. "I always sleep well on planes, even these small ones. Where are we?"

Travis pointed out the lights ahead on the left as Scott let down the landing gear and adjusted his speed.

"Did you sleep at all?"

"I must have", he said. "I don't remember it, but my mouth feels like yesterday's garbage."

She reached in her purse and grabbed a couple of mints, handing him one and helping herself. "This is the first plane trip I've been on in at least a year, I like traveling."

"I wouldn't be thinking of this as a vacation. Chaz is going to have us each doing specific jobs to get this done. I won't be able to enjoy myself until the money's back."

"I've been wearing these same clothes since early this morning, trust me... I know we're not on vacation. We'll be in such an exotic place, I want to at least feel like I can enjoy something I've never seen before."

"I wish I could."

"Do you and Beth travel a lot?"

"Not really, a few trips up to the coast, wine country or down to Carmel, but nothing like this."

"I'm just wondering what they'll think at work when I don't come in."

"Are you going to call?"

"I guess in the excitement of all this I didn't think about it. Even though this is a terrible mess and we have a job to do, it feels good to get out of the office, out of the country even. I needed this." She looked at him an extra few seconds as she said this, and Travis could once again feel the stirring of an attraction between them. If it was any other situation on any other day he would have kissed her hours ago.

That was the last thing on his mind. The task at hand had taken over his thoughts and focused his energies in a laser like intensity, all else falling to the side to be dealt with later. The wheels hit the runway in a smooth landing, and Scott glided the plane to the end, heading towards a dark hangar separated from what looked like the main terminal.

Outside to the left the central area of the airport glowed under flood lights, Travis couldn't tell whether they were a few hundred yards away or a mile. To the right, as Scott pulled closer he could make out the humped shape of a smaller hangar with several utility trucks parked around it. It looked like a freight terminal, the large doors were partially closed, fluorescent light glowed from inside dissipating quickly in the black night.

Scott pulled around to the rear of the hangar where a larger jet came into view. Interior cabin lighting shined through the small windows, sleek wings flared back, and the smooth hum of the engines distorted the air behind the wings with its exhaust. A man in blue overalls was removing the chocks from the wheels and opening the luggage compartments underneath.

Travis leaned forward, "Are you taking us the whole way?"

Scott turned his head towards the rear, "Yep, next stop is Miami, then the final leg to San Juan." The plane rolled to a stop a few yards away from the other jet. The man in overalls had a nameplate on the back that said "Exec-Jet Services."

Scott cut the engine, "Let's unload, we're on a tight schedule."

They descended the small stairs out of the plane, the air much thinner and colder than Napa. They retrieved their bags from the underbelly and tossed them onto a cart, the man in overalls wheeled it to the larger jet. They boarded. While the last jet was comfortable, this was opulent. Cherry wood trim surrounded leather seats, large arm and headrests, a marble counter bar sat to the rear complete with wine and cocktail glasses suspended from a rack above, and a lush burgundy colored carpet below. There were fold down conference tables, projector screens, a computer terminal in the rear, a small refrigerator, wide screen television in the front, and seating for a dozen. This was nicer than most houses Travis had seen.

Outside near the entrance of the hangar, Scott was talking with the man in overalls, going over something on a clipboard. He went into the hangar and came out moments later with a large Styrofoam cup of coffee and a bottle of water. He boarded and settled in to the plush pilot seat.

Scott went through the flight plan on the radio and rolled the aircraft slowly up to the runway. They sat there for several minutes. "They're clearing our flight plan," Scott said.

The minutes dragged on, Travis could see no other planes on the runway ahead, and it started to weigh on him exactly what it was he was doing; leaving the country under cover of darkness, marked a fugitive, using the resources and connections of an ex-con. He convinced himself he would end up in jail before the night was over, wondering how they had made it this far.

Scott put a hand up to his earphone and leaned forward. "Cleared for takeoff, over." He increased the rpm of the engines, the body of the plane shifted in response as it accelerated down the runway.

Scott leaned his head back towards Travis, "We're off, sit back and relax."

Travis sat back, popped open a coke he'd retrieved from the fridge on the way in, and tried to get more sleep. Daphne was digging for something in her purse, and the last thing Travis remembered was a vague feeling that the plane was taking off. His sleep came in fits, jumping and gasping suddenly, then falling right back to sleep. The jet climbed out of the mountains surrounding Salt Lake and began the slow arc towards Miami.

Chapter Seventeen

Turbulence jolted Travis out of his slumber, he looked at his watch, he'd been asleep for only ten minutes or so. The sky was dark, no lights were visible on the ground and the cabin lights had been dimmed. Daphne was awake staring out the window.

"Where do you think we are?" he asked her.

"I'd say ten minutes out of Salt Lake."

"Funny."

"You snore, anybody ever tell you that?"

"Beth."

"What do you think is happening with her? Is it like her to just vanish like this?"

"No, we've only been going out a few months, but this is a new one for me. I thought things were going pretty good. She's a little high maintenance, well actually, *a lot* high maintenance."

Travis rubbed the sleep out of his eyes, "But it's kind of weird, in a way it made me want to be better at what I do, to pull in enough so I could keep her living the way she wanted."

"Why do you guys always fall for that?"

"For what?"

"For high maintenance types. It's like there are all these down to earth girls roaming the planet that would make great wives or even girlfriends, yet you guys go for the sun-tanned, bleach-blonde trophy with the fake tits, then whine when they turn out to be high maintenance."

"Beth doesn't have fake tits."

"I know, I mean I don't know…but I'm speaking in general terms."

"I think guys are looking for the woman that will make them a better man. For some that could be one of these down to earth types you mentioned. For others I think deep down inside if they have a woman that spends too much, and always has to look good then that makes them try harder to become a player."

"And you fall into that category?"

"Which category?"

"The player, the wannabe to impress your trophy."

"You put it that way, no. But I have to admit, the way Beth acted made me want to be bigger, play at higher levels, and maybe that's what I was looking for. It's too bad you never met her."

Travis threw his head back to finish the rest of his soda.

"You are so shallow."

"I'm a guy, we all are. I just admit it."

Daphne went back to her magazine while Travis tried unsuccessfully to get some sleep. The turbulence calmed down, and they were silent for several minutes. Daphne let her magazine drop to her lap and stared straight ahead.

"What is it?" Travis asked. "You look like you just thought of something."

Daphne looked over at him, "Don't you think it's a little bit too much of a coincidence that the money *and* Beth happened to disappear at the same time?"

"What? I wouldn't say Beth has "disappeared", and anyway how the hell are the two related?"

"The timing, it's just too close. I mean here you have this devastating thing happen to you, and for the first time in your relationship you can't reach her at work, on her cell, or at home. Trust me, there's a connection."

"You know what I hate about women?"

"This ought to be good."

"They always talk bad about one another, even though they have no clue what the real story is. I mean if I could tell you how many times I've had a girl tell me how the girl I'm seeing is wrong for me…it's so obvious. Why can't you come up with something more original?"

"Oh, so now you think I'm talking Beth down so I can have a shot at you? I mean don't get me wrong, you're very attractive," her eyes glanced down at his neck showing through his open collared shirt, and back up to his eyes. "And I think about the possibilities, but you've obviously not been listening to a word I said."

"How's that?"

"I didn't say Beth was wrong for you…I said it's too much of a coincidence."

"Beth's got nothing to do with what happened."

"What happened the night you found out the money was gone?"

"I already told you that…we went to a club, I dropped her off, pulled up the account from my computer at home, and poof," Travis flicked open his hand to show it empty as he said this, "the money's vanished."

The plane bounced through a downdraft, Travis grabbed his armrest, letting go once they settled back into cruising mode. Daphne pulled another mint out of her purse and offered it to Travis.

"What was she like the last time you saw her?"

"The same as always I guess, a little pouty like she wasn't getting enough attention or something. I made kind of a big deal about getting back to check on Reg's trades, and I think she took it personally."

"Has she acted like that before?"

"Not really, she's always so independent."

"And the last night you saw her, which also happens to be the night the money disappears, she acts different?"

"You're saying there's a connection?"

"I see one. Did it seem like she was trying to keep you from checking on Reg's trades?"

Travis swallowed as he thought about what this meant. The ramifications were ominous, something he hadn't put together.

"You think she was trying to delay me seeing what Reg did because she knew it was happening?"

Daphne looked at him and raised an eyebrow.

"No way," he said. "I'm having a hard time thinking she would do that."

"And you can't explain where she is or why she's not answering her calls. How well do you really know her?"

"See, you women have this way of thinking everything's a conspiracy, you make connections where there aren't any. Why can't this just be a coincidence?"

"The term you're looking for is women's intuition. We see things you don't. Tell me this doesn't bug you enough to think it's possible."

"I just don't see what her role would be." Travis crossed his arms defiantly as he went on, "I mean did Reg put her up to keeping me away from checking the computer long enough to give him time to flee? And if so how did he get to her? Did they know each other before hand or what? I think this is going to turn out to be a wild stab in the dark and when it's all over there'll be no connection."

Daphne picked her magazine back up and looked at it, but didn't read.

"There already is an explanation, you're just in denial."

"Let's change the subject, I'm not up to this."

"Okay, but one more thing…how did you two meet?"

"It was at an art show, one of those trendy galleries was showcasing a new artist and I went to the reception. I remember thinking it would be a good way to mingle with some art collectors, they usually have money."

"How did it happen?"

"We kind of bumped into each other, started talking."

"Did she make it easy for you to talk?"

"What do you mean?"

"She obviously gets hit on a lot. She must screen out most of the guys that approach her, how did you get through?"

Travis shrugged, "I guess she thought I was her type."

He sat back and closed his eyes, his mind replaying the events of the previous night in light of what Daphne had said. Beth *had* seemed different, there was a needy side to her he'd never seen before. At the time he chalked it up to a predictable female response to a guy on the fast track wanting to check his hedge fund instead of being with her. But looked at under the prism of deception Daphne had laid out, it twisted his mind, played with him.

Daphne looked over at Travis, he looked pale. "It's starting to make sense to you isn't it?"

"Let's change the subject."

The plane shifted in speed slightly, they had hit the smooth cruising altitude that would get them to Miami.

"Okay, what made you get into this business?"

"Hmm, that's a good one. The quick answer would have to be uncle Phil."

"How?"

"He was always at family gatherings, used to come over to the house or he'd have us up to his cabin at Lake Tahoe. He's not really an uncle, but we called him that anyway. He was a friend of dad's, they went to school together. He dated my mom but dad married her; they all stayed in touch, it might sound kinda weird but it worked.

The thing I always remember was my dad always seemed to need money, and Phil was there to help him. I think he felt sorry for mom, and wanted to do what he could to help. What hit me most was the confidence; dad was kind of meek, subservient, whereas Phil came off knowing he had the world by the tail and there wasn't anything he couldn't do if he wanted it bad enough. He gave you the feeling he wasn't afraid of anything, and then you had my dad wandering around afraid to get up in the morning."

"What did your dad do for work?"

"He was a plasterer, tried starting his own business, but the workmen's comp costs almost buried him. After a while he got so he had to slow down, a guy in his early 60's hanging drywall, it can get a little hard on your bones, and that's when he kept going to Phil.

Anyway long story short is my dad got lucky with some real estate he inherited from his mom that she bought down in San Mateo back in the forties for around twenty-grand, and my dad sold it for a one point five million during the dot-com boom."

Travis stared out the window, his voice getting quieter, "I just wish he could have started enjoying life a little younger."

Daphne nodded, "Finish your story."

"I always wanted to know how uncle Phil made his money, so one day he took me to his office and I was hooked. I knew within an hour that was what I wanted to do. He had clients who loved him, had conversations with people like they were old family, then he'd do a few trades and make some money. He helped put kids through college, helped people get ready for retirement, even acted as executor for some estates. The guy was like a family doctor for people's money. But the most important thing, the one trait I noticed above all others when he talked to his clients…"

"What was that?"

"He didn't ask them if they wanted to buy this stock or that bond, he told them what to do and they did it. It was Phil's way or no way, his clients needed that from him and it meant he didn't have to put up with any bullshit. Sounds so much different than calling my clients up and pitching them GE or some overseas bond fund, but I think it's something that comes with time and experience."

"You tell your clients what to do, I hear you on the phone."

"I know, but it's different. With Phil there was never any question, it was all so natural. When I try to do that it sounds forced, and they still question me."

Daphne patted his knee in a gesture of mock encouragement, "You'll get there, you're still young."

"This mess I'm in is starting to make me realize something. To an outsider this looks like a numbers business… make money, earn a certain percentage, outperform an index. But all that is just a side show to what it's really about, it's about people. Clients want someone they can trust so they can live their lives spending time with their grandkids and traveling. If they didn't need me they could easily go online and buy stocks, but they want me not so much as an advisor, but as a partner."

"You're passionate about what you do, I can feel it when you talk like that. Here you are flying to the Caribbean to get your client's money back, I'd say your clients are pretty lucky to have you."

"I don't feel like that right now."

They still had a long flight ahead and Travis wanted to keep talking, keep distracting his mind from what was happening, turn the conversation to something other than him and his plight, "So what made you decide to work for Hastings & McCloud?"

Daphne laughed, "They had an ad online. Seriously, I know this sounds funny but I almost became an actress. I went through acting school, got signed on with an agency, but it never went anywhere. I always thought I would be like Jennifer Tilly in '*Bound*' or that girl in '*La Femme Nikita*', her name was Anne something, I felt comfortable in the noirish, evil role of a foreign femme fatale. But I kept getting these auditions in soap commercials or these lousy sitcoms that never aired and it didn't work for me. So I decided to get a real job to pay the rent."

"You do kind of look like Jennifer Tilly."

"So I've heard."

"Were you in LA?"

"Yes, I moved to San Francisco because I hate it down there, it should be named Shallow City. Hey…maybe you ought to move there."

"Ooooh…" Travis bent over in imitation of taking one where it hurts.

The conversation lulled, Daphne couldn't get off of her earlier thoughts, "Didn't your dad say that they found phone and e-mail records at your house also?"

"Yes, but I never made those."

"Well who did, or could, or had the opportunity and the motive?"

"What are you Miss Marple now? I have no idea, Reg probably hacked in somehow, who knows? In any event, I'm screwed."

"Do you think Beth could have done it?"

Travis didn't want to go there, it was too much to deal with and it depressed him to feel like he'd been played all along. "No."

"Did you also notice that the money was wired out to the account in your name late Friday afternoon, but didn't hit the Cayman's until early Monday morning?"

"So?"

"So…the money was in your name the whole weekend. If you had gone in the office and found it out sooner, you still could have done something with your name on the account. They were totally exposed, and it was her job to keep you out of there all weekend. Were you with her Saturday too?"

"Come to think of it we spent more time together this last weekend than any other. We chartered a sailboat with Tim and Donna, rode mountain bikes on Mt. Tam, I thought we were really hitting it off. If what you're saying is true she played it very well. I never saw it."

"You're a guy, your mind is on other things."

Travis looked out the window again and saw only his reflection against the glass. "I just have one thought right now, and that's to get the money back and make sure Reg gets nailed for this."

"That's two thoughts."

"You can add a third…there is no way I'm going down for this. I don't care if I have to run around the rest of my life, I'm not taking the fall for something I didn't do."

"This is what I like to see, a man with confidence."

"There was something else uncle Phil used to say that I've adopted as my own."

"Buy low, sell high?"

"No…'*The most powerful weapon on earth is the human soul on fire*'. I take it to mean something more concrete."

Daphne cocked her head.

"There's *nothing* I can't do."

Chapter Eighteen

T he tires hit the Miami runway hard snapping Travis awake. Daphne was leaning forward putting lip gloss on using her small mirror. Outside the glow of dawn crept over the horizon. Scott leaned his head back, "I think a Puerto Rican sunrise might be pushing it but we're almost there. Here's where it gets a little tricky."

Travis's head perked up, "What do you mean a little tricky?"

"We're not going to switch planes like we did in Salt Lake, we're simply going to refuel and take off. What we need to be careful of is they're pretty tight here with private jets heading for the Caribbean. We're set up with the control tower, we've already gone through the necessary check in process at Salt Lake and Chaz has registered a flight plan. But we have to make sure we don't do anything to raise their suspicions. We're also lucky in that Puerto Rico is one of the few islands around here that you don't need a passport to get into."

"What do you want us to do?" Travis asked.

"Just stay in the plane, this won't take long."

Scott rolled the plane to the end of the runway where he made a sharp left and headed for an area with several small hangars and gas trucks parked at various angles. Fuel tanks with company logos dotted the area around the hangars, and further beyond that a row of decorative palm trees separated them from the main terminal.

Travis looked out his window. The rising sun cut a beam through the scattered, looming clouds that swirled around the airport. Scott pulled up to one of the hangars and came to a stop. He cut the engine, unbuckled his seat belt and opened the door. A wave of humidity enveloped the inside of the plane.

Travis got up and walked around the cabin, pulling his collar away from his neck and wiping the beads of sweat off his forehead that were already forming. Looking outside he saw two police cars parked next to the hangar, top lights flashing, and another policeman talking to a worker in overalls pointing in the direction of the jet. Travis looked over at Daphne as she watched out the window, the open compact still in her hand. Scott was exiting the jet down the stairs.

Scott and one of the drivers of a fuel truck began the refueling process, the jet rocking as the locking connection of the fuel hose was attached and twisted into place.

Travis bent over, leaning close to Daphne and looked out the same window as her, "What do you think they're doing here?"

She shrugged, "It's out of our hands now cowboy. No use getting worried at this stage of the game."

"I wonder how much Scott knows," he said.

"I say we keep quiet, let him do his job and see where the chips fall."

The fueling process continued, the orange glow of sunrise distorted by gas fumes rising over the wing as the hose filled the jet's tanks. The policemen got back into the vehicles and drove away. The flashing lights were turned off, and Travis let out the breath he had held since watching them.

Scott came back up the stairs as the fuel truck driver shut the pump off and unfastened the hose from the jet.

Travis walked over to Scott, "Why were the police out there?"

"There's always a skirmish or two going on somewhere in an airport this close to the border. Could be anything." Scott said this as he closed the door, latched it and walked back to the cockpit.

Travis searched Scott's face for any sign of shared secrets, but found only the look of a man doing his job. Travis sat back down and Scott cleared the plane for take-off.

Once in the air Travis tried to read a financial magazine he'd found in the seat pocket next to him, the articles which dealt with things like saving for retirement and college funding meant so little compared with what he was going through. The daily grind of his past existence felt remote as the realization he'd become a fugitive overnight pressed down. The flight to San Juan was short, Travis occupied most of it by staring at the blue water out the window as it caught and reflected the morning sun. Daphne was quiet and looked like she was trying to catch some sleep.

The plane landed at Isla Grande Airport which sat on the tip of a peninsula on the northern side of the island. The capital city of San Juan was on the eastern part of the peninsula, and to the south on the large bay of Bahia de San Juan floated oversized cruise and cargo ships.

The plane was met by a black limousine with tinted windows, a driver standing motionless by the door. He had on the requisite uniform, hat and sunglasses, but the way he held himself made him look like more than a driver. Travis decided not to think about it, he was in somebody else's hands right now and had to let go of any preconceived destiny he had in mind for himself.

Scott walked over to the driver and shook hands, then leaned down and peered through the driver's side door and waved towards the back seat. Travis and Daphne grabbed their bags and walked to the waiting limo. The driver grabbed the bags, put them down by the trunk, and opened the back door. "Let me introduce you to Chaz," the driver said. He had opened the door with a flourish, and they looked into the dark interior of the limo.

A puff of cigar smoke hid the face of the man sitting in the back seat. All Travis could see was a cream colored tropical suit, Italian loafers with no socks, and a black Rolex that cut through the hairs of his tan wrist. He sat like he belonged, he sat like a man at ease with the world and everything in it. The cigar smoke slowly cleared, revealing a tan, lined face, receding salt and pepper hair, and jet-black eyes. They shook hands and Travis let Daphne in first, then joined her in the seat across from Chaz.

"Welcome to San Juan folks, enjoy the flight?" The accent was slightly British, cultivated, strong and thick.

"Yes, everything seemed to go smooth. A little scary here and there, but, we made it."

"I've got you booked into a hotel just outside of town, The Wyndham. You'll like it."

"So no checking in with anybody here? We can just get in the limo and drive off?" As Travis asked this the driver finished loading their bags, slammed the trunk, and started the engine.

"The local officials are a special breed down here," Chaz said. "If you aren't trafficking drugs or killing people, they'll let you get away with almost anything as long as there's something in it for them." Chaz rubbed his thumb and fingers together in the universal sign of cash.

"The thing you need to worry about are the US authorities, they don't get bought off the same way. But you're in San Juan now, and even though it's still US territory it will be easier for us to get the job done down here than if we were say, in New York." Chaz inhaled another drag from his cigar, letting the smoke spill back out of his mouth in a lazy, gray cloud.

"Speaking of this job, can you tell us how it's supposed to work?" The driver pulled away from the plane, drove down a side service entrance and pulled out onto the main thoroughfare that wrapped around Isla Grande airport.

"If I told you the details you wouldn't believe me, it has what every great job like this requires, simplicity."

Travis shifted in his seat, "So we're supposed to go into this not knowing what we're doing?"

"I'll tell you what you need to know when you need to know it."

They drove out of the airport terminal and along a coastside highway that took them on the outskirts of the center of town, passing the mangrove studded Parque Central to the right where morning joggers and walkers were starting their day. The clouds Travis saw earlier in Miami had started to break up, and the mid-morning sun was setting up the hint of what was to come. The sky opened up into patches of blue and palm trees waved in the slight breeze as they rounded the south side of the peninsula.

The shops along the waterfront of the bay were what you'd expect in a tourist destination; pottery vendors, candle makers, blown glass artists, wind chimes, wood carvings, and outdoor cafés here and there. Above most of the shops were what looked like living quarters, each window facing the street had ornate wrought iron grates over them, large window boxes were attached with bougainvillea cascading down in fountains of bright pinks and reds.

Chaz was silent. He looked out the window, eyes narrowing as the smoke from his cigar rose into his face. Travis had already decided to follow Chaz's lead, and kept quiet. They exited onto a narrow side street and pulled up to the imposing entrance gates of the Wyndham San Juan.

It dripped with the ambience of a paradise sparing no expense. The lush front lawn swept up to an immense spidery banyan tree wrapping around itself in a twisted display of gnarled ancient bark. To the left were three swimming pools interconnected with canals, lined with boulders and waterfalls to give each of them a natural lagoon appearance. In the trees lining the flagstone walkways the faint, persistent chirp of the coqui frog pierced the air while the thick canopy of green above cast a rain-forest climate over the grounds.

The driver parked in front. Young dark-skinned doormen in red blazers approached the limo from either side ready to help. Chaz got out, followed by Daphne and Travis, and they walked through the tall frosted-glass front doors. To the left was a sunken circular bar, overhead hung an immense oval shaped chandelier. The concierge saw Chaz and immediately waved them over.

"Chaz, always a pleasure to be of service." The concierge handed him a room card and signaled for a bellhop. There was no paperwork, no credit card imprint, no signature. "Enjoy the room sir, as always please let us know if there is anything you need."

As he finished saying this a middle-aged man in a suit and tie walked over and took Chaz's hand, pumping it with overdone two-handed enthusiasm of someone wishing they had more customers like him. "So pleased you're with us again, here's my cell phone number." The man reached in his breast pocket and pulled out a card. "Anything at anytime, it is yours." He followed this with a barely perceptible bow and stepped away. Chaz nodded and took the two towards the elevator where the bellhop was waiting with their bags.

Travis looked at Daphne as they boarded, "Guess you've been here a few times huh Chaz?" He said this with the awkward laughter of someone who's not sure if what they just said was funny or not. Chaz nodded, and pushed the button to the 5th floor.

The windows in room 525 opened out to a view of the bay outside to the left, and looked over the three connected pools down to the right. It was a deluxe suite with a small entry area, followed by doors on the left to the bath and closets, a sitting area with a wet bar and small refrigerator, opening to a king sized bed placed diagonally to take full advantage of the view. Chaz put his hand on Travis's shoulder and leaned close, "I'll leave it up to you to work out the sleeping arrangements." He winked as he said this. Daphne walked over to the window pretending not to hear.

Chaz looked at his watch, "I'll let you two get settled in. It's 10 a.m. now, let's meet downstairs at the main restaurant for lunch at 11:30."

Travis took off his watch to adjust for the time change.

Chaz continued, "I'll go over everything then."

The door latch clicked behind him.

The room air-conditioner turned on, through the open window they heard the laughter of kids playing in the pool below.

Travis walked to the window and closed the thin curtains.

Chapter Nineteen

Reg took the elevator to his room from the hotel gym, a towel hung around his neck, his t-shirt wet with sweat. He inserted the card key in the lock, went in and dug his laptop out of the carry-on satchel laying on his bed. He booted it up, went into the bathroom to dry off, and put on a black pair of warm-up sweats.

Connecting to the hotel's Wi-Fi he tapped the keys, making his way to the SFGate.com home page of San Francisco's main newspaper.

He stared at the front page.

Reg leaned back and breathed deeply, picked up the phone on the bedside table, and dialed Donovan's room. "Get over here, you'll want to see this."

Donovan knocked a few seconds later, Reg let him in.

"What's up Reg? I don't know whether to be curious or nervous."

Reg smiled, "Be entertained."

Reg took the laptop off the bed and brought it to the table in front of the window, motioning for Donovan to take a chair. The computer screen was dominated with a headline in large, bold font. Reg stood behind him as they read the feature front page article:

San Francisco Stockbroker Wanted in Connection with $54 Million Scam

In what appears to be a premeditated scheme to steal his client's money, local stockbroker Travis Black is the subject of a nationwide manhunt after disappearing with over fifty million dollars of client funds.

According to Hastings & McCloud branch manager Dick Callan, Travis approached him claiming one of his hedge fund investments had been mysteriously cleaned out Sunday night. "Why he came to me I have no idea, maybe it was his way of seeing how close he could stay to the scene of the crime before it all unraveled, the whole thing is very bizarre," Dick said.

On further investigation it was learned the funds had been wired to an account in Puerto Rico and from there to a shell corporation in the Cayman Islands. The account in Puerto Rico turned out to be in the name of Travis Black. When authorities uncovered this Mr. Black disappeared.

The FBI agent heading the investigation, Greg Wilks, commented that if he were going to wire funds out of the country like this he certainly wouldn't put it in his name. "The guy is either really dumb or just toying with us, only time will tell. Meanwhile we have enough evidence for a solid conviction, we should have him in custody within 24 hours."

Local authorities acted quickly as search warrants were obtained for Travis's phone and computer records at work as well as home. According to FBI statements these records contained numerous entries and communications with the bank in Puerto Rico as long as two months before the actual theft took place. "It was obvious this was a planned, methodically diabolical move Mr. Black put into place, but he left enough clues and tracks for us to put him away and recover the money," agent Wilks added.

Branch manager Dick Callan was quick to point out that this was the act of a rogue individual and in no way reflects the way Hastings & McCloud does business. "All of the accounts are SIPC insured against these kinds of unforeseen events, and there is no reason for our clients to be alarmed or panic."

Several co-workers expressed shock over the events that had taken place. Travis was described by associates as energetic, driven, and had all the makings of an elite financial advisor on the rise. "The fact that this was going on right under our noses, it's hard to believe," said one employee who preferred to remain anonymous.

Authorities aren't saying where they're conducting the search for Travis. Latest reports had him headed north over the Golden Gate Bridge in his late model black BMW. His assistant Daphne DiMarco is also missing. It isn't clear if she is involved in the crime or is an unwilling accomplice. Her apartment and phone records have been searched with no incriminating evidence as yet.

Travis began his career with Hastings & McCloud over two years ago, and began a steady climb up the chain of top flight brokers the firm is known for. He graduated from Cal Berkeley in 2008, and worked in the accounting profession briefly before becoming a stockbroker. His parents in the Mendocino coastal community of Sea Ranch would not comment other than stating that they know nothing of Travis's whereabouts, or the accusations against him.

Travis was recently seen attending high society social events and other gatherings frequented by the city's wealthiest patrons. On his arm lately has been his girlfriend Beth Wagner, who has been unavailable for comment.

"He was very skilled at talking to people with money, getting them to trust him, and now this. It's a tragedy, it undoes decades of trust our firm has built up," Callan said.

Authorities have stated that the manhunt is extensive. Airports, train stations, marinas and rental car agencies have all received copies of Travis's photos, as well as those of Daphne and Beth. "He won't get far," agent Wilks said. "He was quick and smooth when it came to moving the money, but he's been sloppy in his escape."

Hastings & McCloud was founded in 1985, has two branch offices in San Francisco, as well as offices in Los Angeles, Sacramento, and Seattle. They cater to high net worth individuals, and specialize in seeking out undervalued investment ideas.

"Do you love it or what?"

Donovan nodded, "It looks like the scent's been thrown off for a while. How long do you think it'll be before they catch on?"

"I'd say it's a good week before the cops finally figure out Travis isn't the thief. By then we'll have the money back in the states, in places no one knows where to look, and we move on to the next one."

Donovan looked up, "How much before we quit? I mean isn't this enough to set us up so we don't have to keep putting ourselves at risk?"

"You know what I wish was different about you and half the people I end up dealing with?"

Donovan stared blankly.

"You think too small Donovan; the world is full of mediocrity. Too many people set goals based on a myopic view of what they know from past experience. Think big, get outside of that little brain of yours."

Donovan was taken back, unsure of what to say.

"Don't get me wrong," Reg continued. "You're a great partner in this, you do an excellent job of being a front man, a heavy when I need one and I pay you well for it. But leave the big picture thinking to me. If you ever want out, get out, no hard feelings… but when you're in, you're in on my terms. Got it?"

Donovan retreated from the table and walked to the door. "Got it, I'll see you later on."

Reg went back to the computer and read the story again.

He reread the line that said, '*It was obvious this was a planned, methodically diabolical move*'. He reread it three more times. Reg knew that most crimes like this went wrong when an oversized ego got in the way of a masterful plan, subconsciously craving credit and recognition. He silently repeated his personal vow to never be weak enough to fall into that trap.

Chapter Twenty

Daphne came out of the bathroom patting her face dry. She grabbed her bag and knelt down in front of the hotel room dresser next to the armoire. Travis watched her folding something lacy, white, and laying it in the bottom drawer.

He walked over to her. She looked up.

She let her eyes come down his torso, and back up. She stood facing him, looking at his mouth. He kissed her gently at first, as she responded he threw himself into the moment pressing hard against her.

They scrambled to get each other's clothes off while still kissing and standing up, hopping over to the bed with clothes around their ankles to finish what they'd set out to do. The window was open slightly, the curtains billowed in to the room. The energy of the last 24 hours swept them both into wanting each other, and it cemented the pact they had made to get into this in the first place. At first they probed, tested, explored; soon giving way to each one taking what they wanted from the other. A ceiling fan turned above them, the air conditioning steadily losing the battle to the humid tropical air. They both glistened with a thin layer of sweat.

"Ever read any Shakespeare?" An afterglow of tropical sensuality reddened her face, her wide eyes unblinking in female vulnerability as she asked this.

"Just what I had to, and the cliff notes at that. Why?"

"You know the term he used for what we just did?"

Travis had nothing to say.

"The beast with two backs."

They laughed, tension had been released, and decided they should shower together since lunch was in 20 minutes.

Dressed in new tropical clothes, they descended the staircase from the mezzanine level which took them to a ground floor restaurant. As they walked down Travis looked up to see an American man in a disheveled charcoal suit.

The man could pass for a business traveler, but there was something Travis noticed in the walk. It was the way he grabbed the stair rail, aiding what could have been a weak right leg. He'd seen this before from a different angle and couldn't place it or the face.

The man didn't look at either one of them.

After a few more steps Travis turned around, pretending to admire the ceiling.

The man was gone. *Where had he seen this guy?*

The hotel's main restaurant, Café del Arozzo, had wide views of the ocean while being conveniently shaded by the huge Banyan tree just outside its windows. High ceilings, large paddled ceiling fans slowly turning above, tall banana trees arcing over the tables, and the tiled water fountain in the center meshed together into a tropical oasis. Tuxedoed waiters darted here and there, towel draped over one arm, champagne bottle in the other, smiling and bowing at everyone they made eye contact with.

The hostess approached. Travis scanned the room for Chaz and saw him at a corner table talking on a cell phone, waving them over. The hostess followed them with menus, Chaz finished his conversation and stood to greet them. He noticed their flushed faces and winked at Travis as they sat down.

After the quick exchange of small talk Chaz indicated it was time to get down to business, "We have a lot to do and hardly any time to do it in. The plan is we eat, no lingering over the shrimp cocktail and talking about the views, then we go to my office. Clear?"

Travis and Daphne nodded. They felt like they were school kids on a field trip to a place they knew nothing about, all they could do was follow directions and nod. The dark world of offshore money laundering was foreign and Chaz was their tour guide.

Their table was located away from the main dining area where strategically placed potted palms obscured the view from even the most dedicated lip readers.

"What then?" Travis asked.

"When we get there I'll be able to show you the trail of money. Where it's been, and where I think it's headed. I'll show you my plan, we'll go over each of your roles in this, tomorrow we make our move." Chaz sat back and took a sip of his coffee.

The waiter headed in their direction. As Travis started to reach for his menu Chaz held up a hand, "Please, why don't you let me order for all of us. I've eaten here enough to know what they do best."

Chaz spoke in Spanish as he ordered ceviche, shrimp cocktails, quesadillas, and a tropical version of what they knew as chicken Caesar salad. Iced teas were served and menus whisked away.

Daphne sat up and pulled her shoulder length hair back, "So tell me Chaz, may I call you Chaz?" He nodded. "Is this what you do all day? Recover stolen money?"

Travis looked over at Chaz, uncertain whether Daphne was treading onto dangerous ground by probing too deeply into the working life of a figure like Chaz.

Chaz smiled in answer, "I like people who ask direct questions, no beating around the bush here. The answer is I do a little bit of everything in this area. I have several corporate clients who pay me a retainer to track illegal money laundering, fund transfers, and your odd assortment of rogue operators, somewhat like your Reginald Crae."

Daphne continued, "Sounds like a game of cat and mouse. These people wouldn't hire you if you weren't good at what you do. Do you always catch the bad guy?"

Chaz put his elbows on the table and leaned forward, "I don't know what kind of people you're used to dealing with, but the reason I'm where I am is that I do my homework. I could tell you more about Reg from what I've learned in the last 24 hours than you could from your entire relationship with him."

Chaz sat back and looked at them through narrowed eyes, "This is my job, I take it seriously, and in this game you either know more about your opponent than he does about you, or you lose the game. Checkmate, smartest guy wins."

"So how did you get to be so good at this?" Daphne asked.

Even the most hardened of men will soften up at the flattery of an attractive woman, and Chaz was no exception. "It's a long story, but mainly I got caught up in the wrong side of it several years ago, and made some contacts that I use to this day. After I paid my debt to society I'm able to navigate that underworld well enough to do what I do, and stay on the right side of the law while not jeopardizing my contacts. It's an ideal situation."

Travis asked Chaz what he could tell them about Reg.

"He's a pro and he's done this before. We're dealing with a man who came up from the shadowy world of arms dealing, and when that got too risky he decided to become a thief, but a thief of the highest order. His first attempt at this only netted him a few hundred-thousand, and it wasn't the stealing the money that almost got him caught, it was trying to get it back into the US. He had made the mistake of converting the cash into diamonds, and then trying to smuggle the diamonds into Florida. It would work as a money laundering step, but he hired the wrong diamond merchant. The jeweler was working both sides, thought he could take a fee from Reg and get a reward from the police for turning Reg in. The jeweler underestimated Reg however. Reg had set up a smoke screen in the form of a courier named Donovan who carried an empty briefcase onto a plane under the name of Reginald Crae. The authorities followed the courier while Reg boarded a ship bound for Panama. From there he flew to Seattle, pulled off the same scam only a little smoother. The Seattle job apparently netted them about 18 million, then off to San Francisco. This is the part in the story where you come in."

"What happened to the courier?" Travis asked, "How did Reg get the diamonds into the US?"

"The courier was apprehended at Miami airport, they searched his briefcase, his person, and came up with nothing. It was a perfect bit of misdirection on Reg's part," Chaz said with a touch of professional admiration.

"What about the diamonds?"

Chaz laughed, "It's brilliant. Reg painted them a metallic color and fastened them to a leather belt which he wore on the plane."

Daphne held up a finger, "Wait, you said the word 'them' when you talked about the Seattle job, he has partners?"

"We know he still works with Donovan, and there's word that there are others behind the scene but that's only speculation."

"How do you know all this?" Travis asked him.

"International thievery is actually a fairly close knit society. There are only a few people in the world who have the skills and resources, let alone the balls, to pull this kind of stuff off and get away with it. The people you read about in the papers that get caught are for the most part amateurs, the pros are always one step ahead of everybody else. As I mentioned, I have maintained some contacts in very strategic places. We'll leave it at that."

The food arrived, conversation faded as the two travelers realized how much of an appetite the last day's events had built up. Chaz ate methodically, slowly and deliberately chewing to make each bite an event, while Travis was on a mission to refuel with gusto.

Daphne wiped her mouth with the cloth napkin, "Chaz, I hope you don't mind my asking, why are you doing this? It seems a big risk on your part, and I haven't heard about any fee you're taking."

"I assume you've met Uncle Phil?" Chaz answered.

Daphne shook her head, "I feel like I have the way Travis has talked about him, but no."

"Well, he called me and told me the kind of trouble his protégé here was in, and it gave me a chance to repay an old favor."

"What do you mean?"

"Back when I was working in the trust department for one of the big banks…this is a few years before I …" he looked around the room in an exaggerated sideways glance "…before I joined the dark side in a matter of speaking, I got myself into a bit of a scrape."

"How so?" Travis asked.

"Back in the early 70's things were a lot different. At the bank when we wanted to trade a stock we did it through the broker that referred the account to us, at that time brokers didn't offer trust services. So we would manage the account and direct the trades through guys like Uncle Phil. Anyway, we were buying 10,000 shares of IBM for an account, at that time IBM traded around 400 bucks a share, so we're talking about a single trade worth over $4 million.

The way I remember it, I wrote up an order ticket which I gave to my assistant, she time-stamped it, and phoned it in to Phil. He writes an order ticket on his end, time-stamps it, buys the stock and everybody's happy. Only problem was I had two other clients I was talking to at the same time, one of who was selling IBM. Long story short is that I mistakenly sold 10,000 shares of IBM instead of buying. I must have been distracted when I filled out the ticket, and checked the wrong box."

"So couldn't you just correct it? That happens all the time."

Chaz pushed his plate away and washed down the last of his iced tea. "Trouble was I didn't realize it for an hour, by then IBM had climbed seven points."

"Why so much?" Travis asked. "Did they announce earnings or something?"

"You have to remember, this was before all the stock-splits it went through in the 80's. It was over 400, which would be like one of your 40 dollar stocks jumping by 70 cents. Not very noticeable, except that with 10,000 shares we're talking about over 70 grand. The account who wanted it had been quoted a price and were the kind of people who would hold us to it. He had placed a fill or kill order, and…"

Daphne held up her hand as high as her shoulder, "Excuse me, what's a fill or kill order? Sounds dangerous."

Travis put his hand out to Chaz, "Allow me. What it means is the client wants the stock at that point in time *and* at that price or not at all. It's used when the client thinks they might move the market with one order. Back then it was common for an order of 10 or 20 thousand shares to bump a stock up and make it difficult to fill the order at the price they were willing to pay. It's a way of putting a large order in and not leaving what they call 'footprints', or signs that there is a big buyer out there. Today it would be used only for thinly-traded stocks or for orders of several hundred thousand shares."

"I heard one of the traders on the phone say 'all or none' with one of the orders, is that the same thing?" She asked.

"It's similar. 'All or none' means they want the whole block of shares instead of a partial execution. In other words, if you place an order for 10,000 shares at a certain price, and the trader can only get you 5,000 shares, an all or none order tells him not to get those 5,000, but to do it all at once or not at all. The main difference is fill or kill has the element of time involved..."

Chaz went on with his story, "Bottom line is that in a matter of hours I was on the hook for what at the time was over two years salary for me."

"You would have to pay that?" Daphne asked.

"Back then we would have always been on the hook for those errors," Travis explained.

Chaz continued, "So here I am, a young trust officer trying to do his job and I'm about to lose a huge chunk of money that I don't have."

Daphne was shocked by this, "How do they make you pay it if you don't have it?"

"They take it out of your salary. Indentured servitude until it's paid off."

"So how did Phil help you?" Travis asked.

"Well, the way we stood, there was this purchase of 10,000 shares that needed to be filled, only the price was seven points higher. We could fix it and I get hit for the 70 grand, or we could buy the stock from somebody that doesn't know it's a bad price."

"But that's illegal," Travis said.

"Of course it is. But Phil found a way that made it workable. Back then he dealt with several charitable foundations as well as large estate settlements. It turns out on that same day there was a large foundation that was gifting large blocks of stock out to churches, a major university, and several other charities. One of the churches was set to get 20,000 shares of IBM. Phil had taken care of the transfer, and then called the church receiving the stock.

They were so grateful for this unexpected gift that they were speechless, Phil simply told them he was selling the stock for them and to expect a check shortly. They didn't care that half the trade was bad, didn't know it, and frankly were so happy to get the money that it never came up. So Phil just put the bad trade in their account and I didn't have an error hanging over my head."

"So your account essentially bought 10,000 shares of IBM from the charity at a price that was seven points below the market?"

"Good Travis, I see you're on the ball. The church got their money, the client got his stock, and nobody ever knew what happened."

"So Phil saved your bacon that day and you're doing this to repay him? That was so long ago I'm surprised you remember." Daphne said.

"It was that job at the bank that got me the contacts I have today. It's not Phil's fault I went down the path I did. Shortly thereafter I was in prison, when I got out I still had my contacts and once I got started in this consulting business I've felt I owed Phil something for what he did that day. This came up and I'm here to help."

Travis and Daphne were silent.

Chaz looked at his watch, "We need to wind this up," he held up his hand and motioned the waiter over.

"What's next?" Travis asked.

"We'll go to my office and work out the plan, I'll also show you where your clients' money is."

Chapter Twenty-One

Outside the hotel Chaz waved his limo over and the three of them got in. Daphne was sitting next to Chaz, and Travis across from them.

"Tell us about this plan," Travis asked.

"It's better if I tell you what you need to know as we go along. Besides, it will be easier to run through it when we're in my office in front of the computer screens."

Travis looked out the window. They pulled away from the hotel, out the long driveway and underneath a row of palm trees back to the main highway. The billboards were still in English coaxing tourists to hotels, restaurants, casinos and shops. Travis thought they could just as well have been in LA instead of Puerto Rico. This changed as the driver took his exit and started heading up a winding road towards the center of the island.

Views of the ocean opened up in front as the limo gained elevation. On both sides of the road iron gates stood in front of bungalows barely hidden under draping bougainvillea framed by thick patches of palm trees.

The limo continued to wind up the side of the mountain, increasingly showing higher viewpoints of the island around each turn. Pulling up to a wrought iron gate with thick greenery on either side the driver rolled his window down and punched five numbers into a keypad.

The gate slid open.

"I take it you work out of your house?" Daphne asked.

Chaz nodded. "My office is on the left side of the ground floor, over there." He pointed out the window as they drove down to the end of the stone covered driveway.

Travis lowered his head to get a better view out the window. The driveway ended in a wide flagstone area in front of the house, green moss growing in between the stones, and overhead the shade of swaying palms, banana trees and vines covered the property in a rain forest canopy. The house blended into the surrounding landscaping with ivy growing up the stone façade, a massive porch laid with oversized bricks, and a gray ceramic tile roof sat on top of the two story structure.

It looked like a massive rock growing out of the hillside. Looking closer, however, the details of a dwelling came into view. The plantation shutters on every window, small iron railings in front of each one, large potted plants dotting the porch and driveway, and small brick paths leading to either side of the house.

On the right side of the house was an upper story deck that appeared to hang in the trees like something out of a Tarzan movie with old wooden chairs, rolled up blinds and a small table. On the left where Chaz had pointed out his office, disguised in the many winding vines that hugged the house Travis could make out twisting black cables snaking into an outlet on the side. He followed these to what he first thought was just another skinny palm trunk, but on closer look was straighter than anything in nature. As he followed this up he realized it was a utility pole, and perched on top, far above the highest trees, was a massive satellite dish painted in camo. If you weren't looking for it you would have a hard time finding it, from the periphery of your vision it would look just like the top of another palm tree.

They stopped in front of the house and got out of the car.

"This is a great spot Chaz, how long have you lived here?" Travis asked him.

"It's been a few years. In normal circumstances I'd have you stay here, but the police know where I live, and on the off chance they decide to pay me a visit it would be best if you weren't here."

Travis wanted to stay here, he wanted to live here, retire here, run money from this building, eat his breakfasts on the top deck and cruise down to the harbor for dinner or nightlife. When he saw people who lived like this he remembered why he did what he did.

The money.

The money to buy the toys to lead the life he saw for himself. With all the money sloshing around Wall St. he was determined he could earn enough to make this life happen. As he dreamed this dream he'd dreamed many times before, he knew in the back of his mind there was something wrong with it this time. He was a fugitive… he had a job to do. It was not a time to dream big dreams; it was survival, it was getting out of the deep end before his breath ran out.

Daphne walked up the porch behind Chaz, and he opened the solid teak front doors to a large front room covered with oriental rugs, an Italian chandelier above, and wide, curving stairs straight ahead.

He led them down a hallway to the left.

The slate colored walls were textured to look like old stone caves, and though the floors were hardwood and stone throughout, the house still felt warm. They walked through an open archway which led to a hall on the left lined with three solid teak doors with black iron locks. Chaz took out a key and opened the one on the far right.

Faint light came in from the front windows, illuminating what looked like a financial cockpit. A U-shaped desk sat in the middle facing the windows. On the desk were four 19" flat panel monitors with keyboards in front. On the blotter of the desk was a laptop, several tablet computers, folders and notepads, a remote control and an ashtray with a cigar butt in it. The screens of the monitors were black as slate, this changed as Chaz reached under the desk and turned on the computer system.

Two of the screens blinked to life.

Travis took it all in. He'd been taught how much of an impression an office makes on a client, and he always took care to make his look solid, sophisticated without being intimidating, and it was a fine line that he liked staying on top of. But this, this was an aspiration. It was science fiction movie and corporate titan wrapped into a legend.

The walls were lined with bookshelves, some of the titles Travis caught were stories of larger than life fugitive figures of the financial world such as Vesco, Frankel, Leeson, Marc Rich, Milken; throughout were political titles condensing major coups as occurred in Romania, Cuba, Haiti, and the Philippines. On the walls between the shelves were framed portraits of Chaz shaking hands with recognizable figures; Marcos, Noriega, Rich, Castro. Underneath these were framings of older versions of third world currencies. Handsomely decorated, centered with the portrait of a previous dictator; the currencies either didn't exist in their present form or were now a laughingly devalued version of their former existence.

The computers bleeped to life, Chaz sat in the black leather chair at the center of the cockpit and called them over to the desk.

The screen on the far left of the desk showed a series of entries, each a specific dollar amount highlighted in blue digits against a cream colored background. Row after row of transactions were listed with the sending institution shown on the left column, followed by the amount, then on the next column the receiving bank, the wiring number and in some cases the names on the accounts. Most of the account names were innocuous sounding such B & T Trust, Jackson Imports, Takeda Shipping; as well as several major banks that were household names.

"How is it that you have access to all this data?" Daphne asked.

"As I mentioned at lunch, I'm on retainer by most of the bigger international banks, as well as most of the regional ones based in Florida. I'm paid to monitor money laundering activities so the banks can catch it before the feds do. If a major bank's internal controls catch this it makes the bank look good to the regulators, but if the feds see it first then the bank gets its name plastered all over the papers and a tie in with money laundering takes years of PR to get over, not to mention what it does to the stock price. It's become a several billion dollar a year problem, and the feds make these banks put in all kinds of safeguards and policies to try and prevent it. I have, in a nutshell, become their outsourced money laundering control center. They give me access to these databases in real time, I've set up different alerts that come up when certain parameters are hit, and bingo they can call the feds and let them take it from there."

Travis put his hands on the desk and leaned closer to the screen, "What is it we're looking at here?"

"These are all the transfers either from or to my client banks. It's safe to say that 99.9% of these are routine business, but I'll see a familiar name pop up, or a series of transfers from the same account that looks to serve no purpose other than covering something up, and then we have something.

The banks retain me because it's much easier for someone to look at this from a bird's eye view and spot something, than it is for a clerk in New York to notice that the money he wired this morning to Nassau is in Florida the following day."

Travis looked up and down the screen, the names and numbers blurring together in a maze of jumbled digits.

"Can you see the wire Reg did?" Travis asked.

Chaz scrolled further up the screen, hundreds of transfer entries spinning by as he continued into earlier transactions. "Let's start from the beginning of his moves." Chaz highlighted an entry near the top of the screen, Travis leaned in and saw the familiar name of Hastings & McCloud's bank, followed by several account numbers and routing data, then the amount of $54,367,955.35.

He kept reading to the right, what he saw next pulled the blood from his face, forcing him to hold on to the edge of the desk while the room started to spin.

He knew it would be there, but seeing it brought on a convulsive reaction reminding him exactly how serious this was. On the far right of the entry, listed as the receiving account, the name *Travis Black and Associates* glowed in a taunting display of guilt.

Chaz pulled a chair over next to him and Travis, starting to recover from the shock, sat down and put his head in his hands.

Chaz and Daphne exchanged glances.

"We'll need you with all your facilities tomorrow," Chaz said. "So get this out of your system now. By this time tomorrow we should have everything taken care of. Be strong Travis, this man took you and he's done everything possible to make it look like you did it. He's no better than you, just more devious."

Chaz rolled his chair back away from the desk to look at Travis.

"This is one of those times in your life…this is when nothing else matters, when you need to suit up and do battle. It's now or never, we screw this up and you take the fall for Reg…poof, the money's gone. We win this and your clients get their money back, you stay out of jail, and you go home a hero. Every battle is won in the mind before it's won on the battlefield, and believe me, I wouldn't do this with you if I didn't think you had it in you. It's like I said yesterday, if you're going to go down, make it for something you did, not Reg."

Chaz searched Travis's face for a sign of confidence.

Travis pulled his hands away from his face and looked at Chaz. "I see it in your eyes Travis, this is a mission…stay focused."

Travis stared at the computer entry. His eyes heavy, his face turning into the face of a predator.

Daphne watched him. The Travis she knew last week was not in this room, in his place was a cobra. They were silent, the hum of the computer the only noise as they watched the lifeless numbers on the screen.

"Why can't we take the money while it's sitting in my name?"

Chaz smiled. "Good idea sport, there's just one problem. The money's not in that account anymore."

Daphne sat down next to Travis, "Where is it?"

Chaz scrolled further down to the following days' activities, which would be yesterday, and pointed to a line on the screen, "See this entry here? That's an account in the Cayman's. The money went there last night, then it goes back to San Juan tomorrow, and from there to the US. Once in the US it will be spread out so far we'll never know where to look."

"How do you know what will happen tomorrow?" Travis asked.

"Reg has done this before, and he follows a pattern. The money laundering world is one of 'if it ain't broke don't fix it'. The contacts are too valuable to discard, the accounts, once they're set up, can be used over and over… and Reg hasn't been caught yet. This works for him."

"Why haven't *you* caught him?" Daphne asked.

"Good question. When he last did this I alerted my client bank to his activity. That's where my job ends, and they go to the authorities. The thing is that it isn't a problem for the banks since nobody is stealing money from them. The only people who want to catch the launderers are agencies like the IRS, FBI, DEA or the SEC. Reg was able to slip through their nets both times because his previous scams were smaller. Anything less than 10 or 20 million in money laundering is too small for the feds to set up an operation and gather evidence. Reg is at a level now where he'll attract some attention regardless of what you and I do. The banks retaining me are doing it to keep the regulators off their backs more than anything else. Sure, it's bad business to get caught helping someone launder money, but it's really because of the feds that I'm able to do business at all."

Travis nodded, "So the banks comply with the regulators by hiring you, but if it doesn't involve their money they don't waste a lot of time on it."

"Precisely. You see, money laundering by itself isn't necessary unless a crime's been committed. You and I could move money around the world all we wanted, and to what purpose? But, if a crime is the source of the money then the trail has to be erased, washed away if you will.

What most people don't realize is that these guys usually get away with whatever crime is being committed, but where they get caught is when they try and clean the money. Money laundering is what you might call the necessary residue of another crime, and is often the only thing that can be pinned on them. That's why if you and I move money to the Bahamas it's legal, but if Reg does it's not; money laundering laws were put in place to make the fed's job easier."

Travis continued to stare at the screen. "So what's our next move chief?"

"The money's in the Cayman's now, in an account that can still be linked to Reg. From there, if he follows his pattern, he'll wire it back to San Juan. However, there is still a trail, the feds can follow wire transfers with their eyes closed. So he has to get the funds into an unrecognizable account before he scatters them back to the US."

Chaz leaned back in his chair and folded his arms over his chest, "This means one more transfer, and it's the weak link in his strategy."

"Why doesn't he just wire the money from where it is now to the US?"

"Still traceable, he can wire it to a different bank every day for a month and that won't solve his problem. The essence of money laundering is that it needs to get out of the system, even if only for a day, and then come back in under another identity. Some drug rings actually buy computer or bicycle parts with the money, sell them back, generate phony invoices, buy and sell businesses, anything to take the cash out so it can lose its scent. The way Reg does it is a little less involved than what I've just described, but he'll most likely need an accomplice to help. Fifty million in cash is cumbersome, even in large bills."

"What do you mean?" Daphne asked.

"Fifty million in hundred-dollar bills weighs 1100 pounds and will fill four or five large duffel bags. If the currency is new it will take up less space but it's still a problem, older bills pick up moisture and actually expand, making them thicker. What we have working in our favor is every money laundering operation has one vulnerable spot, and that's the time at which it has to come back into the system. The very essence of laundering money means it has to leave the safety of the system for a brief period of time, and then come back with no trace of its source."

Travis and Daphne were silent as they learned the intricacies of a world they'd never knew existed.

Chaz continued, "It's not very common knowledge, but drug dealers have a more difficult time handling currency than smuggling drugs. Hiding a few hundred-thousand is child's play, but when you start talking millions it becomes something you need to treat as a separate business; the storage, laundering, moving and hiding of currency. You know who Pablo Escobar is don't you?"

Travis answered, "Sure, wasn't he some big-shot Colombian drug lord?"

"Right, his operation was huge, we're talking billions of dollars in hundreds, fifties and twenties circulating through his organization. A friend told me it got so out of control at one point that Pablo had a two-thousand square foot building constructed behind his house specifically for storing currency. After a few weeks he had to have the building walls and ceiling lined with sheets of glass to keep the mice out...they were eating the money."

Chaz snapped back to the moment, "We're off subject here, let's get back to Reg. He has already started a pattern he's ready to repeat, and as I said his weak point in the laundering process happens tomorrow when he has to take the fifty million physically out of the system, then put it back in."

"So what are we going to do, jump him?" Travis asked.

"No, nothing like that."

"What do we do?"

Chaz laid out a brief sketch of his plan to retrieve the money from Reg. When he finished the two stared at him, blinking.

Daphne was the first to speak, "Have you done this before? Can it really work?"

Chaz pulled a cigar out of his breast pocket, and reached for the brass clip sitting next to the ashtray. The leaf wrapping the cigar looked black in the low light of the room. He touched it to his nose, moved it back and forth, inhaled and closed his eyes. He clipped the end off, put it in his mouth and took a gold plated lighter out of his pocket. He snapped open the lighter, put the cigar in his mouth and leaned forward in his chair. The flame danced, the end of the cigar became a red glow and the lighter snapped shut. He took in a deep breath and sat back letting the smoke drift around his face and up to the ceiling.

He looked at Travis as he spoke, "I learned it from a guy in prison."

Chaz pulled another drag on the long, dark cigar. "There were four Romanians who pulled this off in a bank in Italy; it doesn't take any special equipment, just balls the size of watermelons. The four never got caught, the guy I met in prison was one of the bank employees and when he saw it happen decided to do it himself at a bank down the street. He blew it, got arrested, and I met him while I was inside. I'd heard about the Romanians through the grapevine, but actually meeting a witness filled in some holes for me."

Travis stared at Chaz, trying to absorb as much as he could. "What did the guy you met do wrong that got him caught?"

Chaz smiled and took another drag from his cigar. "It's not what he did, it's what he didn't do. He didn't do his homework. The Romanians made it look easy, but what you never saw was the preparation that goes into something like this. Hours and days of watching, planning, researching, you only see the tip of the iceberg when a crime goes off smoothly. The Romanians made it look easy, he tried it without doing his research, and got caught. That's where we differ. Not to worry." Chaz's confidence was unwavering, he sat there smoking a cigar, exposing them to an alien world that they were about to step into as if it were as natural as getting into an elevator.

Travis's face showed a brief flicker of apprehension, hearing the wild stories sounded cool until somebody that did what you're about to do, ends up in prison.

"There's something you need to accept about this business we're involved in Travis."

Travis looked at him.

"Nothing is certain."

Chaz continued to work on the cigar, "If you want predictability you might as well get on the next flight home. But if you want to win this game Reg has asked you to play," he took the cigar out and looked at it, holding it in his hand as if it were a rare jewel, "it will take a leap of faith larger than any you've made before."

Travis stayed silent.

"In your mind Travis, you have to see the successful outcome of this as your destiny."

Chaz put the cigar back in his mouth.

Chapter Twenty-Two

"Take my limo back to your hotel," Chaz said. "There are some things you'll need to do while it's still daylight.

He briefed them further on minor preparations needed before tomorrow. They agreed on a time to meet in the morning, and the limo took them back to their hotel in central San Juan.

The two were quiet on the trip, each contemplating their role in what Chaz had called '*a plan beautiful in its simplicity*'. Coming down the mountain they had a view of the harbor in the distance. The breeze had picked up, whitecaps formed and several sailboats were taking advantage.

Travis's cell phone rang.

He mouthed silently to Daphne, "*It's my dad.*"

"I'm just taking a little trip, that's all."

Daphne could hear the sounds of his father's voice from where she was sitting but couldn't make out what was being said.

Travis sat up straight, "The police came? What did they want?"

The color drained from his face, the limo driver glanced back at him in the rear view mirror.

"Oh God, are you and mom okay?"

Travis listened.

"I'd rather explain it to you when I get home, I've been set up and by this time tomorrow I'll be in the clear."

Travis looked at Daphne, he felt powerless.

"The newspaper?" Travis went on. "No, I haven't seen it."

He looked over at Daphne again, his eyes showing her the alarm at this new development.

"No, don't read it to me, it's all lies dad. I wish you could just believe that."

He slouched in his seat, feeling the weight of the deep water he was swimming in push the air out of his lungs.

"My picture's in the paper? And Beth's? Do they quote Beth?"

Travis kept listening, unsure of how much more information he could ingest.

"I'm sure mom's upset…but please trust me…I'll explain everything tomorrow." He hung up.

"The cops went to see my parents at their beach house up in Sea Ranch. Dad said mom was pretty shaken up by the whole thing, and the police wanted to know if I'd been in touch with either of them."

"This thing is bigger than we thought isn't it?"

Travis nodded, "You should know your picture's in the paper, right next to mine and Beth's. The police think the coincidence of you missing means you might have something to do with this. Dad said they've been getting all kinds of phone calls from the press, friends, and even other clients of mine that are threatening them if they lose money. If this doesn't work I'm not sure what'll happen. It's like I've left this hurricane up there to wreak havoc with everyone involved and I'm down here in a limo chumming around with an ex con, who the hell have I turned into? What do I do if this doesn't work?"

Travis looked out the side window not seeing what was out there, only images of his thoughts.

"I feel powerless, but I can't stand by and watch, I have to be down here doing something about it."

Daphne waited until he was finished, "Your parents might seem upset, but I'd bet deep down they want to believe you if they don't already."

"They've never even gotten parking tickets. They want to spend their retirement playing golf and traveling, now this." Travis was silent the rest of the trip.

The limo pulled off the main highway onto the exit for the hotel, and turned right into the lush driveway they'd seen earlier. The driver pulled up to the front entrance and as he did so Travis looked out the window and saw the same man he'd seen earlier on the stairway. He was still in the same suit talking to another man in a suit, and holding a cell phone to his ear.

As the limo pulled closer both men peered in trying to get a look at the passengers through the tinted windows. A flicker of recognition crossed the face of the man holding the phone as he looked at the driver. His hand came up and he started pointing them out to the other man.

"Don't stop here! Keep going, we've been spotted." Travis yelled at the driver. "Come on, get out of here!"

The driver turned his wheel to the left and sped back out of the circular driveway. Travis looked behind him, the man was talking rapidly into his cell phone while the other looked like he was flagging down a car.

"They're trying to follow us, you have to lose them. Can you do that?"

"I'll handle it."

He turned the limo to the right, went under the freeway overpass and onto a frontage road passing a row of coastside shacks sheltered by palm trees. Travis kept his eyes glued to the rear window.

The limo swerved to the right between a beat up café with locals gathered on the front porch and a brick structure that looked to be some kind of government facility.

They pulled into an alleyway behind the café, engine running…waiting.

"They'll think we took the highway, Max said. "Most people don't even know this road exists."

After several minutes of no other car in sight, Max maneuvered the car back to the coast road.

They continued on the frontage road until there was a long stretch of pavement behind them. When Travis saw nothing out the back window he had a little more respect for the driver. The road took them past old brick buildings on the left that looked like they were once military outposts, while on the right the ocean went on forever.

Max reached for his cell phone which was mounted on the dashboard and pushed a button, "Chaz…listen, there were two plainclothes out front of the hotel when we got there and they recognized us. Right now we're headed up the old coast highway and we seem to have lost them. Any ideas?"

Max listened as he drove, then hung up.

"What did he say?" Travis asked.

"New plan. We're sending a guy over to your hotel room to get your stuff, and you two are going to stay on Chaz's boat which is moored at the harbor up here." As he said this the beefy hand resting on the top of the steering wheel raised a finger and pointed straight ahead. "Chaz wants you to call him once we're on the boat."

"Don't you think it would be safer at his house?"

Max didn't answer.

Further up the coast highway shadows grew longer as the sun dipped behind the swaying palm trees lining both sides of the road. Travis stared at the back of the driver's head. The hair was thick in places, but the faintest traces of an attempted comb over were starting to show. His cheeks were pockmarked, sideburns long and uncared for, a diamond pierced his right ear.

The driver looked in the rear view mirror and caught Travis's gaze.

"Something wrong?"

Travis looked at him in the mirror. "Just not used to this, that's all."

"Don't worry, Chaz is a pro at this." He adjusted the mirror to make better eye contact with Travis, "and he only hires the best."

The limo rolled up to the marina and into a parking lot jutting out from the shoreline facing a small inlet lined with boats. On the right was a tourist strip of craft shops, outdoor cafes and art galleries. Across the inlet was a small park where a local farmers' market was just starting to dismantle. Tables stacked with fruit under blue tents, wheeled carts, and kids on scooters all jostled around each other while steel drum music played.

"Let's go." The driver cut the engine and got out. "See that one with the blue trim on the side?"

Travis looked at the boats, the biggest sailboat in the water had a dark blue streak going down the sides of a white hull. It sat on the other side bobbing up and down with the current, near the stern the name *Moneta* was painted in a dark italicized font.

They walked down the pier towards the boat.

The metallic sound of halyards slapping against masts, the wooden dock creaking, sails being put away as they flapped in the warm wind, and seagulls crying gave Travis and Daphne the brief sensation they were far from home. The sound of steel drums from the nearby park dipped in volume with the heavier breeze over the water.

Max caught up to them and walked over to Chaz's boat.

At 48 feet long it was luxurious without being ostentatious. You could live on it, cruise on it, day sail or race other sailboats. The dark teak decking was immaculate, the sails neatly rolled up and tucked under dark blue sail covers, and the white hull glistened against the cobalt blue trim.

Max stepped up on the decking, then put out his hands, "Give me your bags."

He helped them on board, unlocked the cabin and showed them around. "This will be your home for the next day or so, you could do worse."

The boat was beautiful, polished dark wood trim, tiled bars and countertops on the inside, remote controlled panels opening to television monitors and computer screens, and a thick burgundy carpet. The head had a small shower, the beds fore and aft were made up with throw pillows, and strategically placed mirrored walls made the surroundings seem more spacious.

The essentials of sailing; fire extinguishers, first aid, flares, life vests, all were tucked into visible but out of the way cubbies under the benches and counters.

Travis ran his hand along the dark wood trim, "Chaz never does anything halfway, does he?"

Max pulled out his phone and pushed a key. "We're on the boat."

He nodded. "Gotcha."

"Chaz says to go ahead with what you need to do this afternoon, make yourselves at home. He'll come down here for dinner with you around seven to make sure you're all set. Meanwhile, give me the keys to your room and we'll send someone over to get your things."

It was the way he said the last part about the keys that made Travis cock an ear. For the first time on the trip Travis had a doubt about the people that were here to help him. He'd spent the last day finding out who he couldn't trust, and the list kept getting longer. When did it stop? Was he being paranoid, or just aware? The driver looked at him and held out his hand. "Keys? We don't have a lot of time here."

Travis glanced at Daphne, who was oblivious to what was going on in Travis's head. He fished in his pocket and handed them over. The driver left. As he walked along the pier he shouted over the roar of a nearby engine sputtering, "Help yourself to anything, Chaz will be here later."

"Daphne, do you trust that guy?"

She was standing on the steps leading to the master bedroom, "I think so, why, you don't?"

"I don't know, I got a funny feeling when he asked for our room keys."

"You trust Chaz don't you?"

Travis nodded. "I feel like I have to."

"I think if we trust Chaz we have to trust who he has on his side, otherwise we'll get paralyzed with fear and get nothing done. I have to go over to those shops and get some kind of outfit for tomorrow. Why don't you wait on the boat here and I'll be back in a little while. Then we can watch the sunset together before our big day."

She kissed him and walked off the boat.

Travis sat on one of the benches and watched her leave. *Why did she want me to stay here? We've been sticking together the whole time, what's going on? Can I trust anybody?* He stood up and leaned on the railing, looking down at the water, *I'm going out of my mind, I feel like this is a house of mirrors.*

Looking out over the water, he thought how he wished he would be able to enjoy the sunset from here, what it would be like to live like this without having to look over your shoulder or dread the events of tomorrow. The wind continued to pick up, buoys swung back and forth, their bells ringing.

Travis went down below and poked around. There was nothing personal in the boat, it looked like it could have been on display at a boat show. Clean, inviting, it was another reminder of why he had originally wanted to do what he does.

This was the toy of a player, someone who was liquid and knew there was more coming in. Travis wanted to be on this side of the ledger, he knew he'd tried too hard to get it quickly and ironically, that's why he was on the boat right now.

He sat at the table, leaned back and put his feet up. This was the first time he could relax by himself in hours. He'd slept in fits on the plane, his mind had been racing ahead of his body since Sunday night. It was Tuesday evening, and the last 48 hours felt like a montage of computer screens, car chases, men in suits… and lies.

He closed his eyes. The gentle rocking of the boat lulled him. His head nodded down towards his chest as he wondered how long Daphne would be.

Sleep overpowered him.

Chapter Twenty-Three

Small wakes of passing boats rocked Travis, he was half-conscious, knowing he was waking up but wanting to drift back to sleep. The last wake felt stronger than the rest.

He opened his eyes.

The sun had begun its descent and was shining through the small, round windows in the cabin, thin curtains doing little to block out its glare. Sitting up, wiping his chin and trying to stare through the dense fog of drowsiness that had overcome him, he jerked his head back.

A dark shadow moved between him and the window. He focused his eyes, cutting through the haze, and stared down the barrel of a handgun. Behind it stood the man he'd seen at the hotel.

The man cocked the hammer and stepped closer. "Not one move sleepy head, got it?"

Travis swallowed. His throat felt like dry sand.

In the doorway to the cabin stood another man, Travis recognized him as the second man he'd seen from the limo in front of the hotel. He stood leaning on one side of the opening, his feet crossed in a relaxed, cocky stance matched by the sneer on his face.

"Thought you'd go for a little boat ride with all your new money?" The man in the doorway followed this with a drag on his cigarette.

Travis looked at the man holding the gun in his face.

He looked every part the G-man; close cropped hair, white shirt, thin tie, dark suit, and the freckled, boyish, well-tanned face that seemed to be a birthmark of astronauts, lifeguards and FBI agents. Where this guy looked athletic, spry, and alert the other agent looked slothful. He had a large pot belly, the grey pallor of a lifetime smoker, and the greasy wisps of hair on the side of a bald head belonging to a man who stopped caring long ago.

The man with the gun reached into his breast pocket, took out a leather billfold and snapped it open. "FBI. You're under arrest for the embezzlement of funds from the clients of Hastings & McCloud. Put your hands on your head and stand up slowly."

Travis couldn't move, his brain wanted him to talk but his mouth wouldn't move. "We... we don't have time." His voice felt dry, tight, unsure.

"Excuse me?" The man with the gun stepped closer.

"Time...the money is going to disappear after tomorrow, I need to be somewhere to stop it."

"The money's already disappeared, you're going to get it for us, and then you'll go to prison. It's very simple, now hands over your head and stand up."

"But I didn't take the money, I'm being set up."

The fat man in the doorway laughed a sputtering smoker's laugh and bent over in a fit of reactive coughing. "Oh Jesus, I love it when they say that! Don't you Ben? It's my favorite part...most of 'em wait a little longer before pulling *that* one out." His coughing calmed down.

"It's the truth..."

He was cut off by the man holding the gun, "Shut up, and do what I said."

Travis put his hands on top of his head and stood up slowly. The slight rocking of the boat made him unsure on his feet.

The agent backed up slightly, "Turn around."

Travis turned and the agent went through his pockets with one hand while holding the pistol in the other. All he got was a cell phone, wallet, and some receipts for things Travis had bought earlier.

The agent put the gun into Travis's back, "Now, keep your hands on your head and walk out into the cockpit."

Travis awkwardly tried to climb the three steps of the ladder leading from the cabin while holding his hands on his head and the boat rocking. He instinctively grabbed on to a handrail, which made the fat man reach under his coat and come out with a handgun at snakelike speed. Travis leaned back, put his hand back over his head and kept walking.

The agent followed behind, "Now grab that shroud and pull yourself onto the dock. You make any moves and we shoot, is that understood?"

Travis did what he was told and reached his left hand up onto the cable stretching down from the mast to the decking of the boat, and pulled himself up and onto the wooden dock.

He stopped. The agents stepped off the boat one at a time, each pointing a gun at Travis.

Travis looked into the detached face of the younger agent, "I mean it, we have no time. The money is in one bank on its way to being laundered, and after that we'll never get it back. We've found a way to get it back but you need to let me go before it's too late."

Travis thought he saw the briefest flash of empathy dart across the agent's face. It vanished as quickly as it came.

He had to get him on his side now, or never.

"Who is 'we'?" The agent asked.

"Me and Chaz."

"Who's Chaz?"

The fat man put his gun back in his holster and moved closer to Travis, the dock rocked back and forth with the shifting weight.

"He handles things like this, I hired him to help me get the money back. We're going downtown tomorrow to recover the money."

The fat man stuck his face out and leaned into Travis, "You hired somebody to recover money that *you* stole?" His foul breath made Travis lean back.

The fat man moved closer, Travis stared at the gray, bloodshot eyes, the spider-web capillaries covering his nose and cheeks, and stepped back. "That's smart...reeeaal smart. Think that makes you look innocent? Let's have him spend a night in the can with the boys and we'll have that money by noon tomorrow. Come on Ben, cuff him."

Ben kept looking at Travis.

Travis searched Ben's face for the slightest glimmer of trust. He felt like someone who'd just said he'd been abducted by aliens...there was no one on his side, he needed someone to come over, someone who could help him now.

"Ben, you've got to believe me, I was set up by this guy Reg Crae, have you heard of him?"

No response.

"An uncle of mine knows this man who tracks this sort of stuff from his house on the island. I flew down here with the idea of meeting up with him, recovering the money and getting it back where it belongs. It's all set for tomorrow, and if we don't get there then Reg will have transferred all the money into these small accounts back in the US where we'll never find it. I'll work with you guys but we need to move fast."

Ben put his gun in his other hand and stroked his chin. "Why didn't you call us first?"

"For this very reason. While you guys are busy trying to put me away the money vanishes and we're all screwed. Chaz thought it was best this way. Now that you're in it work with me and we all win."

Ben looked at the fat man, then back at Travis. A few yards off in the distance the familiar hum of an outboard motor revved up and changed speeds as the operator tested the throttle. Travis was standing at the end of the dock, the two agents between him and the rest of the marina. Travis's hands were on his head, Ben's gun still aimed at his chest.

Cornered against the end of the dock he felt squeezed, vulnerable. He was under pressure to get Ben on his side and wasn't sure if it was working. The fat man opened his mouth. "Sounds like a well-rehearsed cock and bull story to me...you buy this one Ben I got some property to sell you."

The fat man's voice was unmoved, a lifetime of cynicism behind it. If anybody was going to come over to Travis's side it would have to be Ben.

"I couldn't make this shit up if I tried," Travis said. "I'm begging you, I'm trying to help you for God's sake. Can't you see what's happening here? This is exactly what Reg wanted to happen. The bad guy is winning!"

Travis threw his head back in frustration, "Is that your job? Just give me the benefit of the doubt, I'm down here working this angle and you can screw it up and lose your jobs or you can go with me for the next 24 hours and get the money back. You are making a decision for dozens of innocent people's life savings; I know what I'm talking about."

Ben looked at Travis's face, searching, examining.

"It's time to fill or kill Ben, do it your way we all lose, give me a break and we restore a piece of the dream to a group of people who have no idea they've been nailed to the wall."

The sound of the motor drew closer. Travis turned to see a small sailboat motoring out of a slip a few spaces down the same channel. The skipper was too busy with the details of navigating the busy marina to notice what was going on. Beyond the marina was a short breakwater and past that the evening cruisers were underway. Party boats, night sails, night scuba charters and drunken Jet Skiers filled the bay. At the entrance to the marina the harbor patrol boat was refueling.

Travis looked back at Ben in time to see him reach under his jacket with his right hand. He noticed the metal bands of handcuffs as Ben fumbled with getting them out. "You already made the decision with these people's life savings. Turn around."

As Ben said this he looked down to see what was hanging up the cuffs.

Travis knew the rest of his life would hinge on what happened in the next few seconds.

The fat man told him to turn around.

The motoring boat pulled closer on its way out to the main channel.

"Put your hands down behind your back."

Travis lowered his hands slowly, watching the boat come up from the left, still several yards away.

The decision was instant, Travis dove off the dock.

A split second before he sliced through the water he heard shouts from the two agents, but no gunfire. The diesel fuel lingering in the water burned his eyes and stung his nostrils. The underwater sound of the boat came closer from the right, Travis kicked and stroked his arms straight ahead through the murky depths.

On the dock the two agents began shooting at the water on both sides. They split up and began shooting under boats, in the slips, looking for bubbles or any other signs that they had him.

Travis continued to struggle against the water, his clothes slowed him down as he kicked furiously against the natural urge to rise to the top. His ears rang from the sound of the bullets, he had no idea how close they were coming. All he could hear were muffled pops and the slowly increasing sound of the outboard as it drew closer.

Ben and the fat man scattered over the marina like sniffing dogs catching no scent and not having a clue where Travis was.

The younger one started shooting indiscriminately at the water.

The fat man shouted, "Meet me back where he jumped off!"

They ran back to the slip Travis had leapt from and peered over the water. "When he dove he went straight out," the fat man said. "Maybe he's swimming to the other side."

Ben looked out beyond the motoring sailboat to the other side of the marina. "It's over 150 yards, if that's what he's doing he's either dead or he'll come up any second."

Travis pulled his arms through the water and fought the gagging in his throat, lungs wrestling to override the urge to hold his breath. The mixture of salt-water and diesel runoff stung his eyes, visibility was less than three feet in the muddy, green marina water.

The boat motored closer, Travis kicked and pulled harder.

Just a few more seconds.

The long shadow of the boat came up on his right as Travis started to ascend while still swimming to the other side. He heard the cavitation of the propeller as it pulled water through itself.

The timing had to be precise.

He looked up and saw the dark shadow of the bow directly above him. His breath was running out, his vision clouded as his brain started to shut down all body functions not crucial to getting oxygen in his lungs.

His hands and feet felt numb.

The struggle of covering more distance as the boat went over him became a dreamy, unconscious fight of mind over body. He felt his right leg hit the long keel underneath the boat as it bore down on him.

He kicked to the surface.

"I don't see anything. If he went straight he's either got incredible lungs or grabbed onto that little sailboat over there."

The fat man put his hand over his brow to shield the setting sun. It glared in his eyes and cast a sparkled reflection on the water. "You radio to that harbor patrol boat to follow the sailboat just in case, I'll keep watching the water and see if he comes up."

Ben pulled out his cell phone and went to work making the connections, while the fat man continued to scan the water. Glistening diamond shaped points of light danced along as the small clouds parted away from the sun; he reached in his pocket for sunglasses.

––––––––––

Travis's head broke the surface with the boat inches from his face. It was between him and the dock moving at a speed of 1-2 knots. Travis gasped for air at the same time that he lunged for anything to grab onto the side of the boat.

Tube-shaped inflatable fenders that cushion the boat from the wooden dock dragged in the water hanging from a line tied to the railing around the boat. Travis's hand came out of the water and in a death-grip clenched onto the nearest fender, gasping for breath as quietly as he could.

Over the railing he could just barely see the top of the skipper's head. Travis lowered himself as much as possible back into the water, while moving his grip to the metal railing around the boat. The driver of the boat picked up his pace as they came to the end of the channel and steered towards the main exit to the bay.

The fat man kept looking straight ahead for any sign of a body. The glare of the sun made things tricky and for a second he saw a head bob in the water. He aimed his gun at it. The black head of a sea lion lolled in the water before submerging again.

Travis moved hand over hand towards the front of the boat, holding onto the deck railing as the boat dragged him through the water. He wanted to keep the boat between him and the agents while staying out of sight of the skipper. The boat headed towards the breakwater and made a wide right turn around it. Travis went around the front of the boat to stay out of sight, and as it finished its turn he was on the opposite side, still out of view of the agents.

Clinging to the railing, his legs dragging in the water, Travis looked over his shoulder at the bay behind him. He realized that while the agents couldn't see him, everybody else could. The boat was on a straight course for the mouth of the bay, and Travis felt the boat shift weight as the skipper went forward to raise the sails and take in the fenders.

Behind him evening party boats were blaring music and heading in the same direction. On the other side of the boat, confused agents pointed, stared, and shielded the sun from their eyes. Onboard the skipper leaned over the railing to pull in a line…and looked straight into the eyes of Travis.

Chapter Twenty-Four

D aphne crept through the aisles in one of the tourist shops along the waterfront, thinking she would rather buy one of the tropical wrap around skirts while she was here instead of the business suit Chaz told her to buy. Exotic prints, hand carved jewelry, artistic renderings of simple objects like door hinges painted to look like children's books were interspersed with bright colored t-shirts, hats and imprinted coffee mugs. On the back wall was a rack of mix and match women's wear. She grabbed what looked like a locally acceptable pants suit, a few printed skirts, some pastel-colored tops and ducked into the dressing room.

The store began to thin out as it neared the 7 o'clock closing time, from the dressing room she heard the clanging of the door chime as tourists turned their attention to outside activities for the rest of the evening. Daphne tried on the pants suit first. The fluorescent lights over the mirror gave her face an unhealthy, dim pallor, and it picked out the flying strands of dark hair she didn't notice in usual lighting. She turned around to see how it looked from the rear. Always self-conscious of her backside, she tried to pick outfits that showed off her legs but slimmed down her butt. This one would do, the olive grey tone was businesslike but casual enough to wear again when this was all over. What was it Chaz had said? *I want you to look like a Puerto Rican banker who has nothing to hide, a sophisticated businesswoman who is perfectly at ease handling millions, with never a doubt as to her competence.*

A thin yellow scarf finished off the look and then she moved on to the fun stuff. After deciding on some of the skirts and tops she went to the register and reached for the cash in her purse when a thick, hairy hand reached out and touched hers, "Allow me, please." Startled, she looked up.

Someone she had never seen before was staring at her with a credit card in his hand. *Was he offering to buy her clothes?*

He was tall, obviously a native from his dark complexion, and wore the local favorite of an off-white linen suit and pastel shirt opened at the collar. Gold chains dangled over a thick carpet of dark chest hair. Daphne glanced at the cashier who only gave her a secretive glance of approval as if to say, *"What more do you want sweetie? Live a little."*

She looked back at the man quickly and said, "No, really, I can handle this."

He smiled. "You look as if you could handle many things. I am merely offering to buy these clothes for you because a woman of your beauty would flatter them more than they would flatter you."

Great, some Latin lover with pick-up lines she couldn't answer. She looked at her watch. Chaz would be at the boat any minute and she had to get going. "No, I'm in a hurry and I have to meet someone right away. But thank you." She forced the bills into the cashier's hands in an overstated gesture of impatience.

The man persisted, "In a hurry? On vacation? What man has done this to you? You may be in a hurry but I assure you no one else on this island is. Please, let me take you to dinner, I know a little place around the corner that serves fish caught this afternoon. You will feel a million miles away from home." He smiled, showing a gold tooth, gesturing with his hands as he described the evening.

"No. I mean it, I have to go."

Daphne stared at the cashier.

He kept at it, "You Americans, you hurry all day, then go on vacation and are still in a hurry. He can't be your husband, I see no ring. Come let a real man show you how things are done down here." With that he put his arm around her waist, gave the card to the cashier and started to pull her away.

"Stop it!" She pulled herself away and put her clothes on the counter. "Can you please give me some change so I can get away from this man?"

The cashier finished the transaction and the man stood there, unsure of what to say. In one moment he had gone from Latin lover to getting yelled at, and his dark eyebrows reflected the scorn and embarrassment he felt. "You shouldn't have done that," he said. The voice was suddenly deeper, not so friendly.

The cashier bagged the clothes and Daphne walked out the door.

The man followed.

She walked quickly off the main road and down one of the side streets that would take her back to the marina. She focused on moving straight ahead, and glanced behind her.

He was still back there, walking slower than her, casually, his hands in his pockets, but his long legs enabled him to keep up with her short, quick trot. Daphne pulled the bag of clothes closer to her and began to run towards the marina.

Chapter Twenty-Five

Travis tightened his grip on the railing and locked eyes with the sailor. A flicker of panic set into the man's heavily-lined face as he put the gunshot activity on the dock together with a crazed man hanging from the side of his boat. The man looked back toward the marina like he was ready to shout for help. Without hesitation Travis pulled himself up, swung his legs over the railing and landed on the deck. He stood there, dripping wet, hair falling in his face, out of breath. The skipper backed away.

Like a cornered animal Travis began to look for anything that would get him where he had to be. People around him had become mere props on a stage as the circle of threats closed in, the clock ticking. *You're a fugitive Travis, start thinking like one.*

The man on the boat would be easy. He quickly recoiled into a crouch against the railing on the other side, "Please senor, don't hurt me, I have a family. Just tell me what you want." He backed up as far as he could without falling over the side. The boat continued to motor in a straight line, the steering had been put on auto-pilot when the skipper had started to raise the sails.

Travis looked at the man, "Just be quiet, don't do anything that looks unusual. Take the wheel."

The man stood up timidly, took the wheel, disconnected the auto-pilot and stared at Travis while keeping the boat on a straight course.

"Doesn't this thing go any faster?"

The man pointed to the rear of the boat. "The throttle, turn it to your right."

Travis crouched down towards the back of the boat and reached his arm out to rev up the outboard engine. He kept one eye on the skipper, who was looking straight ahead, and another on getting the rpm's up.

Behind them he saw the harbor patrol boat start to pull away from the fuel dock, blue spinning lights flashing on top. Travis gunned the throttle, the boat jerked forward and moved only slightly faster. The patrol boat turned towards them, its pointed bow lasering in on Travis like a gun sighting.

He turned towards the skipper, "Is this all this thing's got?"

"Please sir, it's only a sailboat."

The patrol boat turned on its siren and drew closer.

Travis scanned the horizon and saw the beginnings of a plan. He focused on an object fifty yards ahead and pointed it out to the sailor, "Head for that."

"Sir, anything you say, please don't hurt me."

The patrol boat picked up speed and started to come up on the left side. It was still a hundred yards off, but gaining enough ground to be on them in mere seconds. The sputtering, noisy outboard was no match for the powerful chase vehicle, Travis knew it would take more than speed to get out of this. He crouched down in the cockpit next to the sailor, "Keep this heading." Travis continued to point out the object straight ahead.

They slowly closed the gap.

Travis glanced behind him every few seconds, the patrol boat was close enough that he could make out two uniformed men on deck with rifles drawn.

They gained on the object in front, the skipper looked over at Travis, "Please sir, what do you want me to do?"

"Stay just like this, maybe a little more to the left."

"But I don't want to hit him."

Travis used his advantage. "Shut up and do what I say." The sailor was meek, simple, and shirked away from the yelling madman that had crawled aboard.

The sailboat came alongside a couple sitting on Jet Skis in the water, engines idling, talking and pointing. They looked up startled as they saw how close the sailboat was coming to them. Travis looked over the other side at the patrol boat, there was a third man in an elevated cockpit with a microphone in his hand. The speakers mounted on the top crossbar clicked, "Halt your vessel!"

Travis swung his legs over the side of the railing as the Jet Skiers looked at him, unsure of what this wet, crazed apparition that appeared before them was up to.

He lunged at the nearest one knocking him off the Jet Ski. They fell in the water, Travis having the element of surprise wrestled himself free and swam over to the empty Jet Ski.

The girl on the other Jet Ski screamed.

Travis climbed aboard the Jet Ski and gunned the throttle. From the other side of the sailboat the patrol boat kept shouting orders.

In a sweeping arc that shot a plume of water behind him, Travis sped for the other side of the bay, head down, swerving side to side to avoid the inevitable shooting that would follow.

He looked back over his shoulder, the bewildered skipper watching as the patrol boat passed the sailboat and headed right for him. Travis opened the throttle as far as he could.

The Jet Ski bounced off the swells that had increased in size as they got closer to open water. The motor whined and sputtered as it jumped off the choppy bay, Travis felt like he would lose control at any second. The steering wasn't responding well because of the high chop, and he had no idea how much fuel was left.

The patrol boat sliced cleanly through the water.

Travis looked back again and saw a uniformed man on the highest part of the boat bracing his shoulder against the side of the cockpit, holding a rifle aimed straight at him.

Travis ducked down and swerved left.

He thought he had less of a chance of getting shot at if he surrounded himself with innocent people out having fun on the bay. Even the cops down here wouldn't shoot tourists. *Or would they?*

Just ahead on the left was a two level dinner cruiser with dining tables set on the outer decks and tuxedo clad waiters passing out champagne. Behind the cruiser was a large catamaran motoring out with its sails still down, scuba tanks could be seen stacked in rows along the outer benches.

Travis cut in between the two followed by a loud blast on the horn from the catamaran.

He looked behind him.

The patrol boat was temporarily out of sight as the catamaran slowly passed the cruiser. Travis took advantage of this temporary break and hit hard right, coming alongside the dinner cruiser. Its wake sloshed him back and he had to cut in a sharper turn to come up next to its hull. Up close the boat looked much more massive than he thought it would be. Travis maintained an even speed with the cruiser and tucked himself in close enough to be out of visible range of anyone on board.

The wake kept throwing him away from the boat, then sucking him in too close. He found he had to wrestle with the machine just to keep it where he wanted.

The patrol boat pressed on.

Inching closer towards the front of the cruiser he looked back. The patrol boat hadn't yet come into view but he knew it was close. The cruiser was still moving at a slow speed since it hadn't reached the open water, it kept its wake low giving the tourists time to adjust to the rolling motion.

Travis twisted the throttle all the way and started passing the cruiser, as he did so he hit the wake and was thrown in the air several feet, landing back in the water with the engine whining in protest at being airborne. He regained control and came even with the pointed, white front of the dinner boat.

He looked up at the cabin and couldn't see the pilot of the ship, he hoped this meant they hadn't seen him either.

He turned to look back one more time, the patrol boat would be coming in to view any second. When he was a few feet in front of the bow he cut quickly to the right, swerving in front of a 55 foot cruiser barreling through the water. Travis instinctively ducked his head and twisted the throttle, it was already at its maximum speed.

The motion of the cruiser pushed the Jet Ski back to the side and over at an angle to the point where Travis was leaning over, away from the ship, the propeller digging in for traction.

The mass of water the cruiser was pushing was overpowering any momentum the Jet Ski could muster. Travis compensated for this by turning away from the boat which flattened him out a little, giving the propeller a chance to dig in.

He passed the bow again, cut right, angling the Jet Ski around the front of the cruiser, and on to the other side. Another smaller jump as he came over the wake on the other side. He was now on the opposite side of the cruiser facing the rear of the boat.

The patrol boat had just passed behind it, and Travis did a quick 180 degree turn, bringing himself in line with the middle of the dinner boat, traveling in the same direction while using it as a shield between him and the patrol boat. This wouldn't last long and he knew his next move had to be well executed before he ran out of fuel, luck, or both.

Chapter Twenty-Six

Daphne turned onto another side street at the end of a row of shops off of the main street. The building on the corner was an open-air bar and grill with painted parrots hanging in hoops from the ceiling, a blender whirring at the bar, and tables scattered behind an iron railing separating the tables from the sidewalk.

The place was coming alive with the promise of a festive night, and the Latin jazz trio warming up added to the excitement. The lead trumpet player made quick, inside jokes with the other two musicians and riffed a few notes of an old Poncho Sanchez tune. The others followed in, making small adjustments to their instruments. Daphne cut through an opening in the railing and made her way inside. She wanted to lose her stalker in a crowd and get back to the marina.

She looked back, he kept walking towards her.

She made her way through the crowd and up to the bar. The bartender caught her eye as if to take an order.

Daphne leaned forward and smiled, "If a guy in a white suit asks if you've seen me, can you tell him I'm in the bathroom?" She asked this in a perky, flirtatious tone that worked with most men.

He looked at her, blankly, as if he didn't understand a word she said.

"Do you speak English?" She asked.

He leaned forward, put his hands on the bar and smiled, "Very well."

"Can you do this for me?" She looked behind her as she asked this. No sign of him.

He grabbed the wet towel from his waistband and wiped down the bar. "Suppose he don't want me to tell him a lie, and makes me...how you say…an offer I can't refuse?" He looked up at her sideways and raised his eyebrows.

Daphne grabbed a 20 from her pocket and shoved it across the bar.

"Will this work for you?"

He looked back and forth, picked up the bill and leaned back. "Very good."

Daphne ducked her head and without looking back headed out the door facing the other street. As soon as she was out of eyesight of the crowd in the bar, she ran.

The Latin man strode into the bar, wondering whether he would be buying her a drink, or giving up another of his pursuits for the evening. He talked with the bartender, looked over at the bathroom, ordered a beer and waited.

Daphne continued to run, and could see the grassy entrance to the marina ahead. She couldn't wait to be back on the boat with Travis. One more day of this cat and mouse game and her life could get back to normal. She ran through the events of the last 24 hours and began asking herself questions. *Why the hell did I go along with this? What would happen after we got the money? What if we don't get the money and I wind up in jail down here? Why didn't I ask myself these questions before I agreed to go?*

When she could see Chaz's boat out in the marina beyond the brick entrance these questions took on less importance. She was doing this because Travis needed her. Daphne had always gone for men that *she* needed, and this was the first time she felt like she was doing something for someone who needed her. Travis was different from the other guys, he carried a vulnerability that made her realize she had always fallen for the self-sufficient types. The ones who wouldn't call for days and then tell her about a dinner party they had thrown the night before, or the guys who talked about what great shape the new girl in their mountain biking group was in, and then never invite her on any of the rides. She found a pattern in needing guys who didn't put her high on their list, and with Travis the pattern had been broken. He needed her and she could be there for him, in Puerto Rico, helping him at a time in his life when he needed her the most. This was a new role for her and she liked it.

Two men in suits were walking back from the area where Chaz's boat was moored. She couldn't see them in detail because of the angle the sun was setting, but it looked like one was talking on a cell phone, and the other looked like one of the men she had seen standing in front of the hotel. They were walking in her direction, Daphne was sure they hadn't seen her yet.

She changed course and walked more towards the left of the lawn area, this put the brick restroom building at the entrance of the marina between her and them. She slowly made her way around the side of the restrooms, estimating what pace she had to walk to match the pace of the men in suits so they wouldn't see her. She heard a voice just behind her.

"Excuse me, Senora?"

Daphne wheeled around expecting to see her Latin stalker. In front of her was a child in ratty clothes holding the hand of what must have been her older brother, who looked equally ratty. They were holding a bouquet of flowers that looked like they had just been picked from the picnic area closer to the water.

"Three dollars American."

She couldn't think, her mind was on the men in suits on the other side of the bathroom. She had to stay behind the building to keep out of their line of sight.

"No, really. Thank you."

"Senora, these are rare flowers not available in America." The older boy said. "They will turn your husband into a passionate man with just one smell."

She had to get back to the boat to see if Travis was okay, she had to focus. "I have no husband." As soon as it was out of her mouth she regretted saying it.

"Ah, then all the better. The first man who sees you will want to marry you!"

Daphne kept walking towards the boats at the speed she thought she needed to in order to stay hidden from the men.

"Please don't walk away. If you buy these flowers my sister and me can eat tonight."

The sorrowful, brown-eyed look they gave her from their young, dirty faces slammed Daphne with guilt. She reached into her wallet and pushed a five-dollar bill at them. "Keep the flowers, go eat."

She continued her pace, and the boys went over to a young couple just leaving the boat area, held up the bouquet and began talking. Once on the other side of the bathroom she looked around the corner and saw the two men continue walking down the street. She headed to the boat.

Chapter Twenty-Seven

Reg counted out loud as he finished his two-hundredth push up, stood up and looked in the full length mirrors covering the closet doors in his hotel room. Forty-five years old, white hair, black eyes, tanned, built like a sprinter, Reg stared at himself in his black boxer briefs and tightened his stomach in even further. He had decided long ago that gravity would have no effect on how he looked, the things he *had* control over were things he *would* control.

His actions, his health, his temperament; he had groomed himself to do what he does with surgical precision. Reg had his own operation and ran it lean, using only the bare minimum of outside help. Experience had taught him that too many parts of this kind of work outsourced to too many people would not only dilute the earnings, but increase the probability of his getting caught.

That was unacceptable.

One stint in prison was enough to last him a lifetime. One overriding thought governed his every move, becoming the universal theme which he operated under… *never, ever get caught.*

He put his clothes back on and went down to the lobby. He stood taller as he walked, the stakes were getting bigger, his routine and foresight were proving to be exactly what the game required, and he felt what a man feels when he reaches that step in his life that leads to the next level. He felt at the top of his game.

The lobby was filling with tourists returning from whatever outings they had taken, and many were heading into their rooms for a shower or nap before going out for the evening. Reg walked over to the gift shop and headed to the back where the newspapers were stacked on the floor.

He picked up a local one, scanning to see if there was mention of anything unusual. He went to the latest edition of the national edition and realized it was the same story he had read earlier.

He went back to his room.

After logging on to the internet and searching for any more recent developments on Travis Black, it was clear there was nothing new to report. He hadn't been found, no leads were reported, and the rest was just a rehash of what he'd already read.

He called Donovan's room.

"They haven't found Travis yet."

"I wonder where he is. Could be he decided to run, I mean it's pretty obvious he's guilty. Maybe he couldn't take the heat and skipped town."

Reg was silent for a moment as he tried to think several moves ahead of his opponent. "This is unusual, the guys we've done this to up until now have rolled over and gone through the interrogation room until their lawyer shows up. Travis is different. I'd like to know what he's planning, or if he's just decided to run forever."

"He's run away to collect his thoughts and figure out what his next move is, hiding out somewhere. It's not anything I'd worry about Reg, he's the one that's going to have to get himself out of this."

Reg tapped his finger on the table, trying to put himself into the mind of his opponent.

"There's another option we haven't considered Donovan."

"What's that?"

"There's a lot at stake here, not only the money but his reputation. If he hasn't been taken into custody, or gone to the cops to try and convince them he didn't do it, and if he hasn't run into hiding, it's possible he's down here looking for it."

"Come on, how would he do that?"

Reg sat up straight, his new train of thought gaining momentum.

"Think about this…the other ones we've pulled this on have only been able to raise a fraction of the money Travis raised before we nabbed it. So we have to operate with the assumption that he's good at what he does."

"Okay."

Reg turned and looked at himself in the mirror as he talked on the phone. Preening, gesturing to himself.

"A guy that good doesn't do things like everybody else. We have to remember his assistant is gone too. While at first that may make him appear to have fled the scene, we have to look at it from another angle."

"What's that?"

"I'm making the assumption she knows his business and is able to give him help on the operations side of things. Maybe he's got her helping him…I find myself needing to consider things we haven't had to before."

"I'm sure you're just overreacting. He's a kid Reg, you scammed him and scammed him good. My guess is he still doesn't know what hit him."

"I don't agree. He's smart, he makes things happen, and he's missing with his assistant. I have to say, and it kills me to admit this, but if I were him I'd get my ass down here and try anything and everything to get the money back. If that's what he's doing my respect for him has just taken a huge leap."

Donovan was silent.

"I keep running these questions through my head…*What is he doing? And where is he?* I'd give a lot to know what he's doing *right now*." Reg hung up the phone and stared at his face in the mirror.

Chapter Twenty-Eight

Travis maneuvered the Jet Ski closer to the dinner cruiser. He had successfully kept the cruiser between him and the patrol boat, buying himself some time to think out his next move.

Keeping his speed constant, he pulled alongside the cruiser, unbuckled his belt from his shorts and yanked it out of the loops with his free hand. Travis wrapped the belt around the throttle, keeping it at a steady speed. Cinching up the leather, he fastened the throttle at its current speed leaving both hands free.

He pulled as close to the cruiser as possible.

Holding the handlebars with both hands, Travis hopped onto the seat of the Jet Ski. Standing on the seat, still steering with his hands, he put one foot out on the handlebars and stood straight up, the belt keeping the speed constant, and steered with his left foot.

Just above his head was a grab bar on the dinner cruiser. He would have one chance.

He crouched.

Travis sprung himself in a lunge at the cruiser and flung out his hands at the grab bar.

Its surface was wet, rusty in places, and his feet scrambled to catch onto anything that would take the weight off. All they met was empty space.

The Jet Ski, still under full throttle from the belt twisted around it spun off and motored in a circle around itself.

Travis looked up towards the deck of the boat where a metal railing protected the passengers whose feet would be about three feet above his head. He began to hear voices.

"Who do you think it belongs to? I don't see anybody around, do you?"

"I hate those things anyway, too noisy."

He heard the sounds of music as the on-board stereo speakers were located directly above where he was hanging on. The patrol boat was his first concern. He moved further down the railing towards the bow where an anchor hung, connected by a chain the size of a wrestler's legs. He saw this as a way to get a foothold while climbing aboard.

At the front of the boat he put his left foot on the anchor and reached up for the railing. He was able to swing his foot over the deck and wrap it behind one of the railing posts. He looked to the rear, the very tip of the bow of the patrol boat was crawling around the stern of the cruiser. He pulled his other leg up and threw himself onto the deck.

Not knowing what to expect, he simply laid there for a second, dripping, sweating, waiting for an alarm to sound.

Nothing.

Travis opened his eyes and looked around. The front decking was covered with several long benches pointing towards the front of the boat, it had the utilitarian feel of a commuter ferry. Further back changes had been made to the boat to give it the feel of a high-end dinner cruiser, however the maritime necessities of things like fire extinguishers, grab bars, valves, gauges and access panels still stood out.

Travis lifted his head and took in his immediate situation. The front bench was empty in both directions. He slid under it for cover and looked out the back end of his new hiding place. There were several pairs of feet a few benches back, passengers taking in the fresh air. To the sides were other feet standing, posturing, walking, probably some kind of cocktail area over there.

To the front he could see through the railing around the bow straight ahead, revealing the bay and the approaching opening of the ocean where sailboats were silhouetted against the setting sun. The whine of the Jet Ski mindlessly circling about faded as the boat moved forward.

The patrol boat pulled closer to the cruiser. Travis slid his wet body down the length of the bench to get a look at what their next move might be. As the patrol came alongside the Jet Ski they slowed down and men clambered to the railings on each side, leaning over.

Walkie-talkies held at the sides of their faces, there was confusion on board. The men were pointing into the water, at the Jet Ski, back towards the marina and then again at the water. They knew they were close and didn't want to lose the scent.

Binoculars were passed among the men as each took their turn at searching for the fugitive. The dinner cruiser picked up speed as it came to the end of the 5 mph. speed limit in the marina. Travis froze, peering only far enough around the bench to see the activity on board the patrol vessel.

One of the men grabbed the binoculars and pointed them straight at the cruiser. Travis stared back, unable to move. The man quickly removed the binoculars and signaled another over, handing them to him. The second man looked at the cruiser and handed the binoculars back. The dinner cruiser began to turn to the left, the patrol boat receding from view.

Travis tucked back in under the bench and waited. The sun touched the horizon ahead to his right, and the higher wake from the increased boat speed frothed the water below.

His thoughts moved to Daphne, to the job he had to do tomorrow, and how he would get there. A cooler breeze made its way over the water, and the motion of the cruiser picked it up and slid it under the bench, wrapping it around his wet clothes. Travis huddled his arms closer, pulled his knees in, and waited.

Chapter Twenty-Nine

Daphne hurried toward the boat, the wooden dock creaked under her feet as she navigated splintered deck boards and popped up nail heads. She couldn't take her eyes off the sailboat she had left Travis on. *Had those men in suits been on the boat? Was Travis still there? Was somebody watching her to see if she would lead them to Travis?*

Her mind wandered into these areas, distracting her from the uneven surface she was walking on. She caught her foot on a cleat and lurched forward. An arm came out from nowhere and caught her. She jumped, quickly looking over, trying to break his grip.

"Walk faster," the voice said. "We don't have much time."

The grip tightened, she looked back at him.

His face was in the shadow of a hat, he held her in front of him making it hard for her to look at his face. Something was familiar about him, his voice, the pockmarked cheek she caught a glimpse of.

Then it hit her, and this confused Daphne even more.

Max, the limo driver.

"Face straight ahead and keep walking."

She did as she was told. He sidled up closer, walking by her side at the same pace, still holding onto her.

"Where are you taking me."

"You'll see, just act normal and do what I say."

"We weren't sure we could trust you, now I know why. You're hurting me."

He pulled her closer to him. "Will you just keep walking?"

He guided her past Chaz's boat and down one of the side docks away from the main channel. She looked around, seeing nobody at the marina.

143

The bay was active with the evening boaters but the docks at the marina held an eerie silence as she was pulled by the limo driver. They reached the end of the side pier.

Sitting in the water was a speed boat, engine idling, painted racing lines streaked back in a sweeping wave making the boat look like it was moving fast while it sat in the water. It floated low, its bow pointing like a needle, everything around the cockpit area was swept back in a smooth arc that kept wind resistance down. This boat was built for one thing, speed. The small door to the cockpit under the bow opened and Chaz came out.

Daphne at first was taken back, scared, wanting to run for it

He waved his hand, hurrying them impatiently.

Daphne and the driver stepped aboard, Max taking the wheel while Daphne crouched down and went below to see Chaz.

"Where's Travis?" She searched his face, hoping not to see the clues that would tell her what she didn't want to hear. Instead, his face showed the calm it had since she first met him.

"You should be impressed. Our boy has turned into quite the resourceful fugitive. I might want to hire him on for some other jobs."

"What are you talking about?"

Chaz reached down below and held out a pair of binoculars. "Have a look."

Chaz pointed her in the direction of the main channel beyond the marina. She saw boaters, wind surfers, tourist attractions, she had no idea what she was supposed to look for.

"What am I looking at?"

"See that Jet Ski out there making circles?"

She scanned the water, sweeping back with a sudden jerk. "Yes, now I do."

"See that big boat behind it?"

"The San Juan Dinner Tours boat?"

"That's it."

"Look closely toward the front of it and tell me what you see."

Daphne focused the lenses, closed one eye and adjusted her vision.

"There's someone climbing over the front of it! Is that him? It is him! What the...? Would you please tell me what's happening?"

"You tell me. I've been watching him for the last ten minutes while trying to stay out of the line of sight myself. Last I saw he jumped off the Jet Ski and onto the railing. Is he over the railing yet?"

Daphne peered further, "Yes, he just flopped up there, what's he doing?"

Chaz sat back in the small cockpit of the speed boat as Max slowly motored them away from the marina.

"He's evading the patrol boat right behind the cruiser. I'd say he needs our help. What do you think?"

"What are we gonna do, just speed over there and get him? That patrol boat is following them like they want to get on board."

Chaz pulled a cigar out of his breast pocket and lit it with a gold plated lighter. He used less flourish this time, but still took pride in the craft of igniting what was clearly a passion. He peered out the cockpit hatch as they pulled away from the marina. Chaz looked around, stepped out and motioned Daphne to do the same.

"This is where I'll need your help Daphne. I have to stay out of sight around these patrol boats, if I get associated with Travis before we pull this off tomorrow it'll never work. I'll be with you all the way, but I can't be seen."

"What do want me to do?"

"We've got only one chance to get this right. We blow this and the money's gone, but more important, you both will be on that patrol boat headed for a Puerto Rican jail. This isn't just about getting money back, we're now resisting arrest, hindering the apprehension of a felon, and all that other stuff you hear about on TV, except there's just one thing…this is real."

Daphne looked at him, unable to react to this. The clock was ticking, she was in a foreign country in a scheme to get back 50 million dollars while running from the police. She knew she was in too deep to back out now, any thoughts she had of bailing out should have been acted on hours ago. Chaz put his hand on her shoulder and moved closer.

"It's time Daphne."

"What?"

"It's the time to look ahead, not back. The time to reach inside you and find things you didn't realize you have."

Daphne looked at him, blinking, trying to anticipate what would come out of his mouth next.

The engine roared, picking up from a slow sputter to cruising speed as they entered the main channel of the marina.

Max aimed the boat at the dinner cruiser.

Chapter Thirty

T he shifting vibration of the engines pulled Travis from his thoughts as he lay under the benches in the front of the dinner cruiser. Only moments had passed but the hypnotic lull of the water put him in a state that felt out of body. He felt like he was looking at himself and his surroundings as a detached soul from above. The running, chasing and plotting all taking place like they were on a big game board and he was just one of the pieces being moved by a force out of his control. The engines decelerated at the same time a siren wailed. It was close.

Travis crawled over and looked through the railing. The patrol boat had pulled alongside the dinner boat, its lights flashing. A man stood outside with a megaphone in front of his mouth making commands in a language Travis didn't understand. The voice left no doubt that the intention was to bring the dinner boat to a stop. The music over the dinner cruiser's PA system stopped and a male voice crackled in, thick with the accent of the locals.

"Ladies and gentlemen we have a short delay in tonight's cruise. It seems the harbor patrol wants to board the boat temporarily. They have assured me this will not take very long, and we should be back under way momentarily. Our apologies for this, and please accept our invitation to enjoy the cocktails which will continue without interruption. There is no need to be alarmed, they are merely ensuring our safety. Please, enjoy yourselves."

Some moans and could be heard from the crowd, but the mention of the cocktails seemed to keep everybody from rioting out of control.

Travis needed a plan.

He had to get off this boat. He slid under the benches and made his way to the opposite side away from the patrol boat. Peering over the side, he saw that the dinner cruiser had almost completely stopped, and the distance down was only 15 feet or so. *But then what?* The nearest shoreline was at least a half mile away by now, and it was all exposed open water. He'd be spotted instantly.

The patrol boat crept up next to the dinner cruiser and a folding, cantilevered railing was pulled up from the side of the patrol boat and maneuvered into place so that its walkway could be slid across the gap to the other vessel. One of the crew men on the dinner boat guided the sliding walkway over and fastened it to the railing. Three men walked over, guns drawn. Brown, cold eyes looking back and forth, one of them chewing gum, another smoking, the third held a walkie talkie to his mouth. They boarded the boat and split up in a predetermined plan of searching the dinner boat. With the presence of guns the festivities fell into a hush, a heavy silence wrapped around the ship as everyone watched, and waited.

Travis's mind raced. There was nobody close enough who he could snatch and trade clothes with like in the movies, the nearest shore was too far, and his hiding places left no room for error if he was discovered.

He began to think his time had come, that the noose of guilt over something he had no control over was about to tighten. Capture seemed inevitable. He, Daphne, and his clients would be brought down in an intricate scheme layered with complexities that would take days to sort out. And while it was being sorted out the money would scatter like buck shot into untraceable accounts, and a silver haired man named Reg would hop on a plane and claim his next victim.

Travis heard footsteps against the metal floor he was laying on. Peering under the benches, he watched a chocolate colored pair of polished boots walk between the benches, stop, then walk again.

It was only a matter of time.

Travis inched closer to the railing, knowing that his futile attempt to put more distance between him and his pursuers only delayed the inevitable finale. The boots stopped again.

Travis heard the sound of a motor coming from the side of the cruiser he was on. He peered further over to look and saw a speedboat approaching. He didn't believe it, but it looked like the limo driver from earlier in the day. It was getting darker and it was difficult to make out, but it definitely looked like Max, and he was waving to him. He made a motion with his hands that Travis could only interpret one way…jump.

Travis knew this was his only option. Keeping himself low, he slid out from under the bench, stuck his legs out the railing and turned around facing the dinner cruiser. Holding onto the rails, his feet braced against the hull, he looked down, preparing to kick off as he jumped. Facing forward, he found himself staring straight into the face of one of the men from the patrol boat.

The man stood at the front of the benches, pointed his gun at Travis and grabbed his radio, "I got him, up front."

Travis froze.

"Climb back aboard now, slowly." The man spoke perfect English.

The man rose his gun slightly, and Travis stared into the dark barrel aimed at his head. He looked into the patrolman's eyes. The color of frozen tundra, they stared back.

Travis jumped, pushing off with his legs and pulling his arms in as the man yelled.

He hit the water.

Whistles blew, the other two men came running, and the crowd mobbed around the rails to watch.

Travis hit the water feet first, the slap of it on the back of his head felt sharp, tingling through his head with pain. *Have I been shot?* He stayed under as long as he could, knowing that above lay certain death.

Chaz's boat pulled closer, the limo driver pulled a .38 out of his side holster and fired two shots at the man holding a rifle on Travis. He went down, grabbing his leg, screams erupted from the passengers as they all huddled into a mass crowding the doors to get back inside the boat. Travis popped his head up, swam over and grabbed onto the back platform of the speed boat.

"Hold on!" Max was shouting from the wheel as he pushed the throttle forward, dragging Travis in the water behind them. Daphne came back and helped Travis climb onto the rear of the boat.

"Get in, now!" The limo driver shouted this as he looked back, gunned the engine and peeled away from the dinner cruiser, leaving a rooster tail of glistening water in his wake.

The distance between the two boats increased as Chaz's powerboat opened its engine to full throttle. The boat bounced in response to the waves at the mouth of the harbor, Max keeping down as he veered off to the left while yelling at Travis to keep his head down.

Travis didn't dare look back.

The game had changed, his feeling of being a pawn in a chess game over which he had no control weighed on him. A man had been shot and he'd been shot at, things weren't just happening…they were going down.

The sleek bow of the boat lifted as it bore full speed into the darkening open water ahead.

On the dinner cruiser one of the men stayed with the shot officer while the other boarded the patrol boat and unhooked the railing. They pulled away, lights flashing, siren back on, bearing the full power of the patrol boat down on the speed boat leaving the harbor. One of the men radioed for helicopter backup and turned on the searchlights overhead. The lead colored sky lit up with cylinders of light traced from the top of the patrol boat. The pilot scanned the waters, holding the throttle at full speed, his eyes focused straight ahead.

"We have you now," the pilot said to himself. "Nothing out there but ocean."

Chapter Thirty-One

Max kept his head down while using every ounce of power the speedboat had. He shouted over the deafening roar of the engine, "Get down there with the others, we're not out of this yet."

Travis got up from the floorboards and crawled to the door of the small cockpit at the front of the boat. Chaz and Daphne were sitting in the tight quarters, Daphne's eyes wide with the fright of hearing gunshot but not knowing what was happening. Chaz wore his cool expression, never letting on what he was feeling other than complete control of the situation. As Travis climbed in Chaz stuck his head out and cupped his hands to his mouth. "What's going on out there?"

Max kept his eyes straight ahead as the seas took on the slate colored hue of night water and leaned in closer to Chaz. "They're tailing us in that patrol boat, one of their men is down, I'd say a chopper shows up any second."

Chaz kept looking at him, expecting more.

"Leg shot, he'll be fine. My plan is to do the same thing we did last time, you think he's up for it?"

"Only one way to find out, I'm going in to make some calls, why don't you go on as planned, I'll let you know if we need to make a mid-course correction."

Chaz hesitated, "Are the tides in a good position for this, or do we know?"

Max smiled as he glanced down at Chaz, "We're going on faith with this one boss, tell them to hold on tight."

Chaz gave him the thumbs up and climbed back inside. The boat increased its speed, bouncing off the small waves creeping in from the deeper parts of the ocean. Evening tourist traffic was still heavy and at these high speeds the risk of a collision was as great as the risk of being caught by their pursuers. Max braced himself against the side of the boat to maintain control. He glanced behind him, the penetrating searchlights of the patrol boat were unmistakable. He guessed them to be less than 300 yards away and gaining.

The lights along the coast flickered to life as the sun set and nightfall canvassed the sky. The yellows of the harbor lights looked further away than they really were, and the red and green running lights of other boats gave small and inadequate warnings of their presence. This was even more confusing at 30 knots over a foot high chop. Max scanned the shore for the familiar entrance to Bahia Bar.

The patrol boat had one searchlight trained on the boat, and the other scanning the water just ahead of them for anything they needed to be on the lookout for. The man controlling the searchlights looked at the pilot, "Chopper should be here any minute, can this thing go any faster?"

"This is it. Don't worry, they can't go far. We'll get 'em."

The two men stared out the window at what was looking like a monotonous race with no finish line. The pilot looked out the window and up towards the skies, "Nothing up there yet."

The second man took a drag on his cigarette.

"It looks like they're turning."

The pilot adjusted his course to come in at a sharper angle, shaving a few precious yards off the gap between them.

"Where is that chopper?"

Max began a long, steady turn to the right, passing cargo ships docked at loading terminals, and entering the mouth of another marina. To the left was a fuel dock, supply store and grocer, on the right were rows of smaller sailboats, motorboats, fishing trawlers and dredgers. This marina had the feel of a working harbor whereas the one they just left was mainly the base of operations for tourist activities. They kept their speed up, violating the no wake rule of the marina but didn't plan on staying here long enough to be cited for it. As the speed of the power boat slowed slightly the unmistakable sound of chopper blades beat through the air. Max headed for the rear of the harbor.

"Shit." The patrol boat pilot told his partner to take the wheel, "I need to look at a chart, keep following them."

They switched places, and the man who had been driving the boat reached down and opened a Velcro flap that covered a pocket on the side of one of the leather cockpit chairs. He pulled out a folded chart, put on his glasses, stuck a lit penlight in his mouth and unfolded the map. He peered closer, looked out the front of the boat then back at the map. His brown forehead creased.

"I think we're screwed. Is that chopper here yet?"

The man piloting the boat stuck his head out the side window again and looked up. "Looks like he's just a few minutes away, I see him at about 8 o'clock."

The man reading the map grabbed the microphone from its clip overhead. "Bay chopper, this is harbor patrol, do you have a visual yet?"

Static.

"Bay chopper, do you read?"

Crackling on the line, broken words, *"...read...yes... "*

"Bay chopper, come in."

"Bay chopper here, we're right behind you"

"Our suspect looks like he's heading up Bahia Bar, we won't be able to pursue, can you cut across and get a visual before they disappear under the tree cover?"

"Roger, heading that way now. Will confirm visual when we have it. "

The chopper banked sharply to the left. Once Chaz entered the river system miles of tributaries, branches and natural canopies would make a night-search fruitless. The chopper dropped elevation and zeroed in on the mouth of the river that emptied into Bahia Bar harbor.

The boat engine slowed enough for Chaz and Travis to open the cockpit door and come out to talk with Max. "Should just be another minute or so and we'll lose the boat, the chopper will be tough but I think we can find a good hiding place to lose him before we get to Pedro's."

Travis looked around, unsure of where they were, "Where's the patrol boat? I thought he was following us."

Chaz took over, "They can't go any further up this marina than that grove of trees over there." Chaz pointed to a dark stand of cypress at the back of the marina, beyond it the water snaked through a natural river that bent around to the right before disappearing into more vegetation. There was a slight wake at the mouth of the river, and warning buoys on each side.

He went on, "The name Bahia Bar comes from the huge sand bar just under the water there. Any boat much bigger than this, especially at low tide…" Chaz looked at his watch, scanned the marina looking at the level of the water on the pilings. "…which is what it looks like we're in now, will get grounded and have to wait hours for the tide to come in so they can get off. We got lucky here hitting the tide right, but as a rule they never go past those trees."

Max slowed the boat to a crawl, gliding over the churning water. An outgoing tide and the underwater configuration swirled the current pulling the rear of the boat sideways. Max timed his acceleration to bank the boat back into a straight line, and motored through to the other side. Travis looked behind, the patrol boat circled in the marina, shining its lights at the speedboat as best it could while staying away from the sand bar. Overhead the chopper turned on its searchlights and dropped further down. Max cut the lights.

Chaz stared straight ahead into blackness. Travis continued to look behind them at the patrol boat which was stopped in the deeper water of the harbor. "I think we have a problem."

"Bay chopper, do you have him?"

"*We have a visual, they're heading up the river. He's cut his lights but we can follow him, what's the next move?*"

"Stay with him until you hear from us. I'm getting some air and ground backup but I'm not sure how close we can follow. Just stay on them for now."

"*Roger.*"

Chaz turned around and followed Travis's gaze. The patrol boat faced them, its searchlights trained on the water below. Out to the side a crane was lowering an inflatable dinghy with an outboard motor into the water. One of the harbor patrolmen was in it, the other guiding it lower. The rifle he was holding was clearly silhouetted against the lights of the marina.

Chaz went back down below, "Don't take your eyes off that dinghy."

He came back up holding a rifle with a scope mounted on the top. Travis held up his hands, "Stop, I don't want anyone else shot. This is over, this is where I get off."

Chaz squinted one eye as he sighted down the rifle. He blinked once and put his finger over the trigger. The dinghy was in the water now, the outboard sputtering to life. "Didn't you hear me? It's over Chaz, I'm out. You shoot that gun and I'm dragging you down with me."

Chaz pulled the trigger. He lowered the gun and peered through the dark. He raised it again and squeezed off two more rounds. Travis waited for the man in the dinghy to fall dead from three shots. Instead, the water around the dinghy started to bubble as air was let out from the inflated chambers. The man tried to stand up and shoot but he was thrown off balance by the sinking dinghy. He quickly turned the dinghy around and headed back to the patrol boat before it sank any further. Chaz had only shot out three of the six air chambers, giving him enough buoyancy to get out of there alive.

Travis looked at Chaz, who was back to sucking on a cigar. They stared at each other as Travis tried to process what it was he was feeling right now. Chaz took the cigar from his mouth, "What most people would say in your situation is 'nice shot'."

Travis was silent. Chaz went up to join Max.

Travis looked up and all he could see was canopy. Thick, lush, overgrown trees arced over the water in a natural bridge of cover hiding them well. They could hear the chopper and see its searchlight darting through gaps in the vegetation but couldn't see it, and it couldn't see them.

Daphne looked around, "So how far up this do we go?"

"About a mile up river a friend of mine has a house where we'll dock up. I've already talked to him, he knows what we're doing and is expecting us. We'll regroup there, get you into some dry clothes and then we'll all go to my house, get something to eat and spend the night. I'd stay here but they will be combing this area in the next few hours."

They continued to hug the shoreline, staying well under the canopy and using natural shadows to see which way the turns took. It was slow going but it was obvious by the haphazard directions the chopper search beam was taking that the plan was working. The air grew thicker, heavy, tropical. Sounds of hunter and hunted emanated from the jungle shores. Monkeys, frogs, underwater creatures now above water, unseen eyes watched the boat as it crept upstream.

The atmosphere had quickly changed from one of supercharged intensity and roaring boat motors to a quiet, twisting crawl as the bow of the boat sliced still river waters. The vegetation twisted its way up the banks on each side throwing off a different shade of black than the tar colored water.

"People actually live up here?"

"You have no idea. There's quite a flow of boat traffic since this is used as a main access to the marina and the highway by the people that live up here. It's a lot of ex drug dealers, tax evaders and others who want to be left alone. The locals don't bug them, they don't make trouble, it works."

Travis kept looking nervously towards the sound of the chopper's blades. "How do we know they won't follow us to this guy's house?"

"If they had more warning we were going this way they would have airlifted a zodiac in here or something. As it is, the nearest roads are still a good 45 minute drive, the chopper can't see us, and we'll be there any minute. And just for good measure we'll have our driver here take the boat back to the marina, let them pull him over, see there's nobody with him and we're back in business."

Travis looked at the driver, his unsmiling, tired face still focused only on the job he had to do. "Won't they take him in for questioning?"

Chaz slapped the driver on the shoulder and squeezed, "I pay him very well, wouldn't you say Max?"

Max shrugged his shoulders and for the first time Travis saw his mouth break into the barest hint of a smile, "Depends on what I have to do for it boss. Tonight, I don't know, I think a tip is in the air."

Max slowed the boat down some more, glanced over head, then veered sharply to the left. Chaz got out his cell phone and punched one number. "We're here, just make sure there's no lights that can be seen over head."

He listened for a moment. "Got it."

Chaz peered through the darkness to the left bank, eyes in a laser like focus on something that wasn't visible. Then they saw it.

A brief flash of red light, followed by two shorter blinks. Max turned the boat towards the light.

Chapter Thirty-Two

Max looked up, the light from the chopper was 50 yards ahead. Its beam cut through the trees, crossing the river channel over the water like a pendulum. He took advantage of this to cross the river, exposing them momentarily in the uncovered center. He drifted towards the other side at a low but determined speed. They were dangerously exposed but the chopper stayed ahead of them in a confused search for an unlit boat on a dark river.

They reached the cover of the vegetation on the other side, and once again a red light flashed followed by two shorter blinks. Max cut the engine, Chaz hopped on to the bow of the boat, ducking to avoid the draping moss overhead and grabbed a coiled line. The only sounds were the ripple of the water on the sides of the boat, and a deep, throaty mating call from a persistent night creature. As the boat continued its drift Travis watched as they snaked through a canopy of moss and trees and floated into a partially covered lagoon where the faintest black outline of a house could be seen. They heard a whistle.

Chaz whistled back. The light blinked again in its repeating signal, and Max steered the drifting boat towards it and to the right, accounting for the slight current still prevalent in the river. Chaz tossed the rope expertly at the flashing light. As his eyes became accustomed to the new level of darkness, Travis saw a man standing on a dock catch the coil of rope and begin pulling them in.

The boat came up sideways to the dock, Chaz put some protective fenders over the side, jumped off, shook hands with the man holding the rope, and they both quickly cleated the boat to the dock.

"Pedro Sandoval," Chaz said in a hush, "once again you come to my rescue. It is good to see you."

Pedro hugged Chaz and stepped back, "You look good my friend, always ready to help you. So tell me who you have on board here, I see Max." Pedro waved at Max, and Max, shutting off the engine waved back.

Travis stood up and took in the surroundings as his pupils dilated in response to the dark setting. The lagoon led up to the dock they were on, from there to a series of wooden decks that protruded out from the shore line on large pilings. Seeming to hang from all of this was a tropical looking residence, the faintest glimmer of candlelight coming through some of the windows. The inside walls looked like they were painted the color of ceramic pots, and the windows were covered in the same decorative wrought iron grates they'd seen in town. Chaz turned towards him to introduce Pedro. Travis signaled for Daphne to come out from the cockpit where she'd been hiding since Chaz had fired the shots.

"Travis, Daphne, meet my good friend Pedro Sandoval."

They came off the boat, steadying themselves on the uncertain dock and its surrounding darkness, and shook hands.

"This one needs some dry clothes," Pedro said pointing at Travis. "Why don't you stay here for dinner instead of heading back while they're still looking. Let this blow over and make yourself at home," he held out his hand in a magnanimous gesture of welcoming. "I insist."

Travis and Daphne looked uncertainly at Chaz. He held their lives in his hands, they were on his turf, things *had* to go the way he planned. Chaz stepped forward.

"We'd be honored, only problem is we have to get out of here at some point tonight, get some sleep and an early start tomorrow. We're racing the clock and we've only got one chance."

Pedro smiled, "Not a problem, can I have my driver take you?"

Chaz looked over at Max, "No, I'm having Max take the boat back, then he'll get the car and meet us here later. He's an ace at getting past any trouble, that's why I pay him so well." Chaz winked at Max, walked over and palmed what looked like currency in his hand, leaned in and whispered something into his ear, then helped him untie the boat from the dock. The engine whined slowly at low rpms.

Pedro pulled out a small penlight and lit their way along the ground as he led them from the dock to the stairway leading to the main deck. Travis was grateful to be on solid ground again. Between swimming and motor boating the last few hours, the feel of terra firma was welcome. His clothes were still damp, the heavy tropical air keeping them wet after his jumps in the water.

The sound of the boat drifted away as Max took it back to the marina, and the three of them followed Pedro up the stairs and onto the deck leading to sliding doors at the back of the house. The deck was lined with potted plants, hanging ferns, wind chimes; masks were hung on the walls of the house, the candlelight bringing them to life as shadows played with the artificial eyes.

Pedro slid the door open and they walked into the décor of a Spanish king. In the dining room large black sconces hung on the sides of each doorway, straight-backed black teak chairs surrounded a long wooden table inlaid with ceramic painted tiles. Large ceramic vases with fresh flowers decorated the dining table and smaller side hutches, Matisse and Cezanne decorated the walls.

The floors were dark, thick hardwood and small Persian rugs were strategically placed to soften the feel. A woman descended the staircase timidly, wearing a black dress, laced white apron, hair tied in a bun. She smiled as the guests took their bearings in the new environment.

Chaz got out first and walked towards her with open arms. "Bonita, I'm eternally in your debt for helping out here." They hugged, Chaz discreetly slipping a fold of currency in her hand. "How is the tyrant treating you these days?"

Bonita flushed, Travis and Daphne walked up to her and introductions were made.

"Bonita is the one who makes all this work," Pedro said as he waved his hand over the room as if displaying it to a prospective buyer. "I don't know what I'd do without her."

Travis looked at Pedro as he said this, the inside light giving him his first real look at this next person on the list of people he was supposed to trust on first impression. The man's dark hair swept back in a broad wave behind his ears, dark olive skin, large brown eyes, a thin mustache over a broad smile made him look like everybody's favorite uncle. The gold tooth Travis didn't notice the first time flashed only on the biggest of smiles. He was dressed in a patterned tropical shirt which hung out over the white linen pants everyone seemed to wear down here, with expensive looking loafers over bare feet.

Pedro continued, "I took the liberty of assuming you would stay for dinner, so Bonita has put together a meal fit for royalty. I hope you all like fresh tuna? My neighbor had some good luck fishing today and we have plenty, so don't be shy. Young man…" he pointed at Travis, "Bonita will take you upstairs where you'll have some dry clothes, why don't you all make yourselves at home and I'll pour some drinks."

Travis followed Bonita to an upstairs bedroom where she handed him a folded pile of clothes. He closed the door after her and began undressing. It looked like a guest bedroom with a freshly-made bed, dresser, night stand, embroidered rug at the foot of the bed and bamboo shades drawn over the window. There were black and white photos on the walls of Hispanic looking men and women in outdoors settings. The people seemed happy, gaping smiles under dark eyes in a simpler time. Travis finished changing and walked down to join the others.

He went through a small hallway at the bottom of the stairs with arched doorways. This led to a long kitchen with stainless steel sinks, overhead pot racks draped with copper and iron pots, and Bonita standing at the counter cutting avocados. Past the kitchen, through a set of swinging doors sat the large knotted pine farm table set for five. Above the table hung a round wood and wrought iron candle chandelier half as large as the room. It was suspended by a thick rope which wound its way through a rusted pulley and ended at a cleat half way down the far wall. Pedro was letting some rope out to lower it closer to the table. Daphne took the hint, grabbed a book of matches sitting nearby and began lighting the dozen candles while Pedro wrapped the rope back around the cleat.

Bonita laid out plates of baked tuna, fresh salad, homemade tortillas and a papaya salsa garnished with cilantro. "Please, sit down and pour yourself a glass of wine." Pedro handed them each a glass and pulled out a chair for Daphne.

"So, how do you and Chaz know each other?" Travis asked.

Pedro was passing around the salad and looked up with a quick smile, "You mean he didn't tell you?"

He shook his head.

"Well then, he must not want you to know."

Travis looked at Daphne awkwardly, went back to helping himself to some tuna, when Pedro burst out laughing. "We go back a few years, my son started working for Chaz in the United States at one of the big money center banks. Chaz took him under his wing and showed him the ropes. When Chaz had to leave the bank my son took over his position, and it got him into the upper levels of management. I've always told Chaz that whenever he needs anything he can count on me. My son, my only son actually, he was the first of our family to graduate from high school. He's a success, I'm proud of him, and Chaz was a big help."

Daphne took a sip of wine. "Chaz seems to have a desire to want to help people."

"He does. Since then we've worked together on a few of his projects. As a matter of fact, did he tell you? I'll be working with you tomorrow."

Travis looked up. "I wondered who the other accomplice would be. I'm glad we got to meet tonight, at least this way when I see you tomorrow I won't be shocked."

"Ah, but Travis you won't be seeing me until it's over. I'm sure Chaz has explained this to you."

"I'm still having a hard time seeing how this will work."

Pedro came up and put an arm around Travis. "Trust me, this will go over just fine."

"Have you tried this before?"

Pedro looked down at the floor, "Not exactly. But I have worked with Chaz long enough to know that when he puts something like this together, you want to bet on his team. Please, let's eat."

The dinner was accompanied by more conversation of Pedro's son, some local history, and the many things to do on the island. Any questions about tomorrow's activities were quickly brushed aside by Chaz.

During dinner Travis kept feeling like a college student who hadn't studied enough for tomorrow's test. He could see all the questions... but the answers, they were only at the end after it was too late. He played with his food. The wine began to taste bitter. Travis looked over at Daphne who seemed involved in finding out more about the places Pedro was recommending they visit than whether they would be in jail by this time tomorrow.

He looked over at Chaz. He was the picture of cool, never a doubt, at least none that he let people see. Chaz sat back listening to Pedro talk to Daphne, caught Travis's gaze and winked as if he were looking at his grandson at a family dinner. Travis's stomach burned, he wanted to stand up and shout, "*Doesn't anybody realize we have work to do?! Shouldn't we be talking about this?*" The frustration mounted and he waited for a pause in Pedro's conversation.

He got it. "Excuse me everybody..." Daphne and Pedro stopped, looked his way, Chaz sat there smiling, Bonita got up to clear dishes. The silence hung in a weighty, expectant air.

Travis began nervously, wondering why he was the only one worried about tomorrow. "I think since we all have a part in this, and Pedro says he hasn't done something like this before, that it would really be helpful if we went over this in more detail."

Silence.

Chaz got up, opened another bottle of wine on the kitchen counter and poured some in each of the empty glasses around the table. He sat down.

"I was wondering how much of this you'd take on faith, and when it would get to you. Let me give you a little background on what we have in mind for tomorrow, and how it all fits together. I just have one condition that must be met before going any further."

Travis let out his breath, relieved at the turn the conversation was taking.

Chaz sipped his wine, let it linger in his mouth, put his head back, closed his eyes and swallowed. "You need to hear me out, if you prejudge this thing we won't get to square one."

Travis and Daphne exchanged glances.

"First a little story. A few years back, there was a bank in Italy that had a questionable list of customers. It was an old established bank, and they built their reputation by having the Vatican as its largest client. That may also be why they were never called to the carpet on some of the dealings they became involved with. Their client list read like a who's who of tax evaders, drug traffickers, arms dealers and such. Word got out that a large cash deposit was going to be made the next day. Where this information came from nobody really knows."

He leaned forward to wet his lips again with the crisp Pinot Grigio.

"A group of four Romanians, call them some kind of outpost of the Russian mafia for lack of a better term, happened to be in Italy trying to take over some of the drug trade when they got wind of this. What followed was one of the most daring feats of swindling I have ever seen. If I didn't personally know the head of the bank at the time I would say it was impossible. I only wish I could have seen it with my own eyes, it's something that becomes too simple the more you think about it but when executed in the right setting…is a work of genius."

Travis was the first to speak. "And this is what we're going to be doing tomorrow?"

"Yes. What happened the day that large cash deposit was made has taken on the status of a legend. It's still talked about in the circles I used to travel in, and most bankers either refuse to believe it's possible, or lay in fear that their bank will be next."

The table was silent, all eyes peering at Chaz.

"What we're going to pull off tomorrow ladies and gentlemen has come to be known as…" Chaz paused for effect, enjoying the moment, "…the Romanian switch."

Chapter Thirty-Three

The candles in the overhead chandelier flickered, throwing long shadows onto the textured walls. Off in the distance the now familiar sound of howling tropical monkeys shattered the awkward silence. Bonita stepped in from the kitchen, hands folded across her front, "Sir if there is nothing else I shall go to bed now."

Pedro, not taking his eyes off of Chaz, waved silently.

Travis caught Daphne's gaze, her left eyebrow raised in an expression of skepticism over what they'd just heard.

The thick silence was interrupted by a sharp knock on the door.

Chaz stood up, "That must be Max, I'll get it Pedro."

"No, allow me. Sit and drink."

Pedro went through the hall, past swinging doors and across the hardwood floor. He opened the large wooden door as it was being knocked on a second time, this knock more insistent than the first.

An officer dressed in an olive colored uniform stood there, took his hat off and stepped forward.

"Sorry to bother you Senor, but we are looking for two men and a woman that came up river on a speed boat. We're asking people in the area if they have seen anything."

Pedro smiled, the disarming face of a man used to fending off local inquiries into his neighbor's lives. "No, I've been home all night reading. Nothing unusual, would you like to come in?"

The officer hesitated, tried to look behind Pedro and could only see his own reflection in a mirror against the back wall.

"If you say you saw nothing, I see no reason for that." He reached in his pocket and handed Pedro a card. "If you see anybody matching that description would you please call this number?"

"Of course."

"Thank you." The man put his hat back on and walked towards his jeep sitting in the front drive.

Pedro walked back inside.

"'Would you like to come in?' What kind of balls do you have?" Travis blurted out.

Pedro laughed. "One day my son, you will learn the ways of people like him. They are trained to look for the obvious, the inconsistencies. When they are offered something like that it disarms a potentially volatile situation. Call it using judo with words, taking their own force and using it against them."

"What would you have done if he said yes?"

"I knew you could all hear the conversation and would take the necessary steps before he got here."

"I'm glad you're so confident."

Daphne stood up and went to a reclining chair off to the side, "So Chaz how many times have you done this 'Romanian Switch'?"

"Only once."

"Did it work?"

"Oh yes, it worked beautifully."

"Can you do it again?"

"No, *we* can do it again. This isn't a job for a loner, we're all part of a team here, one fails we all fail. Chin up kids, you'll do fine."

Daphne sneered, "Travis has the easy part, you and I are the ones pulling the whole thing off. We're the ones who should be nervous about this."

"You're entirely right Daphne," Chaz said. "And yet I see no other way, you and I are the only ones Reg hasn't met, and that necessitates us doing it as planned."

Travis stood up. "Okay, sure I have the easy part, and you two are on the front line so to speak. Where I'm having trouble is believing this will work."

Chaz leaned back in his chair. "Which is precisely why it does work."

Travis let that digest for a moment. "Fine, I see your point. But can't you expect a little skepticism when your plan is basically to have Reg hand you and Daphne the money?"

"Of course, but the point is they will think we are employed by the bank, he wants the cash out of his hands just as quickly as we want to get it. If we play this right it will go just fine. It's not a lock, nothing in this business is but it's our best shot."

"I'm wondering why we don't just go to the police now and let them handle it instead of pulling a stunt right out of Hollywood."

"We've been over this before Travis. You, right now are their number one suspect. The evidence is stacked so well against you, thanks to Reg, that it will take you all night to convince them of what's happened. Once they believe you, and set up their own sting, the money's gone…" Chaz made a gesture of blowing on his open palm as if sending fairy dust to the wind.

Chaz got up and paced as he talked. "We're this close Travis." Chaz held up his fingers showing a small gap, "It's easy to have these doubts when we're so close, natural actually. But we need to recognize them as the brain's desire to keep you in a comfort zone, and move on in spite of it."

"What if it doesn't work?"

"Think like it will, and it will. Think like it won't, and it won't. We need to walk, talk and feel like it's in the bag."

He leaned against the back of a chair and looked at the three of them.

"Now, we need to get moving. I'll call Max on his cell and we'll go over the plan another time while we wait. On the way to my place we can work out any last minute details, then get a good night's sleep."

Chaz whipped out his cell, pushed one button and talked to Max. "He'll be here in a few minutes. Travis, go over your role in this."

"Okay, I'm to be posted down the street from the bank with binoculars and an earpiece. My job is to alert you when Reg gets near the bank and keep an eye out for anything else that looks like trouble."

"Excellent. Daphne, now you."

"I'm wearing a business suit, with you the whole time, and am assuming the role of assistant manager. My job is to follow your lead."

"Good. I can't stress enough Daphne that you need to really take on the role. You need to eat and breathe female bank exec, it must feel perfectly natural to you. If you act uncertain, or too paranoid, he'll smell a rat and bolt. As you can both see, I have the lead role in this and hopefully that will put your fears at ease."

"Won't the *real* manager and assistant manager at the bank get a little suspicious at all this?" Travis asked.

Chaz held up his first finger. "Wait and see, the way the bank is laid out is very accommodating to our plan. There is a large lobby area between the bank operations and the reception area. It's almost like it was designed for our purposes."

Just then they heard the sound of a horn, and Pedro went out to make sure it was Max. Daphne then thought of something, "Wait, what's Pedro's role in all this?"

"He's a second set of eyes, and a backup driver. He'll be watching with binoculars from another location, and he'll have a second car that we can switch to if we have to evade somebody following us."

Her look softened into an expression of admiration, "You think of everything don't you?"

Chaz brushed this off with a quick smile, and headed towards the front door as he heard Max's voice through the hallway.

"Any trouble out there Max?"

"No, the chopper's given up, I don't see any cars out there, I think they've called it a night."

Chaz laughed, "Highly unlikely, but it looks like we've lost them for now. We need to stay away from the boat and the hotel room. They still don't know I'm involved in this…and I'd like to keep it that way."

They said their goodbye's to Pedro and began the journey to Chaz's house. The limo took them along palm-lined dirt roads curving down a slight grade, tires crunching over gravel, mud, potholes and other signs of an out of the way road. The luminescence of the city of San Juan poked through gaps in the vegetation.

The road gradually widened, and the trees thinned out as they made their way back towards the center of the island. The streets of San Juan went by the windows on their left as the limo skirted the eastern edge of town and headed up the inland grade leading back to Chaz's house.

Travis and Daphne were silent for the ride, each running through what their role was and how it would play out. It felt like the silence before a world class athletic endeavor, Travis knew that what went on in his mind between now and tomorrow morning would make or break the outcome. He hoped Daphne felt the same.

Chapter Thirty-Four

Travis stared at the ceiling in the guest bedroom of Chaz's house, moonlight blanketed the far wall through the open plantation shutters. His mind was a whirlpool of thoughts as he tried to anticipate what would happen tomorrow, and the small role he had made him feel handicapped, dependent on others for the outcome of his revenge.

Daphne lay in bed, unable to sleep. They talked little and slept even less, morning slipped in as a gradual change in the light outside the window. Sleep had been difficult for both of them, and by the time they had exhausted their minds enough to get some rest, dawn broke.

They smelled coffee.

Travis got up first, did as much of his morning ritual that he could under the circumstances of a foreign environment, a sleepless night, and the small out of the way role he played. He headed downstairs, telling Daphne he'd see her down there. She silently made her way to the bathroom, the business suit hung from a brass hook on the door.

She looked in the mirror, steeling herself for the role ahead, not letting destructive thoughts of doubt creep into her conscious. Chaz's words rung true with her last night…in a sting like this it had to be a total commitment. An actor doesn't just *play* the part, the actor *is* the part. She had to wear this like the suit she was about to put on. It couldn't be an act, it had to be a transformation. She recalled her years of acting school, never thinking it would lead to this. Her part felt the most difficult because Chaz did this kind of thing and had been here before, and Travis was off on the periphery. While she, the assistant bank manager that she was to be, was a rookie, a neophyte, on the job training. She raised her chin in the mirror, straightened her shoulders, pulled her black hair in a hand-held pony tail and stared at the image.

"Never a doubt." She said out loud to the reflection, and jumped in the shower.

Downstairs Chaz was cutting fruit, putting out bowls of cereal and pouring juice. He was dressed in a tropical-weight suit. He looked up as Travis came down. "Sleep well?"

Travis shook his head, "Not really. I can't wait for this to be over."

Travis started in on some breakfast when Daphne came down. She had more makeup on than he was used to seeing her wear and the suit she bought last night made her look like one of the local businesswomen he'd noticed in the courtyard last night. She winked at him as he looked her up and down.

Chaz grabbed a canvas travel bag off one of the chairs and handed it to Travis. He opened it and pulled out a pair of compact binoculars, a wireless earpiece with a slim microphone designed to wrap around the front of the users face, and two bottles of water. He looked up at Chaz waiting for an explanation. "You'll need these. The water is because it's supposed to be hot today, and your job involves a lot of waiting outside."

Chaz looked at Daphne, "Perfect, you look every part the businesswoman."

The two of them nervously ate what they could, picking at their food and sipping coffee. Their stomachs retaliated against working on breakfast as they were too overwhelmed with the anxiety of pulling this off. Travis tried to relate this sensation of his nerves with anything he experienced before and came up empty.

Max walked in the front door dressed in his customary driver's uniform. "All set boss."

Chaz clapped his hands together and rubbed them. "As a brave man once said as he headed for certain death, 'let's roll'."

Following his cue they marched out the front door to the limo. The motor was running, Travis and Daphne crawled in the back, Chaz and Max stood on the porch momentarily and talked to each other in hushed tones. Max looked over at the car while they were talking, and Travis once again felt the unease he'd felt on the boat the day before. He knew it was too late to dwell on anything, the wheels were already in motion.

Chaz joined them in the back seat, knocked on the glass partition and the car moved forward.

He sat across from Travis and Daphne, smiling casually at their nervousness. They fidgeted, looked out the window, avoiding eye contact.

"They say," Chaz began, "that the anticipation of an event like this is much worse than the actual event itself."

Daphne looked at him

"I think if you look back into your life you'll notice the same."

"Only trouble is," Travis added, "we've never done anything remotely like this."

Chaz nodded, "The principle is the same, no matter how high the stakes, trust me." He winked, the car picked up speed.

———————

Travis stood outside the gate of a local cemetery perched on a knoll slightly above the center of town. He looked down the street and had a perfect view of the front entrance of Banco de San Juan. Looking through the binoculars, he guessed he was about 300 yards away from the bank and perhaps a few dozen feet above it in elevation. The road went straight down the hill from the cemetery where it passed some gated courtyards leading to what looked like condos or apartment buildings. Just beyond those stood three and four story office buildings, each nondescript in a gray, official looking sort of way.

The bank building stood out in an eye catching display of tropical architecture. A white, textured archway loomed over a polished flagstone walkway, and on each end a domed cap displayed the US flag on one side and the flag of Puerto Rico on the other. Tall, thin palm trees lined the walkway, their tops hinting at a slight breeze Travis couldn't feel at sea level. The bank was on a corner of the main intersection, and its appearance gave the feeling of strength, a place where money was safe.

Travis sat on a bench in front of the cemetery, positioned himself with a view of the front of the bank, and waited. It was tiring to watch through the binoculars the whole time, but he was several hundred yards away from the bank, and this would be the only way he could see what he was looking for. He looked at his watch, 8:30. The bank would open in half an hour. He put his earpiece on and tested it. "Chaz, testing, can you hear me?"

The response was clear, no static or distortion. "Loud and clear, okay on your end?"

"Yes. Is Daphne okay?"

"She's right here, doing her part just fine."

"Can I talk to her?"

There were some shuffling sounds as Chaz took the earpiece off and handed it to Daphne.

"Hey."

"Hey, I just want you to know how much this means to me what you're doing. I know I couldn't do this without your help, and I want to make sure you know that."

"I told you, I want to help you. Doing okay up there?"

"Yeah, something tells me this is going to be a long day."

"Pass the time by thinking of that first night in San Juan. Hang tight, I'm giving the mic back to Chaz."

The waiting continued. The sun climbed higher, the doors to the bank opened and the street bustled with the activity of another business day. Travis sat with his elbows resting on his knees watching every customer who approached the bank, as well as the street activity in front. There was a certain pattern to the goings on. Cars came in spurts, left in spurts, followed by moments of relative calm. During one of these moments of calm Travis checked back in with Chaz.

"Checking in here, you guys still there?"

"Still waiting. Just keep an eye out for Reg, give us the signal when you see him, we'll take care of the rest."

Travis pulled his hat down further and started in on his water. There were shade trees lining the sidewalk in front of the cemetery but the bench was between two of them, and in direct sunlight. Travis would have to choose between the comfort of sitting or the comfort of shade. He alternated between the two as the morning dragged on. At 10:00 he started wondering how long this would take when he saw a shiny, black Hummer crawl down the street. The sun glared off the windshield, it slowly snaked around the corner as its oversized tires slowed and the vehicle parked in front of the bank.

It was the only Hummer Travis had seen on the street all day, and there was something about its presence that alerted his senses. He radioed to Chaz, "We may have something here, stay tuned."

"Waiting for your signal Travis."

The driver's side door of the Hummer opened and a muscular man with a full head of white hair got out and looked in both directions. Travis's throat swelled up in nervous anticipation, his hands gripped the binoculars to keep from shaking, his eyes glued to Reg.

"He's here, wearing a black blazer and black slacks, his hair is white, you can't miss this guy."

"What's he doing now?"

"He's walking to the back of the Hummer. I can't see everything but it looks like he's getting something out of the back."

Travis panned the binoculars from one side of the car to the other, not wanting to miss any of Reg's moves.

"Somebody's getting out of the passenger side door, it's a woman, she's bl... oh my God."

"What is it? What's happening?"

Travis watched as the tall blonde in sunglasses closed her door, looked up and down the street and headed towards the rear of the vehicle. Another man got out behind her. He was dark-haired and broad-shouldered. Travis could tell through the binoculars he played the part of some kind of bodyguard. This man looked up and down the street as well, both hands in the pockets of a light jacket, even Travis with his inexperienced eye could tell this guy had guns and was trouble.

"What is it Travis?" Chaz hissed through the mike.

"There's a bodyguard of some sort, he's standing on the sidewalk between the car and the bank, and Reg has a woman with him."

"Nothing to worry about Travis, you can't pull this kind of thing off alone, he needs help and I've planned for it. Describe his every move to me."

"There's something else…the woman…she…"

"What?"

"It's Beth."

Chapter Thirty-Five

Travis kept his eyes glued on the three of them as they looked around while opening the back doors of the vehicle. The sun flared, beads of sweat stung his eyes blurring his vison. Travis pulled the binoculars away, wiped his eye, and returned to looking at the front of the bank.

"Okay Chaz, he's out of the car standing on the sidewalk. It looks like the bodyguard is getting the bags out for him...wait, they've stopped, they're pointing up the street."

No answer.

"Chaz, Daphne...you there?"

Silence.

What Travis saw next through the binoculars shot a flaming spear through his gut. Reg and the body guard signaled to Beth and they rushed back into the Hummer, hurrying while trying to look nonchalant. The look on Reg's face was fear, the fear of a cornered animal. Out from the side-street next to the bank building Chaz came walking out with his hands over his head, followed by two men in suits with guns drawn.

Daphne was nowhere in sight.

Two black suv's came through a side street and pulled in front of the bank, the Hummer made a u-turn and slid away in the direction it came from. The black vehicles stopped in front of the bank, the driver of the car in front got out and opened the back door while the officer directly behind Chaz put him up against the car, pulled his hands behind his back and cuffed him.

Chaz was looking up the street, his body pressed against the car, hands being cuffed behind him, and was looked directly at Travis.

Travis focused the binoculars closer on Chaz's face, *what am I supposed to do now? Where the hell is Daphne?*

Chaz's face had no expression as he looked back at Travis. The side of his face pressed against the black metal while being frisked and cuffed from behind. Chaz stared over the distance, his eyes said nothing. Travis looked further down the street at the Hummer as it crept swiftly around the corner and out of sight. He banged his fist on his knee and began talking to himself in a hushed, frustrated voice.

"The money's right under your noses! You've got the wrong guy, look around and do your job!"

The men in suits put Chaz in the back seat, putting a hand on top of his head as they did, and not once did Chaz ever take his eyes off of Travis.

He tried Daphne again, "Daphne, are you there?"

"Yes, I'm outside the bank by the side entrance. They arrested Chaz."

"I know, I saw the whole thing. What happened."

She was whispering, he pictured her hiding behind some dumpster in her new suit while she crouched down out of view. "As soon as Chaz walked in the bank through the side door there were two guys standing there and they just arrested him right then. They walked him back outside and I pretended like I was just going for a stroll, minding my own business, digging in my purse for something, and they walked him out to the main area."

"Did you get any idea what the charges were?"

"He asked them loud enough so I could hear, and they said that he was under arrest for shooting at the harbor patrolman last night, and that they were looking for you. They kept asking him if he knew where you were and he didn't say anything."

"Oh God, what the hell are we supposed to do now? The money's gone, Chaz is in jail…this is bad."

"I think they were FBI, I think I saw something in one of the cars that had the seal on it, you know, the one you see on the TV shows."

"Are you sure you're okay?"

"A little shook up, but I'm okay."

"I'm just sorry I dragged you into this. I'm actually glad it was Chaz that was arrested, at least he can handle it. If that was you I don't know what I'd do."

"Hey, look, cheer up. I'm behind you all the way on this, I told you that from the start. And look at the bright side."

"What's that?" Travis changed his earpiece to the other ear.

"The money, it hasn't been deposited yet. We just got a break on the deadline."

Chapter Thirty-Six

Travis kept to the side of the street near the trees bordering the cemetery. He didn't know where to go or what to do. His coach, the man he depended on was gone; the FBI would still be looking for him…and the money, who knew where that was. As he was pacing, wondering what his next move would be, Max pulled up in the black limo.

"Get in."

Travis looked up and down the street before leaving the shelter of the trees. "Where's Daphne?"

"We'll get her, just get in."

Travis darted onto the sidewalk, jumped in the limo and sat, exhaling in a sigh of frustration.

Max made a slow u-turn on the narrow street and glided the car back down towards the bank. He turned left on the side street where Chaz and Daphne had been stationed, there was no trace of the FBI activity of a few minutes ago. Daphne was standing behind one of the rear pillars of the bank, acting as natural as she could while trying to remain inconspicuous. They pulled up to her and Travis opened the door from the inside.

Her cheeks were flushed, the hair she had pulled back so tightly this morning began to unravel, her eyes showed a fear that wasn't there earlier. Travis put his arm over her shoulder, feeling like it wasn't enough but didn't know what else to do. She leaned into him.

Travis looked at Max's eyes in the rear view mirror, "You seem to have some knowledge of this kind of thing Max, what do you think our next move should be? Or do we flick it in and chalk it up to a huge mistake?"

Max returned his gaze, "Chaz has an old saying."

"I've heard enough of his old sayings, they haven't done us any good."

"To paraphrase Winston Churchill, he likes to say, 'Never, ever, flick it in'."

"Okay, I repeat, what should our next move be?"

"First thing is we get away from here and back to Chaz's place."

"Don't you think they'll be looking for me there? Daphne said they kept asking Chaz where I was, I've watched enough cop shows to know that at the least they'll be staking out his place. Come on, you can do better than that."

"He has a second home on the island. You saw his base of ops, but I'm taking you to a safe house. Not many know about it, especially the cops. We should be there in a half hour or so."

"What happened to Pedro?" Daphne asked.

"I'm sure he high-tailed it at the first sign of trouble. They tend to stick together until things go wrong, then it's every man for himself."

"I'm learning that."

Max pulled the car off the main street and headed away from town, passing a small development of bungalow style houses with chain link fences in front. The yards were scattered with rusty wagons, collapsed inflatable pools, broken tricycles. Travis felt out of place cruising through here in a gleaming black limo. He sunk down in his seat, further reinforcing his feeling he had hit bottom, a place he thought he had reached two days ago.

They drove in silence for the first few minutes, Travis and Daphne deep in thought as they looked out their windows, watching but not paying attention to the surroundings. Max drove as if this were just another day in the life of working for Chaz.

Travis felt caged, things were now completely out of his hands and there was no plan, no scheme, no future sequence of events to play out to its logical conclusion.

He sat up and leaned forward. "Max, you must have some idea of what we can do, you saw what happened out there, are we totally screwed or what?"

Max put both hands on the wheel, scrunched his shoulders up and twisted his head slightly. The cracking sound that came from his neck snapped through the rest of the car.

"The way I see it, we need to assess what we have, what our options are and come up with a solution. If we sit here crying in our soup we get nothing done and have failed. Let's stay on track until we get the money back."

Travis sat back in the seat, his arms limp at his sides, "I'm listening."

Max held up a hand and counted off fingers as he talked. "First, we know the money is floating around out there right? I mean, he couldn't deposit it, and that was our deadline. Second, he's as unsure of what to do as we are, his plans are screwed up as much as ours. He knows something was going down at the bank and like a smart thief he scrammed first and asked questions later."

Travis nodded. "Go on."

"The way I see it his problem is actually bigger than ours. He has $54 million lying around that he has to put somewhere. We are just waiting for the right time and place to take it from him."

"Why doesn't he just fly home with it?"

Max looked in the rear view mirror. "Didn't Chaz go over this with you? The money laundering process is all about trails, and right now there's a cash trail from the last bank it was in to Reg's possession. He flies home with it they can trace the money to him and he eventually gets nailed until he coughs it up. That little trick he pulled of putting it in your name only bought him a little time. Once that gets smoked out he's running from them. But if he deposits it one more time, then moves it to US based accounts he can fly under the radar so to speak and launder the money through the system until it's safe."

"So how do we get our hands on the money?"

Max took off his driver's cap and ran a hand over his head. "The way Chaz liked to operate these kinds of things, he always had a saying before he laid out a plan…"

"More of these pearls of wisdom…where does he come up with this stuff anyway?"

Max turned onto a winding road that led away from the impoverished neighborhood they'd just cruised through.

"Look, stay with me. We've got a threesome running around Puerto Rico with all this cash in bags. They're scared, paranoid, and want to get this over with. They're probably starting to wonder what the hell went down at the bank which means one of them may start to get suspicious about the other two. This always happens when there's too many people involved, one setback and you get somebody who thinks there's a conspiracy against him. We need to consider that angle as well."

"I'm not sure I follow," Daphne said.

"Me neither."

Max went on, "What I'm saying is we need to look at this from a strategic point of view, come up with all the possible angles and possibilities and work them into a plan that we can use against them. What this means is we have one goal to work from, and a plan will develop from that. It's like a lot of things in life; simple…but not easy."

"What goal is that? Getting the money?"

"No."

"What then?"

"It's like Chaz would say, we have to make them *want* to give it to us."

Travis laughed, "Like that's a possibility, how are we gonna do that?"

"I don't know yet, this is where we need some of our collective brain power."

"How the hell do you get a guy like Reg to hand over 54 million in cash?"

"Look, you want answers we need to work together. I don't like your attitude and I don't owe you a thing." Max was looking at Travis in the rear-view mirror as he talked. His eyes had narrowed, the pocked skin of his neck bulging out over his tight-fitting collar. "If you want my help you need to show me a little respect and cut me some slack…are we clear?"

Travis nodded, "I'm just a little shaken up, that's all. "

Max's eyes went back to the road. "We all are."

The three of them were silent as Max drove into the countryside.

After the tension thawed out he looked back in the mirror, "You want to know how you get a guy to hand over that kind of money?"

"I'm listening."

"I'll tell you how…he has to think that the idea of *not* handing it over is a worse decision."

"You mean like point a gun in his face? You saw that body guard right?"

"No guns. He has to think it is somehow in his benefit, that he has the edge if he hands it over, like he's putting one over on somebody. That, my friend is how these guys think. A cunning mind is their strongest point, and also their biggest weakness if you can use it against them."

Travis began to put together pieces of the puzzle in his mind. The basic idea was simple, but execution would be the biggest obstacle. Like a phantom that Travis couldn't touch or seize in a three dimensional form, the germination of a plan was there, slipping in and out of his consciousness, lurking in the edges.

He closed his eyes for the rest of the ride.

Chapter Thirty-Seven

Reg paced the floor of the hotel room. Beth sat on the bed flipping the TV through its mindless channels.

"Shut that thing off, I'm trying to think here."

She pouted, flipped through three more channels and turned it off. Donovan stood looking out the window with his hands behind his back.

Reg thought out loud as he walked back and forth, "What the hell was going on down there? Part of me thinks it would be okay to move the money right now but my gut tells me to stay as far away as possible. Something's up and it smells bad."

"Why don't we call the bank manager and ask him what went down, if it's safe to bring the cash in?" Beth asked.

"I did, he wasn't available, they said he'd call back. I also left a voice message on his cell. I gave him my cell number, this has now turned into a waiting game."

The afternoon sun played on the water outside their hotel room window. From four floors up they had a decent view of the east side of the island, afternoon trade winds were picking up.

Donovan sat in one of the chairs next to the window and looked at his watch. "It's just after 2 now, the bank closes in an hour so why don't we let this blow over one more night. In the meantime if he calls we can make a more definite plan. Until then we lay low."

"Besides, I'm starving." Beth had rolled over onto her stomach and was leafing through the complimentary hotel travel magazine.

Reg went into the bathroom. On his way in he turned back, "When I get out we'll get some food."

"Do we leave the money here?" Donovan asked as he pointed to the gym bags lying silently by the dresser in the middle of the room.

"We can't leave it in the hotel safe, it's too conspicuous. I don't want to leave it in the car, we can't walk around with it. I say one of us needs to be in the room with it at all times."

Reg went into the bathroom. As soon as the door clicked shut his cell phone vibrated. It was sitting on the bed, its persistent buzz the only sound in the room. Beth and Donovan stared at it, Reg came out of the bathroom and grabbed it.

"Reg here."

He nodded, looked over at Beth and Donovan, gave them the thumbs up and silently mouthed, "It's him."

"When we saw someone get arrested in front of the bank by what looked like FBI agents we got nervous and decided to back off. Why don't you tell me *exactly* what was going down."

Reg was silent as the bank manager described his version of events. He sat down.

"There must be a reason for your call, what do you have in mind?"

More silence on Reg's part. Nodding, listening.

"I'll check with my associates and call you back in an hour." Reg hung up.

"What happened?" Donovan asked.

"Seems the FBI was ending up a manhunt at the bank the same time we pulled up. It was all a surprise to the manager and he assured me it had nothing to do with us. He said he could understand why we were so hesitant, his idea is we handle the transaction after hours with him personally."

The three of them looked at each other thinking the same thought.

Donovan was the first to speak, "Sounds like a trap."

"My feeling exactly. We need to be careful here. Our plan has backfired, the FBI's in town and we have all this to deal with." Reg gestured toward the bags.

"What's in it for this bank manager to do this for us?"

"He gets a cut of course, and we've done business in the past, that by itself isn't suspicious. But you throw in the arrest, the FBI, the bank manager wanting to do this after hours and I don't like it. Let's eat and come up with our own plan."

They ordered room service and checked email and phone messages while they waited. They ate quickly, quietly.

"Let's say it's a trap, should we respectfully decline now or show up without the money and see what they plan on doing?" Donovan asked.

"I'm working on that train of thought myself. I don't want to burn the bridge with our contact at the bank over something turning out to be just suspicions on our part. On the other hand we need to be paranoid, we have all this loose cash, no plan, and the arrest today was too close to home for me. I'm nervous and I like feeling that way. In the past when I've let my guard down it's been when I'm about to lose my edge."

Beth put her salad fork down. "So how do we get this money back to the states if our bank guy turns out to be a trap? Do we just sit here or what?"

"Look at the big picture for a moment. We're stuck in Puerto Rico with 54 million in cash, things could be worse. I need to keep thinking, make some calls, get in touch with some of my former contacts and see what I can scrape up. This is where most guys screw up. A plan gets messy, things change and they can't adapt. Panic sets in, reacting rather than planning, impulsive…then they get nailed. I'm not about to let that happen, we're too close and I need more time to finish the job."

"I have an idea," Donovan said.

The others looked up.

"Why don't you send me to the bank manager after hours, and the bags won't have the money in them, he'll just think they do. We can stuff them with newspapers, whatever, so that when I show up it looks like we're going along with the plan. If there's any heat and it's a trap we have nothing they can pin on us. No evidence, you're not at the scene, I probably get taken in for questioning and released the next morning. Meanwhile we see out whether it's a trap or not."

"Go on." Reg was following Donovan's train of thought, trying to anticipate problems.

"If it's not a trap we know we can trust your guy from the bank. If it is, I take the fifth, get an attorney, keep my mouth shut and I'll be back here in 24 hours."

"What makes you so sure you can stand up to the interrogation techniques of an FBI trap?"

Donovan held out his arms, "Reg, come on. I got deep inside during the Gulf War, pulled duty in Afghanistan, I can handle a little Q and A from these clowns in suits."

Reg leaned forward, "Until they decide to put a tail on you, and get led right back here." Reg thumped the table with his finger as he finished saying this. "It has too many holes but we need to keep thinking, brainstorming until we can get our arms around this."

They ate in silence, facing an unseen dilemma shimmering like a mirage in the distance.

"How about Donovan *lets* them tail him and he leads them somewhere else? That takes some of their manpower away from us and the money."

"Not bad Beth, keep talking," Donovan said.

"Well, I'm not sure what we do after that, but it just got me thinking that if you are followed that wouldn't be a bad thing if it was handled right."

"We still need to do something with the money," Reg added. "If they follow Donovan it means the bank manager has double crossed us and we need to come up with something else." He drained the last of his iced-tea. "If not, this could possibly work."

Reg finished his meal, walked out of Donovan's suite and down the hallway towards the main lobby followed by Beth.

Reg froze.

He held up his hand signaling Beth to stop as he stared straight ahead. The door to Reg's room was open.

Chapter Thirty-Eight

Beth looked over her shoulder at Reg. A maid was making the bed and her cleaning cart was parked in front of the bathroom door. Reg pulled some local currency out of his pocket, walked over and handed it to her. "Thank you, but you need to leave now."

She looked down at the money, pocketed it quickly and left the room with her cart.

Reg inhaled, letting it out slow as he sat down on the couch. "Okay, let's go through this thing with a fine tooth comb. We need to look at it from every angle then I'll call our guy at the bank and set up a rendezvous for tonight."

Beth sat down.

The afternoon sun was lower in the sky, casting an orange glow over the room as it beamed through the rust colored curtains. From the sounds coming in through the window it seemed the rest of San Juan was out enjoying the day, while Reg and Beth on the fourth floor put their heads together in the quest for anything and everything that could go wrong.

Room service had delivered a pot of coffee and an assortment of sodas; the empty cans and cream pitchers were strewn about the tables. Reg and Beth were back in Donovan's room holding a duffel bag of money in each hand and comparing their weight, balancing them back and forth using his own feel and intuition until he felt it was a good match.

"Put a few more of those magazines in this one, and then we'll lay real bills over the top in case he looks in. A few thousand strewn over the top is a small price to pay to make this look good."

Beth knelt down and added some more weight to the black duffel bag, she and Reg pulled packets of crisp hundred dollar bills from the other bag and carefully laid them over the top. The look was good, if that's all you did was look. To the casual observer it looked like a bag worth millions. If you dug down and pawed through the top few layers of money all you'd see were back issues of Cosmo, Vanity Fair, Cigar Aficionado, and the odd assortment of papers, books and magazines that were available downstairs. They each had gone down separately and bought what they thought were enough periodicals and books to weigh down the bag.

Reg zipped the bag shut and laid it down next to the other for comparison. "They look the same, feel the same, and by the time our bank guy sees the money isn't here we'll know if we're being set up or not."

"So help me out here, if it's not a set up and we have this dummy bag what are you going to tell the bank manager?" Donovan asked.

"He'll understand why we've taken the precaution. If not we'll make another plan from there. That's not my worry."

"What is?" Beth asked.

"If it *is* a set up that Donovan sees it in time and the FBI's interrogation techniques don't get to him." Reg said this as he looked at Donovan, not so much accusing him of something before the fact, but merely laying out how critical every cog in the wheel of this plan had become.

"Not to worry boss," Donovan said.

Reg picked up his soda and drained the rest of it, squinting his eyes as he threw his head back. He crushed the aluminum can, tossed it in the wastebasket and stood in the center of the room with his hands on his hips.

"All right, let's run through this one more time." The others sat at attention in front of him. "Donovan, you take the bag in the Hummer to meet our bank guy out at the pier as agreed. You follow him to the rear of the bank. He gets out, turns off the alarm system and opens the back door. He takes you in the bank and you two get down to business. All this time Donovan has the bag in his hand. Once the bag leaves your hand is when you're most likely to be taken. They'll want you with the evidence, but once it's out of your hand they'll know they can take you down if you try to make a run for it and grab the bag."

Donovan nodded his understanding of the plan they had gone over so many times.

"If there's no sting operation in place, you make arrangements to have our bank contact call us and set up another meet. If you do get taken you're just a customer of the bank and the manager had agreed to get you some traveler's checks in exchange for casino winnings. It's only a few thousand so it's a plausible story. If they don't like it, which they won't, then you get taken in and they grill you. You'll need to stick to your story because so far you haven't done anything illegal. You're just trying to get some cash converted because you're nervous carrying that much around. Got it?"

"Got it."

"Here's the other thing…once they let you go you need to head back to the hotel room we booked for you across town, the Island Paradise. That keeps them away from the real stash which Beth and I will be staying with the whole time."

The expression on Donovan's face shifted. The barest hint of a tightening in the jaw, the color changing, and as quick as it changed his calm look returned.

"Let me just lay one of *my* concerns on the table," Donovan said. "While I'm out getting grilled by the FBI, you and Beth are here with the money and you've sent me across town. What if I come back and you and the money are gone? I'm not saying you'll do that, but I worry about it. Seems like I'm taking the heat here and have the most to lose."

Reg crossed his arms over his black turtleneck and leaned back against the dresser. "I hired you because I thought you had brains as well as muscles, seems I was wrong."

"Don't you think I have a point?"

"Didn't we just try to stick to the original plan which you've been a part of the whole time? And didn't we have to come up with an improvised version on the fly? We've come this far and you think I'm a double crosser…I think you ought to cut your losses now and leave." Reg slammed his hand on the wall, the unexpected crack made Beth flinch.

"Take a million. Go ahead grab a million and get out of my face, I don't need you to finish this job. I've stared down gun barrels and sweated in front of arms dealers I was screwing from behind…you were just an added bit of protection and now I see I've made a serious misjudge of character."

The silence in the room gelled into a sweaty heat.

Donovan backed off. "I…I was wrong to say that Reg, I was just feeling a little tense with the change in plans, I never do well with deviations from the plan."

Reg closed his eyes, inhaled and opened them slightly. His expression had changed. He was no longer the international thief going over a slight change in plans with his team, he was now something different, something to be feared…coiled, venomous.

"Are we clear now?" Reg's voice was steady. "One more like that and you walk away with nothing, understand? If one of us has the slightest bit of mistrust we fall apart, and believe me as sure as I stand here they are counting on us breaking down as a unit. I need to know you're *perfectly* clear on this." Reg had moved closer to Donovan as he said this, his finger pointing at Donovan's chest.

Donovan nodded, "Clear boss."

"Now as I was saying, Beth and I are here with the money and you are a decoy in case you get followed. We use only cell phones to make contact and if it's a sting we lay low and wait this out. If not, we talk the next day and regroup with our man at the bank. Any questions?"

Neither of them said anything for several minutes.

"Actually yes, I have one," Beth said. "Let's say it's a sting and Donovan goes to the Island Paradise, what do we do then? Just wait? I don't get it."

"Waiting will be the only smart thing. If it's a sting there'll be FBI agents all over the island looking for the three of us and those bags," Reg gestured towards the bags of money. "Anything we do that looks like attempting to get cash out of the country will bring them on like a swarm of bees. We'll be forced to be on an extended vacation while I warm up some of my old contacts.

"Like I said earlier, it could be worse. Stuck in San Juan with 50 mill, most people work their whole lives just dreaming of the possibility. Let's just play this as it unfolds."

The air in the room thinned out as the tension eased. Reg turned his wrist, pulled his sleeve up and looked at the black neon diver's watch strapped to his wrist. "Now, Donovan…it looks like you've got a date with a banker. I eagerly await the results of this."

Donovan stood up, tucked his shirt in and grabbed the bag by the door. He slung the long strap over his shoulder, looked back at the two of them and walked out.

Chapter Thirty-Nine

City lights gave way to darkness at the water's edge, streetlights on the main road down to the San Juan pier glowed as lone full moons. Donovan slowed the Hummer to a stop several yards away from a dark green sedan.

Its headlights flashed twice.

Donovan answered with two flashes of his own and the sedan pulled away. Donovan followed.

The sedan took them back around through the main part of town where the nightlife faded into the familiar collection of financial and government buildings Donovan had seen earlier. The calm of the area was a stark contrast to the colorful ambiance of bars and cafés a few blocks away. They passed the cemetery again, the moon picking up gravestones and bathing them in highlights and shadows. Tall white buildings glowed against the dark streets, void of any life or activity. The sedan turned left onto the side street leading to the rear entrance of the bank.

Donovan followed as the sedan pulled into the rear parking lot and up to the pillars which straddled the rear door. He kept the engine running while he waited for the bank manager to get out and turn off the alarm system.

After a few seconds Donovan saw the man get out of the car, stand up and look back at him. He squinted and held his hands up to shield his eyes from the piercing high beams of the Hummer, and waved to Donovan to come out.

The headlights showed the glaring face of the man Donovan knew as their contact at the bank. He looked in the back seat of the sedan to see if there was anybody with him, and he scanned the parking lot for any unusual moves or anything out of place. His years as a bodyguard had trained him to spot irregularities in a seemingly non-threatening environment, and with stakes this high he couldn't be too cautious. He got out of the car and walked over to the bank manager standing at the sedan.

"Aren't you forgetting something?" The man's accent was Asian yet he looked South American.

"Excuse me?"

The man leaned closer, "The money. Did you bring it?"

Donovan shrugged an embarrassed smile, "Hold on."

Donovan went to the rear of the Hummer and opened it. He pulled out the bag, flung the strap over his shoulder, closed the door and activated the car alarm.

The bank manager started laughing. "It's funny, you didn't set the alarm when the money was in the car, but now that it's out you do. Are you nervous? No need to be, Reg and I have done this before. Come in." The man extended his arm in a gesture to come to the door.

The man pulled a ring of keys out and selected one with a tubular shaft with small fins on each side. He pulled open a small flap covering a keyhole on the side of the door, inserted the key and turned it halfway. Donovan quickly turned around and scanned the parking lot. Nothing was different, yet his heightened sense of awareness made him hear sounds where there were none, see things at the edge of his vision that weren't there when he turned to face them.

The skin on the back of his neck crawled with the anticipation of a trap.

Nothing.

He turned back to the door.

The manager was holding the door open, "Come, we only have 30 seconds to turn off the alarm once that door is unlocked. Come in." Donovan followed him into the vestibule between the exterior door and the entrance to the bank. The manager walked over to a keyboard and punched in a 9 digit code, flipped the cover of the keyboard back down and unlocked the second door.

The manager gestured in mock grandeur, "Welcome to Banco de San Juan, where your hours are our hours." Donovan quickly scanned the interior, expecting to see agents squatting, guns held with both hands yelling 'freeze!'

Nothing.

Nothing but the eerie glow of phone lights, dimmed computer monitors, indicator lights over the emergency exits and the sounds of an office at night; overnight faxes coming through, ticking clocks, relay switching noises coming from the electrical systems.

"Follow me, we have a counting machine back here. The way this works is we run the currency through the machine to get a final count. The machine also bands the hundreds into packets of $10,000 each. We put that in the vault, and then I wire it per Reg's instructions he gave us the other day. The whole process should take less than an hour."

Donovan nodded, silent. His eyes darted, senses pulled taut to high alert.

"Don't think I'm doing this out of the goodness of my heart. My fee for helping Reg in the past has put my kids through college and bought my wife enough diamonds to keep her happy."

Donavan followed the manager to the back room, his ears tuned to any change in the drone of an office at night.

The manager led them to an unmarked door that opened without a key. He leaned forward and turned on a light switch. Donovan held back, if it was a trap this would be the time to spring it; cornered, money in hand, nailed like a thief in the night.

The manager stood looking at him, "What are you waiting for? Put the bag on the table here and we can get started."

Donovan walked slowly into the room, crossing the threshold as if it were a point of no return. He moved to a large table in the center. Sitting on the table was what looked like a copy machine standing on its side. A wide tray stuck out from one side, a digital readout glowed red numerals from a small window on the front of the machine. The manager reached over to the side and powered it on.

Looking around Donovan saw the predictable trappings of a room where money was treated as just a part of the job. Shelves lined the walls with bundles of paper straps, specially fitted boxes and containers to carry the currency, and different sized feeder trays to accommodate the variety of international currencies travelling through here. Donovan did as instructed, putting the large duffel bag onto the table next to the counting machine. He looked around the room, headed back to the door and looked out both ways.

"Is something wrong?"

Donovan came back inside. "This has so far been a test to see if there was a trap set for us. Reg is very cautious, and he didn't want to go through this change in plans until he was absolutely sure it was safe. Everything looks in order, I think I'll call Reg and tell him everything's okay."

"I don't understand? If it's a test, what's in the bag?"

Donovan unzipped it as he dialed his cell phone. The manager pawed through the top bundles of currency and shook his head as he came to the piles of magazines and books. "I should have known, Reg has been paranoid since the day I met him."

Donovan stood up straighter as his connection went through. "Yeah Reg, look we got as far as getting ready to put the money in the counting machine and the coast is clear. Nobody in the bank, the parking lot is empty, looks good to me."

Donovan nodded, then handed the cell phone to the bank manager. "Here, he wants to talk to you."

"Yes?" he answered into the phone.

The bank manager listened momentarily, "Of course I understand Reg, I would have done the exact same thing. I would hope however, that eventually you will come to see I am a man of my word."

Donovan couldn't hear Reg's words over the phone, but could tell by the cadence of Reg's voice that he was deferential, almost subservient to the bank manager. He was a key player in this and if he didn't follow through on his end then they might as well turn themselves in.

The bank manager went on, "Yes, tomorrow night, same time, same place. Very well. Goodbye."

He handed the phone back to Donovan. "Yeah, I'm sure, it looks fine. I'm talking to you aren't I? I'll make me way to Island Paradise, see if I pick up a tail, looks pretty clean though." He hung up, took his bag and bid the bank manager a good night.

He walked out the door, through the entryway past the alarm system, and as he was partially out the exterior door he stopped and looked to his left.

Nothing.

To his right, silence, no movement. He walked back to his car, put the bag in the trunk and started the engine.

Chapter Forty

Killing time in San Juan would normally be no problem for the average tourist. When you're waiting to see whether or not there's an FBI sting around the corner, time slows to a dripping, torturous crawl. Each passing minute got them closer to uncertainty, and brief moments of relaxation and enjoyment were overshadowed by an undercurrent of apprehension. Reg and Donovan rescheduled their flights to leave that night, while Beth put a wrap over her olive colored bikini, inched her feet into sandals and headed for the pool.

The tables and lounges around the pool were set in random groupings with umbrellas, side tables, cocktail waiters, towel vendors and swimming pool scuba lessons all going on at the same time. Most of the vacationers were starting the morning off with Bloody Mary's or Pina Coladas, while the braver ones went right to the clear stuff on ice in plastic cups. Beth picked a lounge chair as far away from the centrally crowded area as possible and decided to work on her tan. As she walked by men tried to look while looking like they weren't looking, while most of the wives told them to go ahead and look, silently cursing her for showing up with a body like that.

She folded the umbrella down, put on number two oil, pulled her hair back and moved the lounge chair to the precise angle for what she had in mind. The sun soothed her, and for the briefest of moments Beth forgot what lay ahead, and basked in the tropical sun.

An uncertain amount of time went by, and she decided to roll over and do her back. She expertly undid the back strap, moved her hair to one side and pulled her bottoms up her ass slightly. There wasn't a guy within 100 yards who missed this. She turned her head to the other side and saw a woman on the lounge next to her who wasn't there minutes before. The woman had light sunglasses on making it difficult to tell, but Beth had the feeling this woman was staring at her. Beth threw off a fake courtesy smile and closed her eyes.

"I know who you are."

The voice was Eastern European, somewhere near Russia. A voice born of repression, glaciers and vodka. *Who the hell is she talking to?*

Beth opened her eyes. The dark haired woman had her sunglasses perched off her nose, staring at Beth over the tops of them. She had the faint beginnings of a smile, and looked like she could wait an eternity for Beth to respond.

"Excuse me?"

"I recognize you from the picture in the paper."

Beth swallowed, "I have no idea what you're talking about."

"Sure you do, your picture is in the paper with that guy who stole all the money and fled with his assistant."

The questions came all at once. *What did she know? Who was she? How could she know this? Travis fled with his assistant?*

"You're going to have to excuse me, I have no idea what you're talking about." With that Beth closed her eyes and rolled her head away from the woman.

The stranger persisted. "Beth Wagner." The move was barely there, but she caught it. No matter how hard one tries to move through the world incognito, the unexpected sound of their own name provokes a reaction. Beth was still too new at this game to hide it. The twitch in her shoulders, the raising of her head which she tried to stop too late and too obviously gave the stranger more firepower.

"I see you know your own name."

Beth turned back to face the woman. "Who are you and what do you want?"

The stranger held out her hand, "I am Simone, pleased to meet you Beth."

Beth stared at the hand, Simone left it outstretched. It became a social waiting game that Beth finally won as Simone slowly withdrew her hand without losing any of her poise.

"Now that I know your name why don't you quit playing games and tell me what you want?"

Simone took off her glasses, folded them slowly and placed them on top of the towel next to her. "A little bird tells me you have a problem."

"Your little bird is full of shit, if you'll excuse me I have to go." Beth reached behind her and began to retie the bikini strap.

"Most people wouldn't consider 54 million in cash a problem, but I think you can see how it makes life a little harder, no?" The accent thickened the more the woman talked. It was a deep voice that carried with it the confident air of a well-seasoned international traveler. This was a woman who wasn't afraid.

And she knew too much.

Beth stopped what she was doing.

"Level with me, or I walk away. How is it that you think you know so much about me?"

Simone moved closer, folding her hands between her knees and lowered her voice, "I know the bank…" she looked around to see if anybody was in ear shot, the loudest noises were of the children playing in the pool. "…the bank manager is someone I've worked with before, I am in the business of helping people like you."

"People like what?"

"People who need to move cash…clean, laundered cash out of the country quickly and painlessly."

"And what makes you think that's my problem?" Beth wanted so much to blow this woman off and just get through the day. But there was something about her that went beyond her dead-aim grasp of Beth's predicament; this woman had something she wanted to say and Beth got curious.

"Look, I travel in circles that bring me into contact with people like your Reg and others like him. We're a close knit circle, and I'm not here to bust you but to try and earn some money. My gig if you will, is converting cash to easily transportable diamonds, designing fake passports to get you out of the country, and taking a cut of ten percent. Now I've laid my cards on the table, perhaps we can talk later."

Simone put her glasses back on, stood up, grabbed her towel and walked away.

"Wait."

Simone stopped, turned back and lowered her sunglasses again.

Beth sat up, "I think you can help us."

Simone sat back down.

"Where do you get these diamonds?" Beth asked.

"I don't ask you where you get your cash, you don't ask me where I get the diamonds."

"Okay, what do we do with them once we get back to the states?"

"I can give you some names and numbers, they'll sell quickly. The best thing is to sell them a little at a time in various locations, people screw up when they get greedy and dump them all in a day, that's when things go wrong."

"How long will it take for you to come up with over fifty million in diamonds?"

Simone laughed, leaned closer. "I have them. I am fresh from a new buy and as I said earlier I got wind of your problem. Call it… serendipity, I have always loved that word."

"So your fee is ten percent? I think Reg might feel that's a little high."

"It is no higher than your man at the bank is charging, don't try that with me or I walk. My job is every bit as dangerous as yours and I need to be paid for that risk. Are we clear?"

Beth was used to being a no bullshit woman in a world that was full of it. She'd met her match.

"How do I…I mean how do we know these diamonds are real?"

"I can give you a sample right now and you can take them to any jeweler in town. I am confident they will be appraised as the highest quality."

Beth thought about this for a moment. "Excuse my ignorance, but this is all very unfamiliar to me…how do I know that the diamonds I get for my fifty million are real?"

"I guess that's where you have to make a leap of faith. I can't go around scamming people like Reg for very long and stay in business. My transactions all come from word of mouth, and I work hard to keep my reputation. Once I lose that then I'm out of business, not to mention probably ready to get shot."

"You didn't come to me through word of mouth, you came to me looking for a transaction, what gives?"

"I'm still building my reputation if you will. The man at the bank shared your problem with me as a professional courtesy, if I can get someone like Reg and yourself as a client then my reputation spreads."

Beth stared at the woman, searching her face for something out of place, something she could put her hands on as a reason not to do this. She found nothing except more thoughts racing through her mind.

"How long have you been doing this?"

"A few years." Simone looked at her nails as she did this, apparently checking out a recent manicure. "It has proven lucrative and I enjoy it."

"So walk me through this, how would we go about doing business, theoretically of course."

"Of course. It's very simple, I'm staying at the Wyndham hotel. All you…"

"Wait, that's far from here, what are you doing at this place?"

"Is ten percent of 50 million worth a 30 minute drive?"

"Go on." Beth rolled over on to her side, head on her hand and faced Simone directly.

"As I was saying, all you need to do is show up with the cash, we count it, I give you the diamonds, and we're done. Will you need a fake passport?"

"No."

"Will the others?"

Beth was silent.

Simone waited.

Beth looked down.

"What exactly is the relationship with you and Reg? Do you mind my asking?"

Beth let out a long sigh that sounded like she had been holding in for months. "I guess you could call me his partner, I think of it more as his little puppy dog to do his dirty work for him."

"Like what?"

"Like finding young brokers who want to hit the big time and getting involved with them, putting on the kind of soft pressure that only a high maintenance woman can. It's kind of sick really, but it works."

"Do you have to sleep with these brokers?"

Beth laughed, "Sleep with them? That's the easy part. The hard part is encouraging them, getting them to think bigger, waiting for them to bring up Reg's name and how that could get them to the 'next level'." She held her fingers up in the sign for quotations as she said these last two words. "They all sound the same, and it's my job to get them thinking they need to earn more money to keep me around."

"Sounds weird."

"It is weird, I don't even know if I'm really necessary in these schemes Reg comes up with, but he says what I do is a 'play a vital role' in the process." Again the fingers came up with the quote sign.

"How does he mean?" Simone was an excellent listener and seemed genuinely fascinated in how Reg had decided what role Beth would play in his livelihood.

"The whole thing is that Reg has to find a broker that's not new and struggling, but not a big hitter either. The new guys couldn't raise the money to make it worthwhile, and the big hitters would smell a rat. It's a fine line, and where I come in is in prodding them to get in with someone whose name they can drop at parties, a real live hedge fund honcho. They want to impress me, their friends, and make enough to keep me smiling. Reg has it all figured out and so far it works.

"He has me play a more critical role as well," Beth looked around to see if anybody was within earshot. "My job also entails leaving clues that tie the crime to the broker, this gives us more time to get the money out of the country."

"What kind of clues?"

"Subtle ones, but effective. Making calls to Puerto Rican banks from their home phone, sending incriminating e-mails from their home computer, just enough to keep the heat off Reg."

"Are you good at what you do?"

"If you think about it, it's a very natural role for most women. Be high maintenance, be attractive, be slightly out of reach at times, and be the reason they go to work in the morning. Yes, I'd have to say I have gotten good at it."

"Wouldn't look too good on a resume though would it?"

They both laughed at this, and were silent as Simone processed what Beth had shared with her, and Beth wondered in her mind how much longer she could do this.

"Do you ever fall for one of these brokers? Get to a point where you wish you weren't doing what you're doing?"

"You sure ask a lot of questions."

"I like to know what makes my clients tick."

"Well, to answer your question no. They're usually not my type. I need somebody that this plan wouldn't work on, someone stronger, someone that is already a player."

"What's this latest one like?"

"Travis? He tries so hard and someday it'll click for him. Of the guys we've tried this on he is by far the strongest, which meant he was also risky. But we knew the score would be bigger with him and we were right."

"Did you ever find yourself attracted to him?"

"A little here and there, but he has this focus on the business that's too boyish, all this naïve ambition wrapped up in youthful enthusiasm, he's like a puppy dog. He's obsessed with that movie that came out in the 80's...you know, *Wall Street*, it's got Charlie Sheen and Michael Douglas in it. I swear he watches it every month, it's like he's got the movie memorized and walks around saying things like, 'Greed is good', or 'You're on a roll kid, enjoy it while it lasts; cuz they never do'. It's sweet, but it gets old after a while."

"What's your long term plan? Do you think you'll stay in this partnership with Reg?"

Beth sighed, "I hope not, it's getting to the point where I need something else, something I can use other talents for besides being a fake lover."

They were silent as the words Beth had shared with Simone echoed back to her in a moment of introspection she usually didn't allow herself.

"I get the feeling you think Reg doesn't need you."

"Sometimes I feel that way, but...I guess he does, I mean this *is* working. And I think in his sick mind he likes putting me through this. I wouldn't sleep with him when we first met, and this seems to be his way of getting back at me."

"How did you meet?"

"It was at a party on some yacht in the Mediterranean. He was involved in some high level arms deal and we hit it off."

"But not enough?"

"I respect Reg, I admire his guts, his way of thinking big, but I'm not attracted to him; I think we've reached some kind of understanding that way."

"I think it's really the other way around."

"What? What do you mean?"

"I think, just after talking with you, that it's you who doesn't need Reg."

Beth sat up, readjusted her top and leaned closer to Simone. "You think so?"

"You're a talented, beautiful, articulate woman Beth. You've just made a huge score, go do something for yourself now. How much longer are you going to be his 'employee'? What does he need all that money for anyway? He must have several million stashed away by now."

"He never knows when to quit. Once somebody asked him, 'Reg, how much is enough? How much do you need to stop and do something else?' You know what his answer was?"

"What?"

"He said, 'Just a little bit more'."

They were quiet again, Beth thought she had revealed too much.

"So, how do I contact you?"

Simone gave her a cell number on a card. "I'm in room 724."

"You may hear from me tonight."

"Splendid." Simone held out her hand, Beth took it and watched her walk away. Watching Simone, her worldly manner, Beth felt admiration for another woman for the first time she could remember. Simone was class, Beth wanted to be like her, emulate her, have people look at her like she was looking at Simone.

She laid back down, the images of a new life for her crystalizing at the edges.

Chapter Forty-One

Donovan finished changing the flights to leave San Juan on a red-eye two hours after tonight's transaction. He stayed in the room getting in a final workout of body weight exercises while Reg went down to have an early lunch and catch up on some reading to pass the time. Reg wore a cap, dark glasses, tropical shirt and shorts. He looked more like a tourist than at any time since they'd been down here, and although it would never happen he made up his mind to try and relax today while they were down here.

He headed towards the open air café on the other side of the pool. The tables were covered with logo umbrellas and clean cut looking waiters scampered about looking for any opportunity to earn an extra tip.

Reg passed the news and gift stand and something at the corner of his eye made him freeze.

It was the newspaper a man sitting on a bench was reading.

He looked like he was waiting for his wife to finish shopping. Reg caught himself and tried to act inconspicuous but at the same time he had to see the newspaper again. He strained his eyes behind the dark glasses so as to appear he was looking in another direction, the bold print of the headline draping across the front of the paper.

The man turned the page and folded the paper back on itself, commuter style.

"Excuse me, what paper is that you're reading?"

The man lowered his paper and looked over his glasses at Reg.

"Excuse me?"

"That paper, which one is it?"

"It's the morning edition of the Miami Register."

Reg rushed into the gift shop and scanned the piles on the floor for the paper he'd seen.

Nothing. None of the other papers had the same headline he'd seen. He walked over to the clerk. "Excuse me, I'm looking for this morning's edition of the Miami Register."

"Sorry sir, we just sold our last copy. The evening edition will be out this afternoon if you'd like to try back later."

Reg raced back out and looked at the bench he'd seen the man sitting on, he was gone. He looked around and saw him walking with his wife to the pool area. He didn't have a newspaper in his hand.

Reg looked at the closest waste can and through the flap could see the paper lying on top. The front page was buried under a folded business section.

The headline.

Fugitive Stockbroker Travis Black found in San Juan

The subheading revealed more...

Manhunt Ends in Arrest at Gunpoint, Still Claims Innocence.

Reg felt his worst fears confirmed as he realized how close Travis had come to him.

Reg read the whole story...

After two days of searching for missing stockbroker Travis Black, the FBI reports they successfully arrested him as he attempted to make contact with a bank in San Juan to apparently launder the money he recently embezzled from San Francisco based brokerage firm Hastings & McCloud.

Travis was last seen driving north on the San Francisco Golden Gate Bridge Monday night after fleeing the scene of a sophisticated embezzling scheme he pulled on his unwitting clients. He showed up for work as usual on Monday, and when the scheme started to unravel in front of his eyes, he vanished. Local authorities in San Francisco revealed that Travis seemed to taunt them by staying so close to the scene of his crime. Once it became clear he had wired over $54 million in embezzled funds to an account in his name in an offshore bank, a massive search was put in place.

The FBI agent in charge of the investigation, Greg Wilks, said that while Travis had been very clever in the way he took the money, his method of escape was sloppy and it was simply a matter of following him as he fled to Puerto Rico in an attempt to transfer the money out of the bank it had been wired to.

"He set up an elaborate and complex con, and it seemed he covered his tracks well up until the very end." Wilks went on. "He started making mistakes like they all do, and we put my agents in the right place at the right time."

Authorities say that Travis was arrested at gunpoint as he walked out of his hotel room after visiting a local bank infamous for its discreet clientele. He cooperated, the arrest was nonviolent, and yet Travis continued to insist he was the victim of a set up.

"They all get around to saying that eventually," agent Wilks said. "He has the evidence stacked up against him with e-mails, phone records, bank accounts, I see no problem getting a conviction here."

If convicted as charged Travis could face up to 15 years in prison for forgery, embezzlement, violation of securities laws as well as money laundering. His assistant Daphne DiMarco was also arrested and it isn't clear what her role in the scheme was. "Her being with Travis in Puerto Rico pretty much cements our theory that she was in on it, we'll be able to put the pieces together shortly, right now we're just glad she and Travis are in custody."

Travis and Daphne are being flown back to San Francisco awaiting trial. Hastings & McCloud management reiterated that this was an isolated incident and in no way reflects on their business ethics. Hastings & McCloud is a regional brokerage firm with several offices on the West Coast.

Reg realized he was standing right in the doorway of the gift shop and tourists were jostling around him as he read of Travis's arrest. He put the paper under his arm, walked out to the café and got himself a table away from the main area.

He reread the article. Reg had an even higher level of respect for Travis and continued to fight the feeling he had come so close to meeting his match. If Travis had come down here to get the money that was a first in his experience. Most of these guys just rolled over and let the FBI find out for themselves that it was too late.

He had hit the line with Travis, capable enough to make the operation well worth it but also resourceful enough to put up a fight. Reg, while relieved that this suspicion he had about Travis had been brought to a close, was still reeling from how close he'd come to getting entangled in something that could prove his undoing.

Reg ordered an iced tea, opened his book and tried to read. The minutes passed slowly as he waited for this to be over tonight, and he found himself re-reading the same page over and over. He picked at his lunch of club sandwich and lentil soup, thought about going over to the pool and relax the afternoon away, but his restlessness crawled up inside his skin, making him feel like he had to move, had to do something.

He went back to his room, got the keys to the Hummer, and took a drive to the beach. The afternoon was promising to be as pleasant as any of the others this week, and Reg got out and walked the mile length of the beach, his feet playing with the water as his mind went over the events of the last 48 hours. It hadn't been a routine operation, most of them weren't; yet this one had tried his patience. From the arrest yesterday right in front of their eyes, to Travis in their own backyard looking for him, Reg felt off, his edge had been dulled. His mantra of never getting caught was being pushed into new directions, and he felt the uncomfortable closeness of danger whispering in his ear.

He walked back to the vehicle, his mind wrapping itself around one coherent thought rising above the chatter and questions in his head...*Never, ever get caught.*

Chapter Forty-Two

Reg sat on the sofa in the front guest area of his hotel room and glanced at his watch. Donovan arrived at exactly 8pm, Beth a few moments later.

Reg stood up.

"We're going to play this like we did last night."

"What?" Beth asked.

"We're sending Donovan out first with a dummy bag, and if the coast is clear he'll call us."

"Why? Last night everything looked okay." Donovan asked.

"Think about it," Reg paced as he talked. "We have a bank manager who knows we're coming in tonight, and the FBI has had an extra day to look for us. I feel like any precautions we take are necessary and I want to err on the side of caution. Let's just say my guard is up more than usual."

"But they have Travis in custody," Beth countered. "You showed us the article earlier. Doesn't that take the heat off for a while?"

"We do this my way. I wish I didn't have to repeat myself with you two but the reason we're where we are is because I make sure we don't get caught. If you two want to take chances, go ahead. But not with me and not with my money."

Reg looked at his watch again. "Donovan, you have a trip to make. You're expected in 30 minutes. Do it just like last night and call me when the coast is clear. We'll come meet you."

Donovan grabbed the bag that still was bulked up with newspapers and books and headed out the door.

Reg walked over to where Beth was sitting and stood over her.

She looked up.

Reg's voice was ice, calm, "Anything you want to tell me?"

"What?"

"You heard me."

"I have no idea what you're talking about."

He squatted to make eye level contact with her. "I have a bad feeling, it's like I can sense the hair on the back of my neck warning me about something but I don't know what. Are you with me on this?"

"Why do you have to ask that? I've been with you the whole time, lay off."

"Here's what you need to know… as much as I want to sleep with you and have you as mine, if it comes down to you getting in the way of me and the money, or you taking the fall for this on your own…you go down. Understood?"

"You're such a control freak, get out of my face."

"I mean it Beth. I'd think nothing of throwing you to the wolves to keep me out of their hands. Just hold that in your little brain tonight."

He went into the bedroom, put the bags near the foot of the bed and flipped on the TV. He mindlessly worked his way up and down the range of channels while Beth fumed in the next room flipping through a magazine.

The phone rang.

Donovan.

"It's clear, a carbon copy of last night boss."

Reg started throwing duffel bags onto a luggage cart. At over 180 pounds each the straps were stretching and the bags hung down like they held dead bodies. "I'll get these, we'll have to take your rental car since Donovan still has the Hummer. Get the door for me and let's hit it."

Reg maneuvered the heavy load through the doorway and out into the hall. Beth walked with him to the elevator and pushed the button for the lobby. The door opened instantly.

Beth halted in her tracks.

Inside were two police officers, one smoking a cigarette while the other straightened his hair in the reflection off the shiny metal wall.

They had Puerto Rico insignias on their uniforms, both were South American looking, and smiled as Reg and Beth walked on.

"Going down?"

"Yes, thank you." Reg said.

The doors closed, Reg and Beth stood in silence as the officers continued their conversation. The smoke from the cigarette in the officer's hand drifted offensively into Beth's face. She normally would have brushed it away with a wave of her hand, or even said something. She couldn't move, her breathing short.

"They say it happened right in this hotel," one of the officers said.

The other whistled. "That's a lot of dough for one senorita wouldn't you say? Maybe she needs someone to help her spend it." He laughed, then went back to straightening his hair. Reg couldn't take his eyes off the green lighted numbers over the door as they crept from four to three then two. He took his first breath as it flashed L for lobby and the doors opened.

They exited rapidly, enough to get out of there without drawing attention. "The car's this way, you have the keys right?"

Beth held them up and jingled them as she fished them out of her purse.

"Good, you drive, I hate driving that little thing. Plus, it'll be good for me to keep an eye out."

"Some gentleman you are."

"I'm carrying the goods aren't I?" He patted the bags as he said this and they walked through the revolving door at the side entrance of the hotel.

Beth pointed the key at the car and clicked the alarm off. The car beeped and lights flashed in response. "That was as close of a call as I ever want to get back there."

Reg went around to the rear of the car, looked around the parking lot and stood at the trunk. "Pop this thing open will you?"

Beth got in the driver's side of the silver Mercedes C class, reached down under the dash and pulled the trunk lever. Reg swung the bags one at a time off the cart into the trunk, three of the bags had to go in the back seat. He went around to the passenger door and got in.

They pulled away, Reg gave her directions to the bank as he kept looking around for any other cars pulling out to follow. Nothing.

"So far so good. We could very well be in the ninth inning of this. I'm going to keep an open line with Donovan once we get closer."

Beth followed Reg's directions and made her way through town. As she came up the hill towards the cemetery Reg had his phone out.

"We're just a minute or two away, anything change on your end?"

Reg listened.

"Good, it looks clear from here, you guys are inside still?"

Reg nodded as Donovan affirmed this.

"Let's keep this line open as we pull in, you see anything, anything at all you holler and we'll just pull out. Clear?"

Reg kept the phone to his ear as Beth navigated the slow downhill stretch, past the cemetery and into the financial district of San Juan. She pulled up to the side street, turned left and slowed to a crawl as she came alongside the bank.

"I'm thinking we're in the clear Donovan, you?"

"Good, we'll be knocking on the door in a few seconds."

Reg looked at the shadows the headlights made in the shrubbery surrounding the parking lot. He peered through the windshield up at the roof, looked behind them at the main road. Beth pulled up behind and to the near side of the Hummer. "Don't pull in too close, we may still have to make a run for it." Reg continued to scan the parking lot, "But it looks okay. Keep the engine running until I tell you."

Reg still had the cell phone to his ear. "Donovan, we're here, come to the door and meet me, I'll have the bags."

Reg hung up, got out and headed for the trunk of the car, "Pop the trunk."

He got to the rear of the car, reaching his hand out to open the trunk. The car's rear tires spun in an uncontrolled screeching, the car speeding away. Reg reached forward to try and grab onto the bumper, losing his balance as the car fishtailed. Beth made a sharp turn to the left racing out of the parking lot and onto the main street. Reg ran to the Hummer, it was locked, *Shit, Donovan has the key!*

Reg ran to the rear door of the bank to grab Donovan and chase Beth in the Hummer. As he got to the door, he could hear the tires screaming in the distance as Beth took a side street off the main road. He cursed her to eternal hell, cursed himself for taking her this far. He banged on the door, it was unlocked. He ran in screaming for Donovan, "The bitch ran off with the money, give me the goddamn keys! Where are you?"

The dark bank instantly lit up. Reg froze, *what was happening?* From under desks, around corners, through doors came men in black jackets, guns and rifles drawn and pointed at Reg. He looked down the hall towards the counting room as Donovan was being cuffed from behind by two men. The back of the jacket had bright yellow letters on it. FBI.

The manager came out from the counting room, his hand at his sides as if to say 'I had no choice'. "They threatened to close us down and take me in Reg, I had to look out for myself."

Reg bolted for the door.

"Freeze!" Was all he heard from every direction. He kept running and pushed the door open.

Shots rang out and the glass door that he'd just went through shattered in a crashing waterfall of shards.

He stopped.

The game was up, he knew the next shot would hit. He cut left and bolted for the driveway in an insane last ditch attempt to see which way Beth was heading. The shot came from behind and dropped him instantly. Several more came at the same time, his body writhed in pain, jerking as each one hit.

Donovan was led out by two other officers, their feet crunching on the broken glass as they walked through the door.

Reg looked up at the sky, seeing nothing but the hazy glow of city lights. He attempted a scream, "You bitch!" came out in a gargled last gasp of bleeding spit.

His screams echoed off the granite buildings, mocking him with no answer but his own agony, as the squeal of Beth's tires pierced the night.

Chapter Forty-Three

Beth raced her car through the back streets of San Juan, her mind splashing images of the consequences of her actions in a slide show of fear. The streetlights speeding by, occasional oncoming vehicles, cars she had to pass; these all were interrupted with flashing insights into what lay before her. In a clear moment she tried to rationally go through her fears one by one. The FBI would be looking for her, probably with helicopters; Reg would do everything he could to have her killed and his reach was global; getting through airports; laundering the money; coming up with a new life after she returned to the US...

She lowered her speed to a level that wouldn't attract attention, but still felt like she was getting somewhere. The northern side of the island lay ahead of her, and once there she could meet up with Simone at the Wyndham.

She grabbed her cell phone from the outside pocket of her purse and called Simone.

"I'm ready right now, can we meet in ten minutes?"

"Make it 20.", Simone answered. "Room 724?"

"Got it." Beth picked up speed.

Her first priority was to get off the streets, into Simone's hotel room and make the transfer. She would also need a different car, a different identity and a way out of the country. Simone had said she could help with the identity, but it would be up to Beth to make arrangements to get off the island, she would deal with that once she finished what she had to do tonight. For now, Beth had to do something she wasn't used to doing, focus. Concentrate on getting to Simone's.

The road opened up as it crossed a large expanse of beachfront houses backed up against rolling green hills, her car merged onto the coast highway heading further north. In the distance she saw the lights off the main highway for the casinos, major hotels and clubs... and the Wyndham.

Beth checked her rear view mirror, so far so good. She looked up through the front of the windshield towards the sky, no sign of a helicopter. The night was clear, and the skies were void of any threatening sights or sounds. She thought of pulling over and getting out to look at the money one more time. The idea of her driving around with 54 million in the trunk was still too new to get her arms around, and she felt like if she could just touch it this would all become more meaningful. Her instincts told her this would be foolish, but it was an irrepressible urge at a time when her thoughts were confused. A disturbing thought had lingered in the shadows of her mind and sent a shiver down her spine... *What if Reg had switched bags at the last minute as an extra precaution? I need to know it's there...it'll only take a minute.*

She led the car onto the shoulder, checked the rear view mirror once again, and brought the vehicle to a stop with the engine running. Sitting in the front seat, she waited to see if something or somebody would show up. All she wanted to do was touch it, make sure it was still there, that this wasn't some dream and she'd arrive at Simone's with nothing but a sad story. Beth took a deep breath, popped the trunk and got out. There was no traffic in front or behind as she walked to the rear of the vehicle. The trunk was slightly ajar, she reached down and pulled it up. Laying side by side, just as they were put there, sat four black duffel bags. She bent down to unzip one and check the contents. The trunk light gave her just enough light to see inside, but it was obstructed by one of the bags located near the rear of the trunk. She bent over further to move it, when instantly the trunk was filled with light, only blocked in the middle by her shadow. A truck had pulled up behind her and had its high beams on. Beth's hand had just started to unzip one of the bags, she froze, dared not look back.

She heard a door open, footsteps.

"Hey Chi Chi, you need some help, you need something pumped up? I got a pump."

The sloppy laughter with a thick Puerto Rican accent chilled her, it was the laughter of someone who had all night and nothing to lose. Beth looked down at her legs, she realized she had put on a short skirt and this guy was probably getting a view usually only found in magazines. Another voice joined in, "I think she wants it from behind, look at the way she's standin', she wants it bad man."

Beth remembered she'd left the engine running and it was now or never. She reached up, slammed the trunk shut and bolted for the door. It was still open, she jumped inside, looked in her rear view mirror as the drunken men stood there wavering in their own headlights, wondering how far to push the fulfillment of their desire. They ran towards her, trying to grab onto the back of the car.

"Idiots." Beth picked up speed just enough to stay ahead of them, but slow enough to encourage them. They trotted in a drunken stupor, tripping over each other, each one hallucinating about what they would do once they caught her.

Beth kept driving.

She wanted to get them as far away from their truck as possible to slow them down if they decided to follow. After what seemed like a ridiculous amount of time for two drunk men to chase a car Beth slammed the gas down and sprayed them with road gravel as the rear of the car fishtailed back onto the main highway.

The tires grabbed the asphalt and her journey towards Simone continued. In the rear view mirror the two men were flipping her off between moments of catching their breath. It would be easy enough to lose them before they were able to get going again.

The highway passed the hotel and she had to take the next exit and double back on a frontage road. The signage at the hotel was well lit, she was able to find her way to the main entrance easily and pull into the valet area.

A young, eager man in a tuxedo jumped off the curb and opened her door for her. "Good evening, are you staying with us tonight?" He said this as he watched her thighs under the steering wheel. Beth pulled her hair from her face and looked up, "No, but I will need somebody to get a cart so I can handle the bags in the trunk. I should only be an hour or so."

"Very well." The man blew on a whistle and opened her door further, handing her a ticket. "This is for the car, and a bellman will be unloading your trunk."

Just as he said that an older man wheeled a large, brass luggage cart with an overhead rack for hanging clothes to the rear of the car. Beth got out, handed the valet a twenty and joined the other man. She opened the trunk, "I just need these bags put on here, as well as the ones in the back seat, and I can take it from there. You're very helpful."

The expression on the man's face changed, "Very well, I can take them up for you and help you unload them. That would be no problem."

Beth looked at the man as he tried valiantly to increase his tip by going the extra mile, but she had no time for this. Reaching back into her purse, she pulled out another twenty and put on a faint southern accent, "You are too kind, I wish there were more men like you back home. But seriously, this is all I need you to do."

The man looked confused at first, but then went about the task of loading the bags onto the cart, pocketed the twenty, and tipped his cap to

Beth. She took the cart, wheeled it up and through the front doors which another tuxedoed man held open.

The first sound she heard was one of slot machines; the familiar, banal ringing and clanging. The slots closest to the front door were the big promotional machines, oversized and taking only dollars, they promised millions or the keys to the gleaming red Tesla sitting behind maroon velvet ropes. The machine was taller than anything around it, and plastered on a nearby partition were photos of recent winners smiling as they held up large cardboard checks.

Beth walked past them and headed straight for the elevators. Like all casinos it was difficult to find anything that could help you get out, but when you're wheeling 54 million in cash your priorities change quickly. She was able to scan for the signs and pass the temptations without hesitation. One of the wheels on her cart was wobbling back and forth and kept trying to pull it to the side. Beth found herself having to step up and grab the front railing to keep it straight. *Just get up there and get this over with, you're so close.*

She found the bank of elevators off to the left and pushed the up button. The doors opened instantly, the car was empty, she wheeled the cart in and pushed the button for the seventh floor.

The doors closed. Beth tried one more time to peek at the money, the thought of Reg pulling one last joke on her kept running through her mind. She crouched down, unzipped one of the bags and reached her hand in.

The elevator stopped, the doors opened.

Chapter Forty-Four

T he FBI agents led Donovan to the other side of the bank where one of the black SUV's was parked. As they let him in the back seat he asked, "Reg, did he die? I just need to know."

One of the agents laughed and the other said, "He's dead, and if you don't let us ask the questions you'll look the same. Shut up and get in there." He gave Donovan one last shove and slammed the door.

Over the car radio he could hear the requests for backup to find Beth. They ordered a chopper, the other agents raced to the second black SUV parked across the street on a side entrance and squealed off the in the direction they thought they saw Beth head in. The problem they had was obvious by what Donovan could hear over the radio.

"*Negative, we have no plate numbers. All we know right now is that it's a late model silver Mercedes C class.*"

"*Do we have a location or direction she was heading in?*"

"*She started heading west towards the cemetery, but after that who knows.*"

"*Give us a description of the driver.*"

"*Tall blonde, attractive, white top.*"

"*Sound like if you looked at the car as much as you looked at her we could get somewhere.*"

"*Ease off, things happened too quickly here. We have what looks like the main brains behind this thing dead, and another one in custody. If you get your asses up there maybe you can wind this thing up for us.*"

"*Okay, chopper's on its way. We've got more ground vehicles fanning out from the direction you last saw her, and we've put out on APB to the locals. If we can get a name and a photo then I'll alert airports, ferry terminals and cab drivers, but I need something better than 'attractive blonde'.*"

"Working on it, I'm going over now to have a little talk with our beefcake we have in custody. I'll be back with anything else I can come up with."

With that the radio crackled and then was silent. Donovan looked out his window and saw one of the agents walking towards him, taking off his FBI jacket and hanging it over his shoulder. The man got in the back seat, sat next to Donovan and looked at him, gun pointed at his face. The man's eyes were cobalt, his features gave no hint of any human emotion at all. Short grey hair, tight lips, quick eyes… he saw everything you didn't.

"You and I are going to have a little talk."

Donovan was silent.

"Where's the bitch headed with the money?"

"I don't know."

"I don't believe you."

"I'm telling you, this was not the way it was planned. She screwed us over, Reg is dead and I'm sitting here like a lame duck. I tell you it wasn't supposed to go down like this."

"I smell something…" The FBI agent slowly sniffed around the back seat like he was trying to find the source of a gas leak, "There it is," sniff…sniff, "You know what I smell? Bullshit is what I smell."

He sat back against his door and cocked his gun. "You start telling me what you know or you become a victim of cross fire. Notice there weren't any witnesses other than us good guys out there?"

Donovan stared straight ahead, "I want my attorney."

"And I want your ass in a sling. Now we don't have very much time, and I'm not a patient man. Tell me what you know."

"I'm not a rat."

"You will be when I tell you what happens to little boys like you who don't cooperate in a federal offense. If you start talking, we can cut your sentence, go easy on you. We know you weren't the brains behind this, that's obvious."

Donovan winced. "You're looking for a woman named Beth…"

Chapter Forty-Five

The elevator doors opened and two men walked in. They had tool belts on over jumpsuits, name tags identified one as Jose and the other as Raul. Both hadn't shaved in days, were sweating, and had rags over their shoulders. Beth took her hand out of the bag, zipped it shut and stood up. *Why can't I just look in the bag?*

The men did their best to check Beth out but maintain the professionalism wearing a Wyndham maintenance uniform required. The side glances were obvious, but she could live with them. The car stopped at the sixth floor, they tipped their caps and walked off.

Once again she crouched down, unzipped the bag, and began to slide her hand in. The car stopped at the seventh floor, the doors opened and a family of four stood there smiling, the husband holding the door open for Beth once he saw the large cart. Beth zipped up, grabbed the cart and wheeled it towards room 724.

The wobbling wheel caught on the threshold of the elevator, and once it got onto the thick, plush carpeted hallway it stuck even more. The man in the elevator reached forward to help, Beth awkwardly manhandled it back into position and made her way down the hall.

Stopping in front of Simone's room, Beth knocked.

The peephole in the doorway darkened momentarily.

The door opened and Simone stood there smiling.

"Your timing is perfect, come in."

Simone was dressed in black jeans, a loose fitting maroon sweater, her dark hair loose over her shoulders, and oversize glasses perched on her nose. She held the door open and stepped aside so Beth could maneuver the cart through the door, and she grabbed the front railing to make Beth's job easier.

"God you don't know how glad I am to be in this room," Beth said. "The trip here was stressful, like I told you before I'm not used to this kind of thing."

"Sounds like you could use a drink sister, I've got champagne, vodka, beer, wine…what do you like? Feel like a martini?"

Beth ran her hand through her hair and pulled it from her face. "Actually, champagne sounds terrific."

"Well sit down, take a load off. The business can wait a few minutes while you get used to the idea of being a criminal mastermind." Simone said this with an air of conspiracy among women, followed with a wink. She walked over to the mini bar area between the couch and the TV cabinet. The room was a suite with a lounge area in the front, a sofa, love seat and easy chair were conveniently arranged around a glass topped coffee table. Off to the side was an entertainment center, bar area with refrigerator, and a doorway leading to the bathroom and bedroom.

Simone brought out a dark green bottle of champagne and began unwrapping the foil covering the cork. "So how did it go at the bank, I want to hear all the gory details."

"Why?"

Simone looked over at Beth quizzically, "Just morbid curiosity I guess, after getting to know you the other night I'm wondering how it all went with Reg and everything."

"It went pretty much like I thought it would. They did the test run, which went fine. We got the call from Donovan and brought the rest of the money down because Reg's bank contact had to leave town. I picked my spot, I didn't even have to ask Reg if I could drive, your idea was perfect. He hates that car."

"Let's have the champagne." Simone threw the wrapper in the wastebasket and started to twist the wire cage off the cork.

"How much money did you end up getting?"

"A little over 50 million, Donovan had one of the bags in the bank which must have had a few mill in it. How long will it take to count all this?"

"Usually it's bundled up in packets of ten grand, so that means we should have a little over 5000 packets. If we count forty a minute, which is actually moving pretty slowly, it'll only take us 2 hours. Once we get moving we can shorten the time by stacking them up next to each other, kind of like the way they do with casino chips? That'll make it go faster. Just to keep things so we're both cool with this, I'll do occasional spot checks of the packets to make sure Reg didn't pull a fast one on you."

Beth held back a gasp, "What do you mean a fast one?"

"Come on girl, I've seen things you wouldn't believe. And Reg, from what you told me sounds like the kind of guy that would do anything. He could have switched bags with you when you weren't looking, stuffed newspapers under some real bills, or dumped laundry in there for all you know."

"This is making me nervous, I've been wanting to look in these bags ever since I took them but I never got the chance. While you're pouring that I'm just going to have a look for my own peace of mind."

Simone slowly twisted the oversized wooden cork out of the bottle while Beth walked back over to the luggage cart and unzipped one of the duffel bags for the third time tonight. She jumped as the champagne cork popped.

Simone screamed as the foam washed down her wrists, she ran to the sink next to the wet bar and put the bottle in it while she shook her hands and searched for a towel.

Beth looked in the bag and saw neatly wrapped bundles of fresh hundred dollar bills. She let her breath out. Pawing through the bag, she could see that it was loaded with currency all the way through to the bottom. She checked the others and was satisfied there was close to 50 million here.

Simone grabbed two glasses and poured the champagne, carefully adding to each one slowly while the foam continued to rise with each pour. She wiped her hands on a nearby towel. "Find what you were looking for?"

"Yes, I feel much better now. So where are the diamonds?"

"I suppose since you brought all this cash that's a fair question. Take a look at the bed." Simone gestured towards the bedroom.

Beth walked through the door leading to the king size master bed. Conspicuous on the cream colored down comforter was a gleaming black briefcase placed in the middle at a slight angle.

"Can I open it?"

"Go ahead."

Beth reached down and twisted the latch buttons. The locking mechanism snapped open, the lid lifting slightly.

She pulled the top up and stared.

Against the black velvet interior gleamed handfuls of round and oval diamonds. The entire contents would fit in a coffee can. She reached down and touched them. "I don't know what to look for but these look real enough, they're beautiful."

Beth picked one up, held it to her ear and walked over to the mirror. She pulled her hair back and imagined how diamond earrings the size of almonds would look on her. Simone walked into the room with the champagne and set them on the dresser at the foot of the bed. "Here, I'll show you what to look for."

Simone reached into the briefcase, grabbed a diamond from the pile, reached into her pocket and held a jeweler's loupe to her eye. "What you want to see is clarity, in other words no yellowing and as few flaws as possible. You'll be able to see some flaws once you look hard enough, but this is an excellent batch and I doubt you'll have any trouble getting your money's worth."

Beth took the loupe from her and looked down at the diamond Simone held out for her in her hand. The edges were crisp, the color like blue ice, and the facets were clean, razor sharp lines. "It's beautiful. I think it'll be hard to part with these."

"Then do what most of us do, keep a few for yourself. Fifty million is a lot for one person, keep what you like, sell the rest and live the life you've dreamed of."

With that Simone brought the champagne glasses over to the bed, handed one to Beth, and they held them up in a toasting gesture. "To…what do you want to toast to Beth?"

"The life I've always dreamed of but no one could get for me but myself."

"Cheers."

They downed the champagne and laughed at the audacity of it all.

"I admire you Beth," Simone said.

"Why?"

"It took guts to do what you did. Me, I'm just really a working stiff, I move diamonds for cash, collect a fee, and do it again. My life is just like any other job, I need a network of contacts, inventory, suppliers, a delivery chain, I need to get out and market myself. I mean don't get me wrong it's a different gig all together than say running a grocery store, but still it's a job. You, on the other hand went for it."

"What do you mean?"

"What you did would be equal to me taking these diamonds to the US, selling them and running forever from the man I stole them from, let alone the authorities. I don't have enough guts to do that, at least not yet."

"I guess you put it that way it sounds like you're in a better spot."

"How do you mean?"

"My money is stolen, it's money that Reg stole from Travis's clients using his connections, and using me. It's money I stole from Reg, and I'll end up being not only a fugitive but looking over my shoulder from Reg the whole time. I don't know how to live like that. I'm not complaining, it's what I've wanted to do for months, but it'll take some getting used to. Think I ought to leave the country and go live in Paris or something?"

"I wouldn't be so quick to say I'm in a better spot. You have to remember that anytime I do a transaction like this I can get arrested. Each move for me is exposure, I have to keep doing these to get paid and every time I do one it gets me that much closer to having one go wrong."

"I suppose we each have our crosses to bear. Why don't we get counting."

"One more glass of champagne, why don't you go get the bottle," Simone started walking to the dresser. "I'm ready to party!"

Beth cocked her head... the way Simone said the word party sounded out of place, stiff... unnatural.

The bathroom door flew open and two men ran out, guns drawn and aimed at Beth's head. "Don't move. FBI."

They had on the dark blue jackets and bright yellow writing on the fronts she'd seen on enough TV shows to know this was the real deal. It would have to be now or not at all.

Beth ran through the bedroom door and into the suite, the front door was blocked by the luggage cart. She reached down to grab one of the bags and yanked the door open. The FBI men said nothing, she thought she would have to outrun a bullet as she put her head down and ran. A man blocking the door on the outside grabbed her arms and wrestled her to the floor, two others joined in from the hallway and cuffed her hands behind her back. She turned her head to look up at the man who'd tackled her, something had felt familiar about him and she had to see what was happening.

She looked straight into the eyes of Travis Black.

"You...you did this to me?" she screamed. "I hate you!!" The FBI agents pulled her to her feet, one agent on each arm held her tight as she began to squirm against the cuffs.

"You did it to yourself bitch. And you know the irony of the whole thing?"

Beth didn't answer, her eyes glared in a piercing stare, mascara running down her face.

"Fifty million still wouldn't be enough for you."

Beth shook her hair back, eyes flaring. "You have nothing on me, for all you and these goons know I'm just investing some money in diamonds, there's no way you can tie me to what happened to you."

Her voice had the venom Travis knew all too well. One of the FBI agents walked out of the room holding up his smart phone and tapped it. The hallway echoed with Beth's voice talking back to her, "*My money is stolen, it's money that Reg stole from Travis's clients... using his connections, and using me. It's money I stole from Reg, and I'll end up being not only a fugitive but looking over my shoulder from Reg the whole time... I don't know how to live like that. I'm not complaining, it's what I've been wanting to do for months, but it'll take some getting used to...*"

Simone came out of the room, took her oversize glasses off, walked over to Travis and put her arms around him in an embrace of obvious sexuality, all the time staring at Beth with a wicked smile. He kissed her, reached a hand down her backside and squeezed, "Nice work Daphne, you should be in the movies."

Epilogue

The day after Beth was brought to her knees and the money recovered, Travis and Daphne met Chaz and the two FBI agents at the bar of the hotel they originally checked into.

"So where did the money end up?" Travis asked one of the FBI men.

"It was sorted, counted and deposited into a local bank we use down here. It's ready to be wired to an escrow account while we sort this all out." He looked at his watch, "it should be happening as we speak."

"So what happens now?" Daphne asked.

The FBI agent sat up in his chair, "Once we have people connect the funds with where they're supposed to be we'll make sure that happens, meanwhile you and Daphne are headed home where our people in San Francisco will take over."

Chaz held up a hand, "One thing I'm mystified about, how did that newspaper article appear?"

One of the FBI agents winked, we have a little arrangement with the newspapers in Miami, they scratch our back, we scratch theirs."

Daphne asked, "There's one thing I really want to know, that Romanian Switch we tried, has it really been done before?"

Chaz winked, "I've heard it worked well the first time, I guess we'll never know."

The other FBI agent chimed in, "We've heard of ballsy moves like that, but I have to tell you when Travis called us and said he'd have Beth and the money in Daphne's hotel room I thought it was a trap, smelled like a rat and I didn't believe it. "

"What made you decide to believe it?" asked Chaz.

"Well we got Donovan's story and that made it obvious Travis was the victim here, but also it was something Travis had said earlier on the boat before he jumped. He said 'It's time to fill or kill Ben, do it your way we all lose, give me a break and we restore a piece of the dream to a group of people who have no idea they've been nailed to the wall.' Well I figured it was time for me to have something to be proud of and I took a chance."

Chaz held up his drink and proposed a toast, "To chances…"

About the Author

Jon Gregory is the pen name of a financial advisor with a major Wall Street firm in Northern California. When he's not scuba diving, sailing, spearfishing, abalone diving, cycling or spending time with his family, he's found time to write.

Email Jon: JonGregory.RunForTheMoney@gmail.com

Follow him on Twitter: twitter.com/JonGregoryRFTM